One of the last outposts of the American West, the Montana Territory is filled with promise and adventure for those with brave souls—and open hearts...

Leader of the Timberbeasts, logger Simon Sanders's biggest problem a year ago was deciding which willing woman to seduce. But since being mauled by a cougar he's become a pariah in Missoula's social circuit—and to himself. All he wants is to hide his scarred face and disappear into the bottom of a whiskey bottle. His plan is going well—until his sister's best friend, Carrie Kerr, kidnaps him and forces him to deal with his demons. If he didn't know better, Simon would swear the bossy beauty is a demon herself...

Carrie doesn't like to use the word kidnap. Unknowingly transport, perhaps. In any case, she can no longer watch Simon destroy himself in self-pity. Not since she lost her heart to him as she nursed him back to health. Now, whatever happens between them, she's determined to bring him back to the one place he swore he'd never return to, the place she's sure will reignite his spirit. But if things go awry, will she lose all hope for him to win back his life—much less share it with her?

The Montana Mountain Romance series
by Dawn Luedecke

White Water Passion

Wild Passion

WILD PASSION

A Montana Mountain Romance

Dawn Luedecke

LYRICAL PRESS
Kensington Publishing Corp.
www.kensingtonbooks.com

Lyrical Press books are published by
Kensington Publishing Corp. 119 West 40th Street New York, NY 10018

Special book excerpts or customized printings can also be created to fit
specific needs. For details, write or phone the office of the Kensington
Special Sales Manager:
Kensington Publishing Corp.
119 West 40th Street
New York, NY 10018
Attn. Special Sales Department. Phone: 1-800-221-2647.

First Electronic Edition: April 2018
eISBN-13: 978-1-5161-0344-7
eISBN-10: 1-5161-0344-0

First Print Edition: April 2018
ISBN-13: 978-1-5161-0347-8
ISBN-10: 1-5161-0347-5

Printed in the United States of America

For Denise McNiel.

Thank you for watching my marshmallows (kids) so I could write Wild Passion.

Glossary

Backcut—One of the cuts needed to fell a tree. Located on the opposite side of the trunk from the face.

Bateau—A flat-bottomed boat used to assist the rivermen. Often the men would loosen a log "nest" and then fling themselves into the bateau to avoid being sucked down into the dangerous white water beneath the logs.

Beat the Devil Around the Stump—To evade responsibility or a difficult task.

Big Bug—An important or official person. The boss.

Blowhard—Braggart, bully.

Bosh—Nonsense.

Bucker—A logger who cuts the tree into smaller, more manageable pieces as well as de-limbs the trunk.

Bulldoze—To threaten or bully. Coerce.

Chisler—A cheater.

Chute—A makeshift sloping channel constructed of special treated wood to get the logs from the forest to the lake.

Chute Monkey—Logger responsible for greasing the chute and pulling the logs across the Deck with a team of horses.

Crosscut Saw—A saw with a handle at both ends, used by two loggers to cut across the wood grain.

Curly Wolf—A dangerous person. A real tough guy.

Deadbeat—A lazy person.

Faller—The logger actively chopping/sawing down the tree.

Fisticuffs—Fighting with fists, boxing.

Flannel Mouth—Smooth talker.

Greenhorn—An inexperienced person.

Got the Bulge—Have the advantage over.

Half Turn—A partial supply of logs.

Homeboy—Loggers from the local community.

Hoosegow—Prison, jail.

Lady of the First Water—Elegant woman.

Log Nest—A log jam.

Misery Whip—A slang term for a crosscut saw that doesn't cut well.

Mudsill—A low-life.

Peavey—A logging tool consisting of a handle (30-50 inches long) with a cant hook and metal spike at the end. Used by rivermen to keep the logs moving down the rivers.

River Drive—The movement of the logs from the lumber camp, down the rivers and lakes, and to the mill.

Riverman—A logger who rides the logs down the rivers and lakes to bring them to the mill.

River Rat—A riverman who drifts from lumber camp to lumber camp, working only as long as they want to stay in the area.

Scallywag—A person who behaves badly. Scamp. Reprobate.

Scuttlebutt—Rumors.

Shave Tail—An unexperienced person. A greenhorn.

Shin out—Run away.

The Bull—The boss of the loggers working the Grove.

The Deck—The area between the Grove and the Chute.

The Grove—The area where active logging is taking place.

Timber Beast—A logger who works the timber.

Wannigan—A cook raft constructed with a crude building on top. Often the building would contain bunks for the rivermen to sleep if needed.

Widowmaker—A dead branch balancing precariously high in a tree that could fall and kill a man without notice.

Chapter 1

"I think we should find another way to kidnap him." Carrie Kerr grabbed onto the pommel to stop from bouncing out of the saddle and straight onto the barely used road as her horse lunged up the hill. She placed her free hand over her stomach to staunch the burning sensation deep within the pit of her belly. They had to do something about Simon, but Aunt June's plan resembled a patchwork quilt made of fine silk and threadbare burlap—enticing and solid in one square, but ready to tear apart with each hole-ridden piece in the middle. "Someone who lives this far up the mountain, and isn't a logger, can't be trusted."

"Oh bosh." Aunt June, Carrie's godmother, leaned forward in her saddle—a trick Carrie had used many times to help stay centered on the horse during a steep ascent. "Plenty of people choose to live away from the bustle of the city, and most of them aren't bad at heart. They're simply eccentric."

"I don't think an eccentric doctor is what we need right now. We need one we can trust. How long has it been since he practiced medicine? What if he kills Simon?"

"You and I will both be there. We can ensure that will not happen. In any case, we don't need a doctor who is trustworthy. We need one with no morals. It will be fine. Wait and see." Aunt June smiled in reassurance, but Carrie didn't feel the effects of the grin. Simon wasn't going to be happy once he woke up to find they'd tricked him onto a train. For his own good, of course. At least she hoped it would do him good. These days, there was no telling what might set Simon into a downward spiral of self-pity and irritating surliness. Some days he behaved as he always had—with a jaunty spring in his step—but most days he hid in a deep bottle of amber poison.

If she were going to fix Simon, he needed to get past his scars and trauma from the previous logging season. He needed to find a new passion in life, one that would keep him well for the remainder of his days.

A dilapidated cabin came into view surrounded by equally rough outbuildings. Chickens pecked the ground beside the house, and tucked behind them a mud-bogged pigpen barely held in its overfed occupants. Outside, a large man wearing a yellow-stained cotton shirt leaned into a wagon. Aside from the mud covering the wheel, the wagon was about the only thing on the homestead that looked to be in good shape. The man stood up tall, scrunched his reddened face, and blocked the sun with his hand as Carrie trotted her horse up next to Aunt June's and stopped before the man.

Aunt June dismounted. "Doctor Larry McGuinn?"

"'Pends on who's askin'."

"Are you the traveling doctor who does his business between here and Seattle?"

"'Pends on who's askin'," he said again, and spit on the ground. "Did I sell you my miracle serum?"

"Heavens no." Aunt June clutched the base of her throat. "Do I look like I need a miracle serum? No, sir. When God made me, he made perfection. We're here because we're in need of your medical services."

"Oh?" He spit again. This time the brown stream landed on the front of his shirt, right smack in the middle of the stain. He narrowed his eyes and smoothed his long, greasy hair back. "How'd you know where to find me?"

"Mary Lou sent me. She said your going rate is ten dollars a visit, but I'm willing to give you more. Ten for your services and twenty to keep your mouth shut." Aunt June curled her lip and stared hard at the disheveled doctor. Carrie mimicked her godmother's stare. If this half-cocked plan was going to work, they needed the doctor.

The man smacked his lips together, no doubt envisioning all of the tobacco and booze he could procure with the money. "What exactly is it you're needin'?"

Carrie slid another glance to gauge her godmother's reaction. Nothing about this situation felt right. In fact a hole formed in her stomach and led straight to the bottom of her feet. She probably wouldn't eat until after Simon's inevitable outburst once he got to the mountain. Aunt June's shoulders relaxed and the corners of her mouth twitched as if she held back a smile. "I heard there was a concoction we can get that makes a person go into a deep sleep. We need a bottle of that."

The doctor scratched his head. "Well, now, I don't know about a deep sleep, but my miracle serum could make one pass out, if you take enough."

"What I'm looking for is the potion given to Queen Victoria back in fifty-three. It's still in use today, I presume."

"Well, now, chloroform isn't something I got a lot of and it can be deadly if too much is given. It'll cost ya forty dollars for a dose."

"Thirty," Carrie said, and narrowed her eyes to match Aunt June's hard-bargaining glare.

He shook his head but took a few steps over to the side of his wagon and began to rifle through the contents. "Forty is my final offer."

"We'll give you forty, but you have to come with us to administer it, since it's deadly and all."

"Forty for the chloroform, ten for the visit, plus the fee to keep my mouth shut. I think that tallies up to one hundred and ten dollars." *Good gracious!* To Hades with eccentric, the man was a downright bunko artist. No way Aunt June would give in to such extortion. Carrie bit her tongue against the urge to respond, and waited for the sharp retort her godmother was sure to give.

Instead, and to Carrie's consternation, Aunt June simply crossed her arms over her chest. "Ninety."

"One hundred even." He spit. "I'll need to stay overnight in a hotel."

"Deal." Aunt June extended her hand and the doctor shook it. "Be at 106 Pine Street at nine o'clock tonight. I'll have your money waiting." Carrie followed as Aunt June wheeled her mount around to head down the mountain, but stopped. A part of her wanted to interject, face the dirty doctor and void the deal. The other wanted to see Simon happy once more. The latter won her internal battle, so she kept her mouth shut. Simon was special to Aunt June, but he was also her best friend's brother, and a dear friend to Carrie.

"Nine o'clock sharp," Aunt June said to the doctor. "With each minute you're late, I will take off five dollars." Aunt June ended her statement by kicking her horse to a trot.

Carrie snapped the reins and leaned forward in the saddle to urge her horse to follow.

When they were far enough down the trail to be out of sight from the uncouth man behind them, Aunt June slowed her horse to a walk next to Carrie's mount. "That man is definitely a bunko artist, but he is also the only doctor in the valley who will keep his mouth shut and do what we need, and he knows it."

Carrie's horse stumbled over a rock jutting from the ground, but she caught herself in the saddle without toppling over the top of her bay mare's head. "I don't trust that man. How do you know he is going to be sober by the time he comes to your house? What if he gets the dose wrong and kills Simon?"

"Don't you worry about the doctor. Simon will be fine once we get him to the lumber camp. Wall and Blue will be by my home at eight tonight, and Elizabeth and Garrett are standing by with the train to get us all to the camp by sunup. Only thing you need to worry about is what to cook for them hungry loggers tomorrow morning. I'll be dealing with Simon, who's sure to be as friendly as a skinny grizzly bear in late fall. At least we'll have a few of the Devil May Cares there to help us. Once we get Simon up the mountain, he'll be back to the flannel-mouthed scoundrel we all adore. He just needs to remember who he is."

Carrie nodded and turned her attention toward the steep decline of the mountain trail. If only Simon could find his way back to the man he'd once been, then all would be well. Before the accident, he'd stolen her heart. But she chalked her infatuation up to the days she'd spent nursing him back to health and the fact that he was her best friend's brother. She loved him as Beth did—at least that's what she told herself after he'd dipped into a shadow of self-pity and alcohol. Now she vowed to live as Aunt June— independent and fighting hard until her dying breath. But first, she had to remind Simon who he had been once upon a time. After all, it was her fault he'd become desolate and brash in the first place. If only she hadn't pushed for him to see his wounds. If he had had more time to come to grips with his accident, maybe he wouldn't have changed.

* * * *

Simon paced before the fireplace. The cold, black ashes within were a representation of his soul—once alive with fire and light, but now cold and lifeless. He didn't want company. Hated the look people gave him whenever they saw the ugly scars. Pity. Shock. Terror. Like he was a monster. Mothers shuffled their children away at the sight of him, and men turned their backs when he approached. The women he'd once romanced now whispered behind their gloved fingers. Bully them. They could all burn with the devil for all he cared.

So why did Carrie continue to show up at his home to torture him with promises of balls and social events? A year ago, he'd wanted to take the presumptuous beauty in his arms and show her everything she could be, but not now. She deserved better than to lose her innocence to half a man. He slumped back into his large armchair. "Go away, Carrie. Leave me be."

"So you can wallow in self-pity and bourbon?" She plucked his almost empty bottle of liquor off the small table next to his chair, sniffed it, and then put it on the sideboard well out of his reach. "Fine. I'll have no part of your debauchery."

She turned to leave.

"No. Wait." He stood and reached out as if to grab her, but pulled his hand back to his side. The chair beneath him groaned when he plopped back down as he squeezed his eyes shut. He'd more than likely regret his next words. "You can stay."

He opened his eyes in time to see Carrie twirl around with a grin. One that made him want to shock her enough to put her in a daze of confusion. He wouldn't be opposed to playing games with her, but the one she no doubt planned was not what he had in mind. He picked up the decanter of liquor and held it out. "How about tonight, you partake with me?"

She crossed the room and stood before him. "Sorry, I can't do that. You are coming with me. My carriage is waiting outside."

He stood, bringing his body mere inches from hers.

"No." The answer came out more as a growl than a word, but he didn't care. Her flowery scent filled his senses, and he leaned closer. His eyes drifted shut as the fragrance brought him to a place of calm. Visions of the meadow at Mother Goose's Cottage, deep in the forest near the logging camp, filled his thoughts. In his mind Carrie ran from flower to flower, reveling in the earthly beauty with nothing on but what God gave her. She'd circle around back to him and press her body close for a kiss.

He opened his eyes, but his vision grew hazy as Carrie's chest rose with a deep breath, revealing the deep plunge of the valley between her flawless breasts. Flawless. Perfect. A reminder that she deserved better. God, it had been a while since he had had a woman beneath him.

He let his nostrils flare as his heart plummeted back into the pit of darkness from whence Carrie had lifted it with her breasts. With a growl, he plucked the bourbon off the table where she'd left it, and drew distance between them before he could give into the temptation to put her in her place with a well-placed kiss. Something he would have done in the past. Not now. With his face distorted and hideous, a kiss like that would do nothing more than make her vomit on his shoes. The blasted woman! Why couldn't she leave him be?

He tipped back the drink and let it burn down his throat. His cheek twitched near the scar. "If you won't leave me to my misery, then hike up your skirts and come over here. At least then you can be of some use."

To the damned woman's credit, she did no more than blink in surprise and quickly squared her shoulders. She stared hard and took the remaining distance between them. She pressed her hand to his chest and lifted her chin, bringing her face so close his breath mingled with hers. His heartbeat kicked up and he prayed the thick layers of fabric between her fingers and his heart were enough to hide his response. She pressed her body against him, heating his skin wherever they touched. What was she doing?

He couldn't keep his eyes off her mouth when she pinched the corner of her bottom lip between her teeth. Air dried out his tongue, and he swallowed as she stretched onto her tiptoes and brought her face close. A mere inch separated their lips. The sweet fragranced air from those damned flowers she always left was all that stood between him and the one thing he'd wanted since she nursed him to health—Carrie's mouth pressed against his, her chest panting with the need to have him inside her. At least that's what he hoped she wanted. Like any good thoroughbred, he fancied himself an expert in the art of seducing the opposite sex. Knowing how to take a woman's innermost thoughts and draw out her desires was the first step in seduction. But this was Carrie. She was different.

She lifted one soft finger and traced the sensitive scar on the side of his face, and he flinched. She smiled like a cruel temptress. "You're a fool to think you can scare me away with such inappropriate talk, Mr. Sanders." The long black lashes that had fluttered coyly many times before, tempting him, blinked rapidly as she took a step back. "Now, get your coat. There's a slight chill in the air."

All he could do was swallow to try and force moisture back into his mouth as he made sense of what had happened. Before he could process the moment, she pressed her fingers into his chest like his sister had done many times before and pointed toward the door. He moved despite the nagging voice in the back of his mind telling him to take control. What the hell happened to him whenever she drew close?

Blasted woman!

He neared the door and scooped up his jacket from where he'd deposited it last night. Relief spread through him at the weight of the flask he'd hidden in there yesterday when his sister and her new husband—his best friend—visited. If he was going to be bullied into leaving, at least he had the cheap bar liquor to tide him over.

He slid his coat over his double-breasted vest and yanked open the door, not waiting for Carrie as he took the stairs. The sight of her surrey brought him to a halt. The only women who'd driven him around were his grandmother when he was a lad and later his sister when he taught her how to drive. No way was he letting Carrie take the reins.

Carrie brushed past him, and he could focus on nothing but her small frame as she approached the large horses. "Yes, that's right," she said with a smug gleam in her eye. "I'm driving. That way you can't disappear on me like the night Beth and I attended the Governors Dance. Now. The least you could do is help me up the steps."

"If you would mind your own business, I wouldn't be forced to use such trickery. There's no way I'm going to be chauffeured about like some woman."

She mounted the surrey without help from him. Not that he offered any. Although he would have if she'd waited a fraction longer.

Carrie's narrowed eyes bored a hole straight through him. "Get in or I will put you in myself."

"I doubt you've ever lifted an ax let alone a grown man." There was no way she could force him inside the carriage, but he didn't want her touching him again. He settled into the seat, placed his hand over the flask beneath his jacket, and scooted toward the edge of the bench to put distance between them.

"I'll have you know, I gained a lot of cooking skills from Aunt June last summer. While I may have grown up not having to work, I no longer choose to live in such a way. I quite like Aunt June's lifestyle, and anyway my threat worked to get you in. Now settle down." She snapped the reins, and the buggy jerked into motion. The gentle clop of the horse's hooves over the dirt roads filled the silence between them. Why did he torture himself so much by allowing the little minx into his home on a daily basis? She did nothing but toss demands about and order him to better himself. Well, bully her. He had no intention of improving anything except his liquor supply.

Simon touched the jagged scar running down the side of his face and past his jaw, only to stop at his neck. Beneath his layers of shirt and vest fabric, remnants of the predator's teeth and claws sliced down to dip below the waistband of his pants. Although healed, the scars were still sensitive to touch. Before last season, his face never failed to melt the resolve of every woman he chose to seduce. Not now. Not after the cougar attack that almost took his life. He'd survived, but he'd lost his face and soul. "Where are we going tonight? A dance? Dinner party? Drinks with the president?"

"If President Harrison visited I doubt you'd clean yourself up enough to attend anything in his honor."

"There's nothing for me out there." He motioned toward the far-off buildings of downtown Missoula.

"If you weren't obsessed with self-pity you'd see there are many people around you who love you despite your scars—and attitude."

"What? Like you?" He spit the words out with contempt, but like before his remark failed to make her react as he wished. The moment thickened with silence, neither offering a response.

After a few uncomfortable minutes, Carrie spoke up. "I'm taking you to see a doctor."

"Of course," he snapped. "And that's why we're traveling the back roads, right? Can't be associated with the monster of Missoula."

She snapped her gaze to him. "Where did you hear that?"

"Isn't it on everyone's lips these days? After that reporter in the *Herald* got hold of my story, it's been all the rage."

Carrie focused once more on guiding her horses through the streets. "Let them talk, Simon. They're all catty imbeciles with no grasp of reality beyond the dances and teas they attend."

Simon didn't respond. What could one say to her? To the knowledge that the only woman left in the world who will look at you was searching for a way to be able to stomach your company. "Are you certain this doctor is reputable?"

Carrie squirmed in the surrey seat next to him and snapped the reins, not yet offering a response.

"So, not reputable then? So why in Sam Hill did you bulldoze me into coming? And why did we have to take your buggy? I could have walked just fine."

"Dr. McGuinn comes highly recommended by Aunt June." She yanked hard on one rein and the horses turned onto Pine Street. "And I will not risk you running back to your hole to hide."

Simon searched his inside pocket for the flask. If he was lucky, he could down the entire pint before Aunt June caught him with it. The blasted woman was likely to lay into him like a gospel sharp to the devil. There was no way he could deal with this whole evening sober. Even if the doctor was as good as Carrie claimed, he couldn't fix the scars on his soul.

Simon turned his body to face away from his sister's bosom friend. His elbow bumped the back of the padded seat as he shielded his face with his coat jacket with one hand and took a swig of cheap, back-alley liquor. The buggy shook as it rolled over a divot in the ground, and what remained from the flask drenched the front of his shirt. The booze he'd swallowed burned down his esophagus and he coughed, trying not to spit out the only relief he had for this hellish night ahead. *Dammit!*

He wiped frantically at the front of his white cotton shirt as the liquid soaked into the fabric.

The liquor spread through his veins, and he gave up. He buttoned his jacket as Carrie pulled up in front of Aunt June's home and set the brake. The spring-supported leather bench groaned as Carrie squared her body to his. His pulse raced, whether from the drink or her scent drifting on the breeze past his nose he didn't know. Did it matter?

In the fading daylight, he caught the gentle firming of Carrie's lips before she spoke. "You are going to go in there and give this doctor a chance to help you. Do you understand me? I cannot go to the lumber camp until I know that you aren't going to drink yourself to hell while I'm gone."

"Don't be a fool, Carrie. I've been damned for years. Trying to save me now is like trying to float a log down a dried up riverbed." Without thought to Carrie's sensibilities, he tipped back the flask to take in any remaining drops of booze, then held it out to her. The only woman left in his life who seemed to truly care. *Well, she shouldn't.* "Why don't you be a good girl and fill this up for me when Aunt June isn't looking? She keeps the good stuff in the bottom cupboard of her sitting room sideboard."

She snatched the flask from his fingers and tucked it into a pocket sewed to the folds of her skirts. "I will do no such thing, and neither will you. Now, I hope you haven't forgotten your manners." She flicked her eyes to the steps of the surrey.

Simon grumbled as he leapt to the ground and in a few steps reached up to help her down. Normally he didn't need to be reminded to be chivalrous, but today he didn't feel much like catering to the demanding female desires.

Carrie took his arm and led the way toward Aunt June's door. Simon's stomach dropped at the thought of the doctor and what he could possibly do for him. Could he fix him, or was the man just another bunko artist peddling false hopes and disappointed dreams? Most likely the latter.

Simon couldn't get his hopes up. He wanted to tell Carrie as much, but he knew it was too late with her. She was the only one who truly believed that he could be fixed.

By the time they reached the top step, the door opened to reveal Aunt June. "It's about time, you two. The doctor is in the front sitting room, and he's ready."

Carrie tightened her grip on his arm and snuggled closer. She was like a drug to him. One touch, one smell of her hair, and she could bend him to her will. Once he stepped through the door and into the candlelit room, he yanked free of her confusing grip. She stumbled a step but threw back her shoulders and brushed past. He watched her disappear into the next room, and his heart sank. What he wouldn't give to be normal again. To feel her warmth beneath him as she writhed in passion. He swallowed hard and tugged at the collar of his shirt. The back of his finger brushed against the scar dipping down his neck. No woman in her right mind would be able to stomach the sight of his mangled body, especially not one as innocent as Carrie. This was going to be a long night.

He followed Aunt June into the parlor and glanced around to take stock. Carrie stood, half hidden behind the pillar near the fireplace. Aunt June bustled up to a round man wearing a threadbare suit, slightly stained. In his hand, he held a black bag normally associated with a man of his profession.

Simon's face twitched near his scar again. "Let's get on with this." He walked to the couch and sat.

"Chipper for a man in your situation," said the doctor. "Do you know what I'm about to do?"

Simon flipped his hand through the air. "I assume needles. Poking. Do what you will. You're going to fail anyway." He caught Carrie's gaze and motioned toward the sideboard holding the liquor. "Be a good girl."

All the blasted woman did was shake her head and drop her gaze to the decorative rug beneath the couch. Damn. He refocused on the doctor as he pulled a vial resembling an oversized perfume bottle from his bag. Reaching in a second time, he withdrew a face mask and attached it to the bottle.

"What the hell is that?" Simon leaned against the couch back.

"This is an anesthetic."

Simon let his shock show on his face. "Something more powerful than booze, huh?" He turned to Carrie. "You arranged for me to get something better than booze? Well, then, let's get to it." He grabbed the mask from the doctor's hands and placed it over his mouth. Maybe for a while he could forget about Carrie's distractions and get right in the head after he woke. And by some miracle maybe the doctor would have success with fixing his face, but he doubted he'd have such luck.

He took a deep inhale a mere second after Aunt June motioned toward the door. His lungs filled to their capacity, and he grew dizzy. The last thing he saw as he drifted into blackness was the faces of his old logging crew, the Devil May Cares, as they slipped into the room. What in the hell were they doing there?

Chapter 2

"That was easier than expected." Carrie walked toward the growing group surrounding a now slumbering Simon.

Aunt June hovered above the couch. "Yes, that was. What did you do to him, girlie? He didn't even ask questions."

Wall stood tall, staring down like the rest. "It's like he was running away from something."

"What did you do to him, girlie?" Aunt June repeated and tossed her a confusing look.

Carrie's heart beat faster. What had she done? Besides play his game at the house. Let him see she wasn't afraid of him, no matter what vile obstacles he tossed in her path. She wasn't one to back down, and she had showed him that. Hadn't she? "He seemed fine on the carriage ride."

The doctor cleared his throat from across the room where he'd retreated. "That'll be one hundred and ten dollars."

Aunt June rolled her eyes. "Ninety dollars even. You were two minutes late."

"My money." The doctor held out his hand.

Aunt June faced the Devil May Cares. "You boys get him loaded into my buggy out the back alley. Tell Beth and Garrett that Carrie and I will be there shortly." Aunt June turned toward the doctor. "I've got to settle with the *good* doctor here."

"I'm as good as your money makes me," the doctor said as he followed her toward a brown jar on a bookshelf in the corner.

She shoved her hand in the jar, yanked out a wad of money, and thrust it toward him. "Now don't you go thinking you know where I keep my loose money. I put that in there for safekeeping for tonight. If I find anything amiss in my house I'll know where to go to extract revenge."

The doctor snatched the money and pressed it to his chest. He smiled as he arranged the dollar bills in his hand. Without another word he scurried out of the room, stuffing the bills in his jacket pocket.

As the sound of the large front door shutting reached Carrie's ears, Aunt June returned to Simon's side. "Off you go, boys. Best get him to the train before he wakes up. I'm not confident this doctor didn't give us a half dose, or how long the chloroform sleep will last."

"We'll meet you there." Wall, the new leader of the Devil May Care boys, motioned for Blue to take the feet as he positioned himself above Simon's torso. Within a few minutes the Devil May Cares loaded Simon in Aunt June's buggy and headed out.

Carrie followed them outside behind Aunt June and watched until they disappeared into the night. She covered her aching stomach with the palm of her hand, then faced Aunt June. "There's no turning back now. I just hope he won't despise us when he wakes."

"Oh, you can count on him to be roaring like a bear when he wakes. Wouldn't be surprised if he breaks somethin'." Aunt June motioned for Carrie to step inside the house. "He'll have to get over it. Now, girlie, go upstairs and get the belongins you brought over this morning. We need to get to the train before Simon wakes."

By the time Carrie lugged her overly stuffed bag down the stairs and out the front door, Aunt June had already loaded her luggage in the footboard of the wagon. "Hurry now, girlie, get in."

Her godmother's impatient foot-tapping filled the silence of the night. Carrie set the bag on the floor and slid in beside her. Before she settled, Aunt June whipped the reins to send the horses forward.

The slight spring chill in the air cooled her heated face. The last few hours sent a rush of emotions flowing through her like a white-water river. What had Simon meant by trying to shock her with his inappropriate words? Then again, why had her riotous mind considered taking him up on his offer, even if for a mere heartbeat. For a moment she thought him serious, but that could never be. Simon was a womanizer, well-known to the harlots of Missoula and a few lonely wives. With so many prospects, he'd never look her way. Ever since they were children she'd been nothing but his sister Elizabeth's obnoxious friend.

She needed to get over the way Simon made her tingle inside whenever he drew near, and focus on getting him well. After all, she didn't need more complications at the hands of Simon. Not after she'd finally convinced her parents that she'd be safe and whole at the lumber camp. After the tongue lashing she'd received in regards to her chastity, she had to be on her best behavior or risk getting thrown in the streets. If she came back ruined by a logger, her parents would disown her before she could even walk through their door.

No. She could help Simon without giving in to the temptation of a man who once bragged to her neighbor that on a wager he'd talked the stickler wife of a local banker out of her bustle. Of course, she overheard the whole conversation while spying on him through the rose bushes in his backyard while waiting for Elizabeth, but her bad behavior was not in question. What she needed to do was stay focused on helping her best friend's brother, and keep her heart from falling for him all over again. She'd barely gotten over him.

Simon was trouble. Trouble she didn't want, or need, in her life.

* * * *

The familiar screech of a train slamming to a halt echoed through the darkness and brought Simon's mind to focus. He squeezed his eyes shut even tighter. What in Sam Hill was going on? Closer still, voices whispered in hurried tones. He picked out Wall's and Garrett's voices, his sister, and Carrie. What the blazes?

He lurched upright. "Where am I?"

"Where do you think?" Beth walked toward him and sat down next to him on the couch. "You're in the railcar Garrett gave me as a wedding gift." She stared at her husband in the most nauseating way.

Of course Simon was on a train. One guess as to where it was headed. He turned away from her. His sister. The one person on earth he should be able to trust. A movement behind Beth caught his eye as Carrie stepped into view. What was left of his heart sank to the deepest pit of his stomach. He glanced between the two women—the reason he now lived as half a man in the first place. Hadn't his forgiveness of their antics last year been enough? He lowered his voice to a growl and turned his gaze to Carrie. "What did you do?"

Tears filled her eyes, but he refused to let her frail emotions sway his ire. "You had no right."

"It wasn't Carrie's fault," Beth defended.

He gave his sister a stare designed to frighten her. "Let me guess. It was one of your plans."

"No." Carrie glared. "It was my idea, and it's a good one."

"Good as any I've seen." Aunt June stepped forward and planted her hands on her hips like she was apt to do whenever she wanted the men to feel as if they'd been properly scolded.

Simon glanced between Garrett and the Devil May Cares, but he couldn't say anything. Simply shook his head.

"You need help," Garrett said, and wrapped one arm around his wife. "We all agreed this was the only way."

"Did you think I would wake up and thank you for drugging me and kidnapping me?"

"I wouldn't call it kidnapping," Carrie spoke up. "Maybe if you think of it as unknowingly transporting you to camp then it may not seem so wrong."

"You're a fool like my sister." His heart twisted, and his stomach grew nauseous. Why? Why would she do this to him? He never should have let the damned Jezebel lure him out of his home. What she had done was worse than the moment the cougar ripped the flesh from his chest. This woman tore his heart clean out with one deceiving moment.

"Pardon me?" Beth elbowed him in the ribs, and he flinched.

"No!" Carrie snapped. He stared into her sky-blue eyes, fired with righteous passion. "You're the fool. You have a whole camp full of people who depend on you, trust in you, and need you. Yet because a few people in Missoula are too weak to be comfortable around your scars, you take to the bottle. Lose yourself. We brought you up here to—"

"To what?" Simon lurched to his feet. "To fix me? Nothing can heal me, but apparently who I am is not good enough for a Delilah like you." He turned his attention to the rest of the group. "Any of you."

Without waiting for someone to object, he stomped toward the door. To hell and back with them. He didn't need anyone to *fix* him, and he certainly didn't need anyone telling him what he could do as a man, or where he could go, or in his case, not go.

"Simon—" He heard Carrie's voice call behind him.

"Let him go," Aunt June said as he walked out into the cool mountain breeze. Night surrounded the trees like a cloak to a thief. And it was. This blasted place took everything from him, and left him a wretch.

Off in the distance a fire lit the towering trees surrounding a camp. *Greenhorns, shave tails,* he thought to himself as he stared at the scene. Only new loggers in camp would be up this late instead of catching what little sleep they could.

"Simon." Garrett's voice sounded behind him.

He stopped and faced his friend. If anyone could make right this situation, it was Garrett. "Don't try to stop me from leaving, Gar."

Garrett stopped before him, and he felt more than saw his arms extend. "I wouldn't think of it."

"Then what do you want?"

"Everyone on the rail car did what they did for you. Especially Carrie and Beth. I know how Beth's plans can go, and I don't usually condone them, but we need you here just as much as you need to be here. You're the leader of the timber beasts. Without you, they couldn't get the job done."

"There are other men on the crew who could lead."

Garrett's feet shuffled over the pebbles on the ground. "Not this year. The Devil May Cares took two of your men to fill the open positions, and with the new railroad logging, we've taken on a lot of greenhorns. The beasts need an experienced logger. Especially one who knows how to work the new system."

"What about Earl or Fredrick?"

"Earl didn't come back this year. We've taken Fredrick on, but I don't know if he's going to work out. You're it. You've got a few yearlings and two-year-olds out there, but the rest of your crew is new this year. They need *you*, Simon. Without you, I don't think we could do this. The year-round crew is working overtime, but even that's not enough. It's up to us to get the trees felled and down the hill. The mine we contracted last year needs their logs, and I've placed a new order for my father's railroad company as well. We've got work to do."

"I'll think on it." Simon stepped away from his friend toward the trail at the base of a nearby hill. He needed to think, and there was only one place to do that: the cabin he and Garrett had built their first year here. The one far up in the mountains where no one would bother him.

"Are you going to Mother Goose's Cottage?"

He stopped and turned back to his friend. "Yeah. And thanks for that, by the way."

"For what?"

"Allowing my sister to give it such a silly name."

"You didn't mind last year."

"Last year I was a fool."

Simon felt Garrett move, and at the same time noticed his friend's silhouette shift against the dark of the mountains behind him as if he searched the trees. "It's late."

Simon gave a sarcastic laugh. "What? You think I'm too weak to walk the trail alone at night?"

"Not at all. I simply wanted to let my buddy use my knife." The sound of Garrett undoing his buckle filled the space surrounding them. His hand brushed Simon's bicep as he extended his arm. "It's not a statement of my trust of you. It's simply a weapon in case you run into anything up there."

Simon took the knife, opened his belt, and slid it into place behind his back. Part of him didn't believe Garrett. Tonight proved the people in his life thought little of him. And while Garrett had never lied to him before, he didn't stop the women from pulling off another loathsome scheme. This time at Simon's expense. But Garrett was right. He needed a weapon. As far as he could tell, the only thing Carrie had taken from his house was him. Without supplies, he was vastly unprepared for the dangers of the forest, or the logging season. He buckled his belt.

"Thanks."

Carrie.

The damned woman would pay for what she'd done. He expected this sort of behavior from his sister, but not Carrie. Not the woman who'd come to keep him company every day since they had returned from that fateful season. Not the woman who'd taken up the majority of his thoughts for over a year. She would pay for what she'd done to him. One way or another.

Chapter 3

Carrie searched the group of men hovering near the cook table waiting for the noon meal, but Simon was not among them. He'd stormed out the night before after serving her a justified, yet hurtful, retort. She deserved it. She should have been honest with him.

"Ms. Carrie," a young logger she'd never seen before said as he shoveled a mouthful of the shepherd's pie into his mouth. "Are you courting anyone? With the way you cook, I'm surprised no one has scooped you up like one of your biscuits." He bit into a buttermilk biscuit and smiled.

"No. No suitors here." She waved the suds-soaked spoon toward what was left of the food after the men got to it. Dishes clanked in the wooden wash tub as one of the new rivermen slid his dishes into the water. "Just me and my vittles."

"Will you marry me, then?" The young man smiled. "I could live to be a hundred and never grow old of this pie."

"You'll have to get in line, young Max." Aunt June set a jug of milk in the center of the crowded table. "Carrie here has a string of suitors waiting for her at home. She's a picky one. So far no one is good enough. Gets that from her godmother." Aunt June winked at Carrie.

The young man groaned, clutched his heart, and leaned back as if wounded. "Tell me where the line starts. I'll beat the tarnation out of any fool in front of me."

Despite the nagging worry of Simon in the back of Carrie's mind, she smiled. "I'll warn them you're coming."

"Speaking of, after the big bugs from the mill leave, we'll be deciding who the crew bosses are next to the lake. Cuffs up and chins down." A logger Carrie recognized from the year before sat back and gave a toothy grin while chewing. "Even though you're a greenhorn, you can get a shot."

"I may be a greenhorn here," the young man who'd proposed said, "but I ain't no namby-pamby. I'll clean your plow if that's what you want."

The older logger erupted in laughter. "Is that a bluff, or do you mean for real play? Ain't no one beat me yet."

"There's always a first." The young man turned his attention back to Carrie. "If you'll excuse me, Ms. Carrie, I need to show this old timer a thing or two."

Carrie chuckled and motioned toward the lake. "By all means." The poor boy didn't stand a chance against a seasoned logger. According to Simon, they settled everything with fisticuffs.

She searched the men, but knew he hadn't yet snuck into camp. A hollow pit grew in her stomach. Where was he? "Aunt June, if we're done, I got something I need to do."

Her godmother stared at her with a calculating gaze for a few heartbeats before nodding. "I'll take care of the rest."

"Thank you." Carrie wiped her hands on the apron she wore, untied it, and hung it on the peg next to the door of Aunt June's cabin.

She pivoted to search for Elizabeth when Aunt June spoke up behind her. "If you see him, you tell that handsome man that Ms. Victoria will be visiting with Paul this year. Since she took over everything, even the railroad logging operations, she's been a bang-up boss lady. Make certain he's here. Don't want him to get fired before he even starts."

Carrie smiled. Even though her godmother talked strict, when it came to Simon she turned into a mamma bear. "He'll be here." She spun on her heels to go find Beth.

In a few seconds, she ran up the steps of the railcar and yanked the door open. "Beth?"

No answer. What did she expect? There was no way Elizabeth would be hidden in the railcar. Carrie slammed the door and headed for the railroad logging.

The tracks arced around the section of timber they had cut the year before. The log train rested at the top of the loop that would take the train back home. Beth stood next to her husband near the tall, carriage-like pulley positioned on a flatcar in the center of the train. "Get the pulley to the front!" Garrett shouted at his men.

The machine jerked and started to roll on wagon wheels from car to car, taking the gaps without issue as steam billowed from a stack sticking from the top. She stopped next to Garrett and Beth. "That's quite a contraption."

"Another of Wall's ideas. The man has proved to be much more than peavey and cowboy boots," Garrett said as the train jerked and he snapped his attention to the contraption, and then back at her and Beth. "Excuse me, ladies."

Garrett ran toward the machine, and Carrie adjusted her step to get closer to Beth. "Have you seen Simon today?"

"Garrett said he went up to Mother Goose's Cottage last night. He should be back any minute." Her friend bit her lip and shook her head, but Carrie knew better. Whenever Beth bit her lip, she was nervous or worried.

"Aunt June said he should be there for Victoria and the big bug from the mill." Carrie peeked over Garrett's shoulder to the trail at the base of the hill that led to Mother Goose's Cottage. She'd never been there herself, but Beth had disappeared up there several times last year.

"Carrie," Beth said with a warning tinging the word. "Do not go up there by yourself."

Carrie stretched her hearing beyond her friend to the base of the trail and into the trees. Half-expecting to see Simon climb down the mountain, she barely heard what Beth said, but she waved her hands in the air. "Of course."

Beth grabbed her shoulders and turned her until their faces grew close. "You cannot go up there alone. Garrett took a look up there this morning. The winter team moved the Grove, and now there are trees with widowmakers, not to mention the fact that they are clear-cutting a spot farther up the mountain, near the trail."

Carrie focused on Beth's eyes. "I won't go," she lied.

Her friend studied her until Carrie repeated. "I won't."

Beth let go and stepped back. "Simon will be fine. He's lived among these hills for years. He knows the start of the season is today. He'll be here."

"You're right." Carrie kicked the corners of her lips up in a smile she hoped didn't show her true thoughts. "I'd better get back to help Aunt June prepare for supper. She wants me to make a cherry pie."

"All right." Beth eyed her with disbelief.

Expanding her smile, Carrie pivoted on the green meadow grass and hurried toward Aunt June's house. She waited until she was far enough in the trees at the end of the meadow before she tossed a glance over her shoulder. Luckily, Beth now yanked on a pulley line behind Garrett as they struggled to secure the machine.

Carrie's heart thumped in her chest, and she ran toward the base of the trail. She searched the surrounding meadow and trees, but all of the loggers were gathered by the machine.

Her thighs burned as she raced up the hill and out of sight. When she crested the hill she slowed and clutched her side as she walked to calm her breath. She'd never run so hard. Thank God Aunt June had made her buy the cowboy boots. At least she wasn't tripping over the tiny heel of her only pair of sturdy shoes like last year.

A few feet away a tree creaked as it swayed in the wind, and she studied the top branches as she walked past. High up, a broken branch from another tree balanced in the boughs. It swayed, and the branch moved an inch. A tingle of numbness slid down her legs, and her breath grew rapid.

Another glance around the trees aligning the path proved Beth's words true. Widowmakers like the one she had just seen dotted the branches above. If she remembered correctly, the men would be up ahead in the new Grove.

Keeping an eye through the trees for movement, she ran up a small incline. She was about to take a corner when the sound of two male voices echoed off the trees ahead. Her chest tightened, and she leapt onto an animal trail off to the right. Ducking low behind the brush aligning the path, she headed farther into the forest. Ahead, the trail twisted in the direction she needed, and a quick glance to the treetops above showed no widowmakers. With luck the path would twist around and connect with the trail to Mother Goose's Cottage. It looked like it did, anyway.

Carrie slowed and peered through the brush toward the other trail. To her relief, she stood alone. No one could see her. Now if she could find Simon before Victoria showed up. If only he could find his way out of his darkness. Otherwise this whole debacle would be for naught.

The crash of disturbed brush sounded before her, and she paused. Her blood pumped hard through her body and thrummed at her temples as a deer leapt before her and took off to run away. She pressed her palm to her chest and stopped to search her surroundings.

As expected, she stood alone, but the trail veered to the left instead of looping around back to the path. Behind her, the trail all but disappeared. She spun around and rushed down what she could make of the path, only to stop when it forked two ways.

Dear Lord, which way had she come? She clenched her teeth to ward off the urge to cry. Another sound to her right made her jump, but it was only a squirrel skittering up a tree trunk. She focused on the path, studying both sides of the fork. Which way should she go? With a deep breath, she headed down the one on the right, praying to God it was the right way.

* * * *

The squeal of a train slamming to a halt filled the trees surrounding Simon. He watched as the last load of loggers leapt from the boxcars with their usual whoops and hollers. He'd been one of those poor fools in seasons past, but no longer. Now the charm of a season filled with hard work and male camaraderie felt more like a prison—one with trees for bars, and a small backstabbing beauty for a sheriff.

He pressed his pockets to search for his flask, but he knew it wasn't there. He sniffed his clothes. The stale stench of the bourbon he'd spilled the night before made his mouth water, but he cringed. *Damn.* At least the big bugs wouldn't smell liquor on his breath. The last few hours he'd stayed at the once peaceful meadow to think, but all it did now was remind him that things could never be the same. His life had changed, and not for the better. But what could he do besides stay and work? At least the physical exertion of felling a tree would help ease the constant tension in his shoulders, even if only a little.

Simon rounded Aunt June's cabin to find the start of the season hubbub. In the center, Paul Smith stood with Victoria, barking occasional orders and talking quietly to the cunning beauty in between shouts.

A hollow ache started in his throat and slid past his chest to settle in his stomach. Last year Victoria had showed up like a queen visiting her lowly subjects. Here she stood again with an even more arrogant stance and righteous calculation etched on her face. She certainly didn't wait as long this year to show her true intent. At least she had been smart enough to let Garrett, her then fiancé, go when she found out he loved another. Especially when all she wanted was the company anyway. She had gumption, he'd give her that much.

The skin surrounding the scar on his cheek twitched, and he started toward the woman in question. *Best get this over with.*

"Ah, good, Simon," Paul said as he neared. "Sorry to hear about your accident last year, but glad to have you back."

"I didn't have a choice," he muttered.

"True, true," Paul said. "Once you get the woodsman itch, there's no going back."

Simon opened his mouth to correct Paul's misunderstanding of his words, but Victoria interjected, "This year I'm putting Wall as leader of the Devil May Cares, and he will also be sharing responsibility over the timber beasts."

"What?" Simon snapped his attention to Victoria and her challenging stare. He fought the urge to intimidate her by closing the distance to tower above her, and instead clenched his fist. Inside, the beast within him roared. Although he didn't want to be at the camp in the first place, he was completely capable of performing his tasks without a blasted Devil May Care dogging his every move. "They have their own problems to deal with every year. I mean, hell, you saw what happened last season with the saboteur."

"I've made my decision." Her eyes darkened and dared him to argue. "Wall will lead the Devil May Cares, and he will preside over the railroad logging. The winter crew has downed enough trees to keep the summer team busy all season. Both inland and near the lake. You will take your usual position as leader of the timber beasts, preparing the logs for a river run."

"Goddammit, Victoria. I don't need a nanny watching over the way I do things with my team. I did a hell of a job last year."

"Yes, but look at you. You are in no condition to take over the entire workload. We've doubled the number of loggers from last year to accommodate the new system. We need someone on top of their mountain, not buried under it."

Simon widened his stance and clenched his fists. "You're saying that because I was injured, I'm no longer capable of leading my men?"

"No. I'm saying because you are too liberal with your whiskey consumption, you're not capable of leading your men alone. At least not until you get your mind focused on the job at hand and not the booze." Victoria motioned toward his disheveled clothes, caked in mud from the cottage floor, and shirt slightly askew. "Paul has pushed to let you stay on as leader, and I trust his instinct. But you smell like a pig who bathed in liquor and horse manure. You're not ready to return to work as a leader without help from someone else."

"This may come as a surprise to you, Miz Harrison, but this is the way a logger looks." Simon tucked his shirt into his waistband. "We work hard, and we drink like lumberjacks. Because we are."

"I cannot risk the lives of the men under my employ to satisfy your ego." Her dainty stance widened beneath her lace-ridden skirts. "Paul tells me that you are highly regarded among your men, and a top performer. Which is the only reason I chose to give you a second chance, but I cannot let you do it alone. Either take my offer to share responsibility with Wall, or resign. Your decision."

"I was drug up here to do a job, and I'll do it." He flared his nostrils to take in more air, but all it did was dry out his throat. What he really wanted to do was curse loud enough to startle his prim new boss. This whole thing was a disaster. A mess caused by Carrie and her scheming accomplices. If it weren't for her, he wouldn't even be here. He'd be comfortable at home, away from the curious stares of his coworkers. Where had the little minx gone anyway? He searched his surroundings for a flash of Carrie's blond hair, but without luck. He needed to have a nice long chat with her, maybe even put her over his knee. "Are we finished here? I've work to do." Victoria smiled and inclined her head. "Excellent. Now if you prove that you are capable of handling things on your own by the drive, then I will let you have full responsibility once more."

"How generous of you."

"I'll leave you to it then." In true socialite fashion, Victoria ignored his tone and shooed him away with her gloved fingers. As much as he despised everything she represented now, she was his boss. And whether he'd come here willingly or not, this was where he was. He may as well do his job. Take out some anger on a hundred-year-old ponderosa.

But first, Carrie.

Simon scanned the group of men in the cook camp, but no small figure in a frilly skirt swayed between the filthy loggers. Aunt June's brown, plump body bustled through the crowd and motioned for him.

He took a deep breath and closed the distance.

"Good. Glad you're back. It's getting close to supper time, and I have no serving cook." She searched the space behind him. "Where's Carrie?"

A frown creased his face, and he took a step back. "I haven't seen the little wench since the train."

The crease between Aunt June's brows deepened. "She set out to find you after her chores were done."

"Probably got sidetracked bamboozling some other poor fool."

"Bosh!" Aunt June slapped his arm. "That's no way to speak about a lady. Get your handsome, grumpy butt out there and look for my goddaughter or you won't be eating my bear stew. I need her here in time to serve the men. You've got one hour to find her."

"More than likely she's with Beth."

"Go find her quick, and get back." Aunt June hurried off toward the cook fire, leaving Simon standing alone.

Victoria and Paul had disappeared, and the loggers busied themselves with business. Off in the distance, the train squealed, followed by a loud thump of a tree hitting the flatcar. He headed in that direction. Even if Carrie wasn't there, Elizabeth would be. Chances were she had something to do with her friend's absence, or at least knew where to find her. Whenever there was trouble, Beth was usually at the center of it all.

Just as he'd anticipated, his sister stood next to her new husband as he directed the off-loading of some new machine. Simon gave a quick whistle and beckoned his sister closer when she looked. In less than a heartbeat, she started toward him.

He took the distance between them, and stopped when she drew close. "Have you seen Carrie? Aunt June is looking for her."

Beth took a deep breath and placed her hands on her hips. "She said the same thing about you earlier this afternoon."

"And?"

"And I told her as far as I knew you were still at Mother Goose's Cottage. She promised not to go up there. I assumed she went back to camp."

"She's not there." Simon's heart twisted in his chest, and his fingers grew numb. Had she defied good sense and braved the dangers of the mountain in a vain search to find him? *She damn well better not have.*

"Try the outhouses or by the lake," Beth suggested. "She usually doesn't wander too far away from camp."

"Thanks." If Carrie was anything like his sister, and she was, then she'd gone up the mountain. Regardless, he took a quick look by the lake and outhouses, but as he suspected, she wasn't there.

With a silent curse, he took the trail he'd come down only an hour before. He crested the top of the hill where the Grove used to be located and spotted a small footprint deep in the mud on the side of the path. He searched the ground near the print but found nothing but another, leading toward Mother Goose's Cottage. He studied the widowmakers lining the trail. A chill sent goose pimples plummeting down his skin. "Goddamn woman," he said aloud, but knew he stood alone. The men who chopped trees farther up the trail had long since gone to camp for the evening. Simon studied the sun, halfway submerged behind the Mission mountain range. His chest tightened like an outlaw's neck in a noose, but he didn't know if worry or anger tied the forbidden knot. He'd kill the blasted troublemaker, if she wasn't already dead.

Simon followed the prints up the trail until his lungs burned along with the thick muscles in his legs. With each new bout of pain, he widened his gait—his steps matching the speed of his runaway heartbeat. What would he do if anything happened to her?

Images of her body twisted and bloody beneath a cougar dominated his thoughts. His stomach burned with a hollow ache and suppressed vomit. *Oh, God.*

"She damned well better be alive and well when I find her," he told the trees surrounding him. She was a sharp pain in his backside, but if she were gone then who would visit him in town when no one else would so much as glance his way? Who would bring him those damned yellow flowers she kept arranging in his study, regardless of his insistence that she toss the smelly things?

He shook his head to clear it of foolish thoughts. Most likely he'd find her bouncing down the trail before him, once she failed to locate him at the cabin.

A quick search of the ground for another print made him skid to a stop. Ahead no more little dimples made from a woman-sized boot marred the ground. The only evidence was that of the logger's spikes worn by most men in camp.

Damn. He turned to backtrack. His breath grew to short bursts when he failed to find another sign, almost as if she'd disappeared into the trees above—or from the side. *Oh God.* Had she been attacked by a predator?

Flashes of red followed by the tops of the trees along the river where he'd been attacked took over the imaginative images he'd had of Carrie's bloodied body. The cougar latched onto his shoulder and dragged him into the brush as the beast's body quivered. His vision tunneled. He scanned the ground for signs of blood or drag marks. *Dear Lord, don't let her end in a fate like mine.* She was too good, too pure to deal with anything this cruel.

His brain fogged and he realized he'd held his breath. He took a deep inhale as he searched the vegetation surrounding the last print on the trail. He was about to turn to the other side when the heel of her footprint, tucked beneath a fern, caught his attention.

Simon brushed the plant away, and the blur and panic dissipated. The depth of the indentation mirrored that of those on the road, and no blood soiled the ground. So why had she strayed from the hike? A quick survey of the forest around him showed an animal path, and on it another print. He breathed easier when he headed in the direction she'd taken.

He followed the trail of unintentional breadcrumbs, doubling back a few times, until the land began to grow familiar around him. A hollow pit grew in his stomach, and he headed toward a hidden cliff where his friend had fallen to his death years before.

Simon rounded a large tree as the sound of a woman's sniffle pierced his concentration. Near the brush skirting the cliff's edge, Carrie sat atop a large boulder, her knees tucked up to her chin.

"Carrie!" He cringed when he realized the word vibrated with emotion he didn't want her to hear.

"Simon!" She shouted his name as if he'd pulled her from the icy depths of a raging river. Before he could respond, she flung herself in his arms, and he squeezed her tight. The noose around his heart snapped with her touch, and he let her have her moment. A moment she needed as much as he did.

The rich aroma of her hair tickled his nose, and he dipped his head to take in as much of her as he could, desperate for the small comfort the scent allowed.

He stood unmoving until the beat of her heart beneath his palms slowed. Once he was certain he wouldn't show his weakness, he tugged on her shoulders so she would step back and look at him. What he wanted to do was swoop her up until the heat from their bodies entwined into one. Set his lips against hers in a kiss she would remember the moment she took her last breath.

He needed to fight the urge to scoop her up and comfort her. The damned fool could have gotten herself killed. And all because she couldn't wait for him to come to grips with her deception and make his way down the mountain.

No. The little fool had to know she couldn't traipse about the outskirts of a logging camp. "Why the hell did you leave the path? Had you gone any further, you'd have died. Twenty feet behind you, through the thick brush over there, is Dead Man's Cliff. One wrong step and your perfect body is nothing but vulture food. I've seen good timber beasts die here, and they were aware of its existence. You were not. But I suppose no harm could befall a thick-headed minx of a woman like you. One hell-bent on controlling even the air those around her breathe. The earth wouldn't dare challenge your authority, right?"

She stepped away and her blue eyes darkened to a steel gray flecked with shards of sapphire—the bottom of her eyes puffy and red from the tears she'd shed only moments ago. Tears he'd caused. The thought pierced his soul like a black widow's knife, but he couldn't let her see. Refused to back down when he was right.

Carrie swiped at a wisp of hair that floated across her face with the breeze. She lifted her head and tossed back her shoulders. "If you hadn't stomped away like a bratty child, I wouldn't have needed to look for you."

"A child?" He grabbed her hand and tugged her as he turned and headed back toward the trail. "I suppose you fancy yourself my mother then? There to scold me until I follow the narrow path of righteousness."

"Hardly. If I had a son as difficult as you, I'd take a switch to his backside and force compliance. It seems to be the only way to get through to a hard case such as yourself."

"I'm the hard case?" Simon didn't hide the scoff tickling the back of his throat. Carrie struggled to wade through the thick grass hanging over the barely visible trail. He plucked her off the ground and set her on a dry patch of grass nearby. "I'm not the one who drugged a man and forced him to bend to my will. You are."

She leapt over the muddy ground like a frog on lily pads. "You make it sound much worse than it is. Had you not wallowed in self-pity for the last year, I wouldn't have been forced to take drastic measures."

"Pity is for women and sick dogs. Not men."

Carrie followed him onto the open path next to the old Grove and headed downhill toward camp. "Self-loathing, then. Whatever you wish to call it is on you. The fact is you are a strong and determined man who has not been behaving the way he should. Aunt June and I are here to set you right. Whether you like it or not. We aren't going away, and we aren't going to give up on you."

"You think I'm strong?" He teased, but the words lacked the passion he once had for such a kittenish game. Before he'd play until his feminine opponent melted into his embrace. Not anymore. He refused to let any woman, let alone Carrie, grimace while she felt his jagged scars beneath his clothes. He tugged at the front of his plain blue shirt to pull any material that might touch his torso away. "I'll take a switch to your rear and show you how strong I am if you ever wander off alone again."

"Oh, for heaven's sake. You'll do no such thing." Carrie sped down the trail to leave him walking slowly behind. Her backside swayed with each step and made her skirts dust the top of the ground. She wasn't made for the harsh mountain terrain. Not like Aunt June, or even Elizabeth. God made Carrie to wander the well-manicured town streets while she shopped and gossiped with the local ninnies. She was fragile. If today's excursion proved anything, it was that Carrie was not nearly as strong as she pretended to be. If she had to do anything other than stay in camp and cook, she wouldn't survive.

Carrie rounded the corner and dipped out of sight for a split second before her piercing scream echoed through the trees. A coldness hit his core like a deep winter blizzard, and he launched into a run. He caught up with her in time to catch her as her knees gave out, and that's when he saw the spiked soles of logger boots protruding from the brush near the path.

Carrie shook as he urged her to stand on her own. Unlike him, she'd probably never seen a dead body. If they were lucky, the logger in the brush was simply unconscious, but he doubted it.

Simon knelt next to the person's spiked boots and moved the overgrown fern aside.

"Is it Beth?"

He shook his head. "I've never seen him before."

"What happened?" Carrie peered over his shoulder.

Simon surveyed the ground but stopped at a large branch near the man's head. "Looks like a widowmaker." He shifted to glance up at Carrie as he pulled the whistle from his inside jacket pocket. "Cover your ears."

He studied the treetops, but no more dead branches hung precariously in the leaves above.

Once Carrie shielded her ears from the noise, he blew six long blasts— the lumber camp's chilling signal for an injured man.

She dropped her hands and a tear filled the corner of her eye. "I heard that signal last year, but it's more eerie when you're close to the sound."

Simon gave her a sad smile and made a futile attempt to check the man for signs of life. He didn't know what else to say to her. She shouldn't be here, watching as the team hauled a dead man off the mountain.

Within minutes men from camp came running. Somewhere in the midst a logger with Aunt June's stretcher elbowed his way to the front of the mumbling crowd. "Who is it?"

Simon shook his head. "I don't know."

"Has anyone seen him before?"

No one in the crowd made claim to knowing the man. Who was he? Somewhere high on the mountain, the chilling screech of a cougar echoed off the cliffs and through the dense trees. Simon's blood ran cold, and a lump formed at the base of his throat. "Let's get him down to camp."

Like times before, the men worked to get the logger secured on the stretcher, and then most followed as they hauled the man down the path. Carrie stood crying with Wall, Garrett, and Beth silent behind her. Garrett moved to where the body once lay and crouched down to examine the ground. Wall picked up the branch, weighed it in his hands, and turned it to peer at the broken end. "Does this branch look odd to you?"

He held the object out, and Simon took it. "It looks a bit fresh, but I don't see anything else to make it seem off. Why?"

Wall shook his head and tucked the widowmaker under his arms to take it with. "No reason."

Carrie shivered next to Simon despite the fairly warm forest air. She'd been through enough and needed the relative safety of camp.

"We'd best get back." Simon slid his hand to the small of her back and hoped the warmth would ease her fears even a little. The way she did for him whenever she was around. Even though she was the bane of his existence, she was also the light on a cold winter's night. He'd die if her light was ever extinguished the way his had been.

Chapter 4

Simon plopped down onto the log facing the cook cabin with his tin bowl of bear stew. Somewhere in the night the body of the man lay in a railcar, undisturbed in the condition and clothes he'd died in, ready to be taken down to his family to be buried. At the mill a doctor would examine the body to make the final call, but Aunt June and Garrett were convinced that the first accident of the season happened before it even began. After the winter crew finished moving the Grove, the trees above had become dangerous—more so than usual. If Carrie had wandered beneath a falling branch and been crushed, he didn't know what he would have done. Without her, he'd die too. She was the only thing between him and an early grave.

Carrie's hands shook slightly as she dished the food, and she took a deep breath, the shock of the day wearing on her. Not only the dead man, but getting lost in the forest. Either incident was enough to make a flowery woman wilt for a month, but Carrie wasn't weak like the ninnies in town—despite the tears. She stood tall and worked while keeping her tears hidden behind smiles most thought were genuine, but he knew better. She was scared and tired. She needed to lie down like a wilting Missoula miss.

He stretched his feet out and crossed them at the ankles, taking care not to dip his toes in the fire. Not that the pain wouldn't be a welcome distraction from Carrie. The woman who took up every thought he had. She stood, serving food with false gumption. Each time she scooped another serving, her ladle clanged against the metal bowls. Was it his imagination, or were there a lot more men than normal gathered around Aunt June's serving table?

A lanky man stepped before Carrie and tossed her a wolfish smile, while another stood next to him fingering the hilt on his knife with one hand

and holding a tin plate with the other. The second man stared at Carrie as though he'd never seen a woman before, but the first man surveyed her with a hungry gleam in his eyes.

Simon straightened his back, and sweat formed at his hairline when he recognized the first fool. Why the hell was the chiseler faller from the Bonner crew in the Missoula supper line? He inclined his head. "Oy, Thomas, don't you have a cook back at your camp?"

His words drew the attention of most of the group, but he didn't care. The fool needed to know he wasn't welcome here. The Missoula camp, and the women who graced their cook fire, were not prizes for every logger on the mountain. Especially not a Bonner boy. Carrie wasn't some logging crew perk to be handed out to every man who showed up for the season.

"Sure we do," Thomas said, not even bothering to look at him as Carrie dished food into his bowl. The blasted fool smiled as he moved down the line. "But the women are a lot more pretty in the Missoula camp, and I've heard that the berry pie she makes is the best this side of the divide. Jake and I came here for both."

Thomas motioned toward his leering friend, who responded by widening his lecherous grin and giving a bosh request. "Marry me, Ms. Carrie?"

Carrie gave another false smile, and her face grew red. A color similar to the one Simon now saw as the blood pumped hard through his temples. He jumped to his feet and took one hard step forward. "Miz Carrie didn't come up here to be hounded by a bunch of blowhards looking for a woman. If I see you taking up space at Aunt June's table again, I'll clean your plow until your mule runs away."

"You leave them boys alone," Aunt June interrupted, and dropped a clean stack of bowls down on the table next to Carrie. "There's plenty of space at my table, and more than enough food to be served."

"He's a curly wolf, Aunt June." Simon turned his sight to the plump older woman. "Carrie didn't come up here to be ogled by a bunch of deadbeat blowhards."

"And you cut a swell yourself, right?"

His cheek twitched. *God, I could use a drink.* It wasn't a year ago that Aunt June would never have talked to him in such a brash manner. Cut him down until he was nothing but a hollowed out bag of bones. He fought the urge to let his emotions show as he stared into the old matron's eyes. "You used to think so."

"Still do, but only when you aren't acting like my goddaughter is a new toy you don't want to share. You ain't spoke for her yet."

"That's not what's going on and you know it." Simon pinched his lips together as a dull ache began to radiate from his forehead. He ran his hand over his forehead to help ease the tension and chanced a glance at the small woman in question, still serving the hungry men. She squinted as if concentrating on her job, but after a moment she flicked her gaze to him and they locked eyes. Her long lashes fluttered, and she focused on her task. The damned hounds before her didn't deserve to have a woman as perfect as Carrie dishing their food. She shouldn't be up here in the first place. If it wasn't for her blasted plan to fix him, she would probably be back home with her parents. Safe from the timber wolves of the lumber camp.

"Well, the moment my goddaughter comes to me and says she done run away and married you is the day I'll let you beat the tarnation out of every man who comes a courtin'. Until then, mind your supper and let them men be."

"But Aunt June." Simon took a small step toward the matronly cook, but she shooed him away with a flick of her wrist.

"I'm more than capable of looking after Carrie. Not that she needs anyone to dog her every move. Now, unless you're planning to propose to Carrie right now, I suggest you stop bulldozin' my guests."

"Guests? You invited them?" Simon crossed his arms over his chest and adjusted his stance.

"I did. A few of these boys were asking about Carrie. I invited them to eat with us so's they could meet her."

His neck grew hot and perspiration dripped down the thick muscles in his back. Why in the hell would Aunt June solicit Carrie's romantic attention in such a way? "I wasn't aware you'd turned into a madam during the winter season."

"Get out." Aunt June's face grew red, and her chest heaved with short breaths. "I'll not stand for your bullish behavior in my camp."

"I'm done anyway." Simon stomped toward the wash bin and tossed his bowl inside. The water splashed up and soaked the front of his pants, but he didn't care. With one last glance at Carrie, he pivoted and stomped past the cabin and toward the trees. His cheek twitched near the scar, but the rage within his soul stopped him from turning around.

What the hell was Aunt June's game? Carrie wasn't some whore for her to lend out to every man who showed an inclination. Hell, in a camp where women were sparse, even a priest would turn into the devil for a woman.

And Carrie was more beautiful than any woman he'd ever seen in a logger's camp. Her hair shimmered with streaks of gold, and her eyes made the blue of the far-off mountains green with envy. If Aunt June wasn't careful, she would lead her goddaughter right into the mouth of a predator.

* * * *

"Are you certain Simon is all right out there?" Carrie swiped the rag over the last dish in her bin, set it in the wooden crate, and watched as the last man plopped his tin into the water and headed out of the cook camp. Her nerves from the day's events still caused her hands to shake, but she couldn't think about that now. Simon had been in a right state when he left. "I haven't seen him come down, and he forgot his knife."

"To Hades with him." Aunt June tossed a sour glance in the direction Simon had disappeared an hour ago. "That boy needs a good set-down. Maybe a switch to the backside. Your desserts don't belong to that man. Yet."

"You don't think that little scheme you pulled was a little over the top?"

"What scheme?" Her godmother pursed her lips and moved them back and forth, like she always did when hiding a lie.

"The one where you brought in men to make him jealous. I don't know why you'd do such a thing. There's nothing between him and me but friendship. No need to go making him mad."

"I have no idea what you are talking about. Thomas and his fellow timber beasts are friends of mine, and they love my bear stew. And you are the only unmarried woman under 50 in this camp. I won't be surprised if every river rat and at least half the homeboys stop to look at you. You're certain to get a man or two who wants to court you."

"I was here last year and no such attention befell me then."

"Last year Beth was running around in britches, and Victoria graced us with her presence. They were probably scared of gettin' too close to the boss man's daughter. You need to make certain the only man you fall for is Simon."

"Aunt June," Carrie chided, and crossed her arms over her chest, extending her right foot. The meddlesome woman was dear to her soul, but irritating just the same. "I'm not falling for anyone. Quite the opposite, in fact. And Beth is still in britches."

"If I were thirty years younger," Aunt June responded, "I'd take Simon for myself. Besides, ain't no man been hurt by a little jealousy."

"I beg to differ. A jealous man, especially one like Simon, is a weathered stick of dynamite. Capable of causing all kinds of pain."

"Don't you worry about him. I know what I'm doing. You take care of yourself and don't go falling for a logger, or worse, gettin' ruined by one.

Your mother would murder me on her doorstep the moment I don't bring you home whole."

"Next time I won't hold my tongue." Carrie heaved the crate up into her arms. "I swear, your plans have caused a constant ache in my stomach ever since we went to visit that doctor."

"Then perhaps you should hike up to the mineral pond and drink some of the healing waters. We're in this, and we're going to make the man whole again. No matter what the cost."

"I want to help him out more than anyone, but we haven't done a bang-up job yet. If anything we've pushed him further away." Carrie walked toward the cabin and set the crate inside the door, then stood tall to turn back to where Aunt June sat watching her. "I'm tired of the deception. Simon deserves better than constant lies and trickery."

"Well, then, missy. Why don't you go have a nice long set-down with that man? Get him to see the light. Maybe even school him on the proper way to treat a woman he desires."

"Aunt June." Carrie shouldn't be shocked at her godmother's constant push for her and Simon to be together. It was common knowledge that Aunt June favored the roughened timber beast. The way she'd joked lately, though. As if she had some secret plan in motion. "Are you trying to marry me off to Simon?"

"Only if he comes back to us. Ain't no way I'm marrying you off to that old grumpard when you can have the charming man we used to know."

Oh, good Lord. The woman was notorious for meddling in other people's affairs. "I appreciate the help, but I don't plan to marry anyone. Thank you. I want to be like you. Work up here until I wither away."

"Nonsense. This is no life for you, girlie. Sometimes a girl like you needs guidance in finding a match. And most of the time men need a huge push."

"Don't push too hard. You'll end up shoving him right off a bluff."

Aunt June flashed a toothy smile. "I can't promise anything, but you should go talk to the man. I think he needs a little calming. It's gettin' on in the day. Let him know I still plan to make him his traditional breakfast in the morning."

"Any idea where he might be?" Carrie scanned the outlying area, but only a few young loggers scurrying toward their destinations flashed past her vision.

"Most of the men are setting up their sleeping quarters right about now." Aunt June pointed toward a small but worn trail leading up a gentle slope, but Carrie already knew where the men slept from the previous year's excursion with Beth. Aunt June slipped her worn apron over her head and, in a few steps, hung it on a peg near the door to her cabin outside the dining area. "Be back by dark or I'll come searching for you myself."

Carrie didn't miss her godmother's true intent on sending her to Simon, but the truth was he did need her. She knew how to help him whenever he spiraled into such an angry state. Temporary as her effect usually was on him, at least she could try to give him some sort of happiness in his life. Even if just for a moment.

She scooped up Simon's forgotten knife and headed toward the loggers' cabins, searching the ground as she went. Mud caked the damp trails and deep green ferns surrounding the path, but what she wanted to find was color in the dense brush.

She adjusted her step to take a steep incline in the path when a flash of blue deep in the trees caught her attention. Carrie pursed her lips and searched the trail before her in hopes of catching Simon sauntering down the hill, but only a squirrel skittered in the trees.

Carrie hiked up her skirts and stepped over a large fern and into the undisturbed dirt off the path. Unlike last time, she would go no farther than the flowers and return without wandering. Luckily the flowers were only a stone's throw from the path. Not that it didn't make her nervous to go back into the wild trees again.

She searched the branches above, but no widowmakers hung precariously in the quivering limbs of the vigilant pines. She let a deep breath go she didn't even realize she'd held, and quickened her step. The vibrant hues of the blue flowers made the corners of her lips tip back in a smile. For the last year she'd kept Simon's study vibrant with a dainty yellow thing that grew in her mother's garden, but this was much more beautiful. As usual he would grumble about the smell, but then settle in with a more cheerful mood after he gave in to her insistence. Perhaps this time he'd argue a little less about the cheerful gift.

In half the time it took her to get to the flowers, she was back on the trail headed for the cabins with a knife in one hand and flowers in another. As she rounded a bend, six crude abodes dotted the space between the trees—almost double the amount of cabins from the previous year. Men slid in and out the doors, some carrying their belongings slung over their backs, others exiting to talk with their fellow loggers who lounged against trees or buildings outside, but on first look Simon was not among them.

Near the door of the cabin farthest from her, Garrett stood with arms crossed over his chest, his stance wide and brows furrowed as he conversed with the new leader of the Devil May Cares. She picked up her pace. "Garrett!"

With a nod to Wall, he turned to her.

"It seems to be a common question of mine to you and Beth, but have you seen Simon?"

Garrett motioned with his head toward the Grove. "He's working off some of his ire."

Carrie pursed her lips as she turned her attention to the trail leading from the cabins to the Grove. She clutched the little blue flowers tight in the palm of her hand. After this morning's journey into the wild, she had no desire to wander into danger, but she desperately needed to talk to Simon. Make certain he was all right.

"I see you ended up with my knife somehow."

Carrie lifted the object in question. "Simon forgot it at camp. I'm bringing it back to him."

"Those are pretty flowers. Forget-me-nots?" Garrett brought his gaze from the knife, to the flowers, and finally to her face as a strange glint shone in his eyes. "Are those for Simon as well?"

"Beth and I have kept him supplied with something pretty in his study to lighten his mood. It seems to work," she said pointedly. Although she knew how it must look. A decent, prudish woman would never bring gifts to a single man. All her life she'd been the moralist with a penchant for trouble—brought on by the hands of Elizabeth.

"You *and* Beth have?" He questioned, the corner of his lips twitching.

"Okay, I have. But Beth has been busy with you. So, I took it upon myself to help him while she was away."

Much to Garrett's graciousness, he simply smiled. "I'll take you to him. If you'd like."

The tightness in her chest eased. She dropped her shoulders a fraction and smiled.

Garrett turned toward the trail and motioned for her to proceed. "I hope you and Aunt June know what you're doing, toying with the man the way you are."

"I don't think anyone in this life knows what they are doing. Someday we're all going to wake up and realize no one ever learns from the mistakes they make."

"Is bringing Simon up here a mistake?" Garrett held back a long branch extending over the path, and she eased past.

Once clear of the obstacle, Carrie stopped hiking for a moment. "I hope not."

Her friend's husband let the branch go and paused long enough to nod, then moved up the trail. She followed. Was this all a blunder? Had she brought him up here, only to make him worse with Aunt June's games? And why did Simon care that another man was interested in her? And what in Hades had happened in his study? It was as though she had lost all rational thought when he stalked toward her like a predator. Her breath grew shallow at the memory, and she pressed her hand between her breasts to stop her body from reliving the moment.

Carrie crested the hill. Last year she had thought they might have had something between them as she nursed him back to health, but then he'd spiraled into his own personal hell and forgotten all about them. So she'd given up on any thought of Simon loving her. Frankly, she had no desire to fall into marriage, or even love, anytime soon. Her focus was only on making Simon whole…and in keeping her promise to her parents. If she turned out like Aunt June—adventurous spinster that she was—then Carrie might have a chance at forging her own happiness in life, without needing a man to provide.

The gentle tap of an ax against wood reverberated through the trees. Her stomach knotted. She brought the flowers close to her chest as Simon came into view. His body tensed with each swing of the ax. He didn't hold back the rage evident in his jerky movements and the way he attacked the base of the tree.

"There he is." Garrett waved toward Simon. "You'll be fine from here. I've got to get back to Beth before she sticks her beautiful nose into something she's not supposed to."

"Thank you," Carrie said, and waited for Garrett to disappear back down the trail before facing Simon.

He'd shifted his stance, and turned his back toward her. Did he truly not know she was near, or had he chosen to ignore her presence? In only a few shallow breaths, she walked close enough to see the notch he'd chiseled in the trunk. She didn't know much about felling a tree, but she did know she was in no danger of being crushed by the giant mass at this point in his progress. But nearby a large pine that must have been his first victim lay prone on the ground—the branches not yet settled and tool marks fresh. "You don't seem to have gotten far on that tree."

Simon turned with a jerk, his brows drawn together and blue eyes as dark as a stormy winter's day. "What the devil are you doing out here, woman?" He searched behind her.

Inside she sighed. He hadn't seen her, which meant at least he was approachable. Perhaps he wouldn't bare his pointed teeth this time around. "I brought your knife. Don't worry. Garrett brought me up, but he left. I didn't chance the mountain alone, and I wasn't in any danger."

She held the knife out, and he took it, sheathing it behind his back.

"Up here you're always in danger." The anger in his eyes changed to a glare of accusation, but he shifted his weight to one foot and leaned against the ax. A flick of his gaze toward the pocket of his discarded jacket made her follow his line of sight. The top of a flask peeked from the corner of the pocket. She tried not to rush to the offending object, yank it from the cloth, and toss it into Seeley Lake. He snatched the jacket up from the ground. "It's empty."

"I didn't ask."

"You did with your eyes." He tossed the coat onto a nearby log. "I don't want to be caught in the sights of a cougar without my wits."

Carrie frowned at the memory of his wounds the year before. While she didn't judge a man based on the way he partook of the devil's juice, she didn't condone it either. But he was right. Out here, you needed to be aware of the dangers surrounding you.

Simon stretched his neck to the side, then straightened with a smug smile. "Did your new love's annoying voice make you run back to me?"

"What a petty thing to say. You know darned well that Bonner boy isn't my love. And what do you care? It's not like I haven't had beaus before. You've never had an issue with them."

"I *don't* care."

"Then I assume you're afraid of losing the one person on earth who can tolerate your surly disposition. Even Aunt June kicked you out of her camp."

He tilted his head and glared. "Now who's being petty?"

"I find it's the only way to battle with you."

"Ah, yes, your feisty personality." He dropped his ax and stalked toward her with a predator's stare, causing her heart to beat so fast she could feel it in her throat. He reached up and ran a finger down the side of her neck. "Do any of your suitors make you weak?"

She shivered. He wanted to make her step back. To herd her like men were apt to do—like he'd done before—but she wasn't going to give in. No matter how much her feet wanted to form a mind of their own and obey his unspoken command. She refused to budge. "That's none of your concern."

He stopped with only an inch between them. His hot breath tickled the sensitive curves of her neck when he bent down to her ear. "I'll bet you've never felt that fiery ache in your stomach." She gasped when he reached out and placed one warm palm on the flat part of her stomach just above her womanhood. "The one feeling that can only be satiated by the touch of a man. The one that makes women forget all recourse, and give in to the temptations of a well-stocked man. A mistake powerful enough to bring down nations, and turn friends into enemies."

The sensation of his warmth over her womb caused her breath to fail as an ache began beneath his palm as promised and stretched to even the most sensitive of places on her body. She struggled to gain control of her lungs as her mind fogged, with only the sight of his face, inches above hers, visible to her as he drew back to look deep into her eyes. She had to get control of herself. Simon was a wolf. A predator like the one who haunted his every thought. One well versed in making women swoon. What he did now aimed to scare her. Distract her. Perhaps even punish her.

Carrie swallowed hard to help bring her mind to focus and took a step back. Simon dropped his hand from her stomach as she slammed the flowers against his chest.

He straightened to his normal height and stretched his mouth in a victorious grin.

She lifted her chin. She had to show him he couldn't scare her. "I brought you these, but I don't know if you deserve them."

"Forget-me-nots? Are you trying to say something with these?" He clasped his palm around the back of her hand and bouquet, anchoring her fist to his chest. Tingles shot down her arm as he released her hand and took the bouquet.

How much longer could she take this sort of torture?

Her parents had been reluctant to let her come this year. She had to prove to them that she was capable of going out in the world without being ruined forever, but the one person who could destroy her chance was the man before her. "You can't scare me. No matter how hard you try."

"Is that a challenge, my love?" A smirk formed on his perfect lips.

"I'm not your love." Frankly she was damned tired of his smug looks. Maybe she could slap it off, but then he'd only take her outburst as a challenge to tame her or some such nonsense. *Incorrigible blowhard.* "And no. It is *not* a challenge."

"I think it is. I accept."

Blasted! She held back the urge to growl. The man was infuriating. "No you don't. I didn't challenge you."

"I think you did. You'll find I can be a better lover than any fool you've courted thus far. Even with all my...faults."

"I've never had a lover, and I won't take one now. I'm not one of your strumpets."

He reached out and wrapped his hands around her waist, tugging her hard toward him. "No one said you were a strumpet, but by the end of the season you will be ruined for all men but me."

"You're a monster." She tilted her head to the side and silently challenged him to argue.

He glowered, the glare in his eyes tempered with rage, and with one hand shoved the flowers in the inner pocket of his jacket. With the other he pushed her away and turned to snatch up his ax.

Her heartbeat returned to normal, but a different sort of ache took residence in her stomach, and her body grew cold where they'd touched mere moments before. She'd hurt him with her words, albeit unintentionally. "I didn't mean it the way you think."

He ignored her and chopped the tree. The sound echoed the beat of her heart, quick but steady. "Simon, please? I didn't mean to call you a monster."

He stopped, grasped the ax near the head, and turned. "It's what I am. I just never thought I'd hear you say it."

"That's not true. You're Simon Sanders. A little free with your love of women, but a good man."

He chopped once more, turning his back on her. "I'll never be who I was, Carrie. The world won't let me. You need to accept that."

"Missoula social circuit, perhaps not, but this world." She motioned toward the tops of the trees surrounding them. "This world, and all of us down there at camp need you. Violent moods and everything."

He continued with his work. His gaze focused on only the tree.

After a few moments of silence, she shuffled her feet. "I suppose I should get back. Aunt June wants me to return before dark. She wanted me to tell you that she'll have your favorite breakfast ready at sunup." Carrie pivoted and located the trail.

"Wait."

She stopped and turned to him, only a few feet farther than she'd been. "Yes."

"Stay." He motioned toward the trail with a flick of his hand. "I'll take you to camp once I finish this tree."

The tree towered above her, a notch weakening the base. She grasped her fingers with her opposite hand and blinked a few times. "Is it safe? I don't want to die out here."

"You're safe with me. Always will be."

"All right." She settled on a nearby log to watch. She doubted his words were true. In matters of the heart, he was the most dangerous man on the earth. She smiled as he placed his palm over the pocket holding the flowers as if checking for them, then turned back to his task.

They didn't speak, didn't need to. She waited as he took out what remained of his aggression on the base of the towering pine. If he didn't make good on his promise of lustful bliss, they would be fine. She didn't know what she'd do if he seduced her. As tempting as it was to fall into the arms of a rogue like Simon Sanders, she couldn't give in to his spell, else she'd lose everything she'd worked hard for as a single woman in a wild mountain town.

Chapter 5

Simon stood behind the men and watched as the Devil May Care boys challenged each other in their seasonal pecking order games. In years past he'd have been right there in the thick of it. Perhaps even throwing a few punches himself, just for fun. Not today. While the good-natured row did lighten his mood a bit, his mind wandered elsewhere. Lost somewhere between thoughts of making Carrie pay for her deception with sensual moans and boarding the first train off the mountain. But regardless of her lies and deceit, she was right. This place, with its towering pines and mist-filled mornings, did something inside his soul. It anchored him to the land and the world created within.

A cheer rose up among the men and drew his attention back to the games. As expected, Wall had beat everyone on both the log run and fisticuffs, and the only thing left was finding out who would take the position as his right-hand man. So far, Blue was in lead.

The competition ended with good-natured slaps to Blue's back and a few coins exchanged from bets placed, but work called. Simon caught Wall's eye and raised his head to beckon him closer.

Wall trotted up to him, and Simon motioned toward the rowdy crowd of men. "Looks like you got a fine team this year. Good men to ride the river with."

"If we get to ride the river." Wall turned his gaze to the mountain peaks, barely covered with what remained of the light snowfall the winter before. "The spring runoff is nearly over and we've only just begun with the warm season. If the rivers aren't deep enough we can't get the logs down that way."

"There's always the rails." Simon didn't mean to sound brash, but he couldn't help it. Not that it was Wall's fault Victoria had taken away half of his job, but he'd still been usurped by the leader of the Devil May Cares.

Wall studied his men busy chatting with their comrades. He took a step closer. "I'm going to have to go down the river with the boys and check out the water flow. Maybe clear a few blockages."

"Won't that leave the railroad loggers without a leader?"

He rubbed the back of his neck and stared at the ground. "Yeah, about that, I told Victoria you were more than capable of handling the timber beasts without me, but she insisted."

"I appreciate the confidence."

"You're a good timber beast," Wall said. "Everyone knows it, but there's a little more going on than you need to worry about. Just focus on the job."

Simon nodded. "As long as we're on the same page."

"We are. Victoria is back down at the mill. Aside from me bothering you to keep up appearances for her sake, once I get back I won't bother the beasts as far as work goes at the Rails or the Grove. You can have that. I will be around enough to keep Victoria happy, though."

"Whatever you need to do to please the boss lady."

"And protect Great Mountain."

Simon tilted his head. "Is there something going on I should be aware of?"

"Not anything Victoria and I can't handle."

"If you need me—"

"You've got your own problems. Starting with Miz Carrie, from everything I've seen the last few days."

Simon chuckled. "You're right about that. She's a handful."

"But well worth the effort from what I've seen. You seem to have something between you. Anyone who can put up with Elizabeth's antics, and be brave enough to drug you and drag you up here, must have guts of lead. You can't go wrong falling for a woman like that."

"Or a head full of oats, and there's nothing between us."

"So you say." Wall chuckled. "Either way, she's Beth's kindred spirit."

"I always was a glutton for punishment when it came to women."

"A glutton for something, but I don't think I'd describe your vices for women as punishment," Wall said.

Simon was about to respond when a flash on the hillside caught his attention. Every fiber of his body tensed when flames shot from beneath a log barreling down the new chute. "Sonofabitch! Teddy's done it again." He cupped his hand beside his mouth. "Oy, Teddy, grease the damn chute!"

The chute monkey didn't respond.

Simon shook his head and adjusted his footing. "If you'll excuse me, I've got to go up there. I swear the blasted man is hell-bent on starting a forest fire by not greasing the damned chutes."

"Do what you need," Wall responded and, with a wave, returned to his men as Simon headed toward the Grove.

What was Teddy thinking? Wall might be spouting fables of the past when it came to Simon's love of women—and relationship with Carrie—but he was right about one thing: the spring runoff was lower than usual. A dry winter meant a dry summer, and they now sat in a tinderbox of scorched, overgrown vegetation. If they weren't careful this year, the whole forest could go up in flames.

* * * *

Carrie dipped the bucket into the lake and heaved it up. The wooden panels groaned with the weight of the water as she adjusted her grip while searching her surroundings for a glimpse of Simon, but with no luck. He'd busied himself with work, and she was glad for it. Glad for a start to the rebirth of Simon Sanders, timber beast.

The rhythmic chop of the men busy at work sounded from somewhere deep in the trees on the hill. Closer still, the grate of a log against the chute demanded all who heard watch as a log barreled down the slide and landed with a loud splash into the lake.

Since she'd first entered camp the year before, she'd grown to love the simplicity of life here. There was no one to impress. While men were as prevalent as a worker bee in a hive, they didn't vie for her attention. Demand she have eyes only for them, or even attempt to court her. At least they hadn't last year. She had thought she and Simon had had a spark, but he'd never approached her with anything more than friendship. She'd realized then her feelings were a result of their circumstance and nothing more. It was for the best. And up here she was allowed to do as she wished. To live as she'd always wanted. Free. Single. And simple. Now if only Simon could find himself, she might get over the guilt she felt whenever she watched his soul mourn. She'd been the one to nurse him back to health. If she'd done a better job, perhaps she could have helped him ease into his new life with his injuries. But she'd failed him.

"Miz Carrie," a man's voice sounded behind her.

Water splashed from the bucket as she turned. "Good Lord, Thomas, you frightened me. I didn't know anyone was down here."

"We're taking a break, and came down to fill up our water pouches." He pointed at the man she recognized as Jake from Aunt June's blunderous dinner.

Carrie responded with a nod.

"Can I carry that for you?"

"It's not heavy." She adjusted it in her arms to hug the barrel. After her fight for independence, she didn't need a logger treating her as though she were a helpless, weak female.

"What sort of man would I be if I let you carry that all the way to camp?" Without giving her a chance to argue, he plucked the bucket from her arms as if it weighed close to nothing. He motioned toward the trail leading to Aunt June's cabin and cook fire.

Jake stood with a smile and watched her as though he'd never look away. She turned slowly to follow and hugged her light jacket closer to her body as a shiver ran down her arms. A quick glance behind showed Jake followed, still focused on her as they walked. He adjusted his knife and sheath along his back, and she snapped her head forward.

"Those were some good vittles you made the other day," Thomas said.

"I can't take all the credit. Aunt June is the cook at our camp. I merely help."

"Our cook isn't nearly as good as you."

"Aunt June did most of the work. Really." Carrie gave a forced smile. What was his aim giving her the compliments for something she didn't do?

"I'd like to see what else you women got cookin' over at the Missoula camp," he said.

"Aunt June makes those decisions. I'll let her know you're interested in tasting another one of her meals." If he mentioned Carrie's cooking again she'd scream. The man was incorrigible.

"I'd be mighty pleased if you would," Thomas responded. Thankfully not giving her more false praise.

Carrie peeked over to Jake as he stepped beside her, brushing his arm against hers. She mumbled the expected answer to Thomas as they stepped off the path into the cook camp. She pointed toward the fire. "You can set the water over there. Thank you."

"It was my pleasure, Miz Carrie." He set the bucket down. "If you ever need me to do anything else for you, let me know. There ain't nothing I wouldn't do for a woman who can cook as good as you."

"You're mighty fond of Aunt June's food, aren't you?" Carrie said, not bothering to check her manners. Why should she? She was in a logging camp for heaven's sake.

"I like the food, but I also like the cook." Thomas winked as his friend stepped up beside him, but Jake remained silent.

To Carrie's relief, Aunt June bustled out of the cabin holding a large cast-iron pot.

"Aunt June," she said, trying not to show the relief she felt at the woman's presence. "These gentlemen were impressed by your supper the other night and would like another taste."

"Would they now?" Aunt June heaved the large pot onto the table and stretched her mouth in one of her mischievous grins. "I think I might be able to find a spot at my table for two strapping young lads such as yourselves."

Carrie tried not to groan. The older cook wasn't going to quit. Once the men left, she'd need to have a talk with the meddling woman. She'd agreed to Aunt June's plan to get Simon up here, but that was as far as she went in forced compliance.

Thomas sauntered over to the fire and began to woo Aunt June with compliments, leaving the ever-silent Jake behind.

"Miz Carrie," Jake started, and then cleared his throat. "May I call on you tonight after you're done here?"

"Oh...I..." Carrie fumbled. "That's sweet, but Aunt June usually keeps me busy. I don't have the time to be courted this season. Perhaps if you're in town this winter I can save you a dance at the mayor's annual soirée."

The man's face grew red, and he rubbed the back of his neck. "I understand."

Although the logger made her uneasy with his silence and astute stare, she felt bad. One thing she hated in life was disappointment. "I'm terribly sorry."

He shook his head as Thomas returned. "We'd best get back to the Grove. Wouldn't want to tick off the Bull."

She nodded her goodbye and waited for the men to leave before turning to her godmother. "Please stop inviting them to supper."

"Oh, bosh." Aunt June swatted her with the towel she kept slung over her shoulder. "I'm not doing it to make Simon jealous. That is a happy extra. If the boys love my food, who am I to keep them from the eats?"

"There's something about the silent one that gives me the chills."

Aunt June studied the trail where the men disappeared. "He is a quiet one, but he's new. I suspect he's easing his way into the order of things."

"Or he's a rat." Carrie hung the large cast-iron pot over the fire and poured the water in to heat.

"That boy ain't no river rat. I've been with those men my whole life. That boy has the look of a timber beast. No way he rides the river. There ain't enough meat on his bones."

"Either way, he makes me uneasy. I'd best not be around him if it can be helped."

"After tonight, I promise I'll stop." Aunt June peered over Carrie's shoulder. "Now, while this water's heatin' for the soup, run on up to the chicken coop and get that straggly red girl who don't lay no more eggs."

Carrie's arms tingled, and she sucked her lower lip in to clench it between her teeth. Did Aunt June mean for her to kill the helpless animal? "Catch her?"

Her godmother handed her a small ax and a bag. "Take her to the block behind the cabin and chop off her head. Then yank out the feathers and put them in here. Mind you don't get blood on the feathers. I hate the smell of a rotting corpse when I'm trying to sleep."

"Aunt June, no, please," she pleaded.

"Get to it, girlie. If you're gonna be a cook in a lumber camp, you gotta learn where the food comes from."

Carrie took a deep, shaky breath, grabbed the tools Aunt June held out, and slowly headed toward the chicken coop a few hundred yards into the trees, near the makeshift horse stables. How was she going to get through this? Last year Aunt June would disappear from camp and come back with the meat, ready to cook. This was the first time Carrie had ever been asked to perform such a barbaric task.

In a few breaths, she stood before the small coop and searched for her intended victim, the poor lady. Going about her business, plucking away at the ground, only to be tossed in a pot of boiling water.

The chicken wobbled around from behind the shed, and Carrie's throat closed up. Unable to hold back a gag, she made her way toward the animal. The soft coo of other chickens sounded above her, and she glanced up to see three hens sitting haphazardly on a low-hanging tree branch.

She turned her attention back to the tattered red hen and crouched low as she stalked toward the animal. She had no more than a step to go to get her before the damned bird flapped her wings and ran away.

"Blast!" Carrie cursed, dropped the ax and bag, and launched into a run after the chicken. She chased the hen, running in circles until she grew dizzy and her breath came in shallow bursts. Giving up, she plopped right down into the middle of the white-speckled, muddy hen yard and slouched her shoulders.

Something flew into her hair, and she tangled her fingers into her loose tendrils, only to feel a slimy puddle. She lowered her hand to stare at the white droppings on her fingers as a deep, masculine chuckle reverberated into her thoughts. Simon. Lounging against the horse shed, in all his arrogant glory.

"How long have you been there?"

"Long enough to enjoy the performance."

"And you didn't think I might want help?"

He stood upright as the chicken ducked past him. "Oh, I knew you wanted help. It was more fun to watch you wallow in the filth."

"How chivalrous," she mocked.

In only a few seconds, he scooped up the hen and tucked her into his arms like she was a precious gem he protected. "I take it we're having chicken for supper?"

She clambered to her feet, swiped fruitlessly at her soiled dress, and snatched up the ax and bag. "You're as observant as you are gallant."

"So you're either saying I'm not observant, or that your previous tone was a lie and you believe me to be a white knight."

"Uck," she said, and followed as he headed toward the back of the cook cabin. "You're incorrigible."

"I thought you loved that about me."

"I do." She stuck her tongue into her cheek. The way he carried himself, the smile flirting with his lips when he'd poked fun at her. He seemed lighter. Happier even. But if the last year had taught her anything, it was that his moods could pivot like a spinster in a room full of ruined debutants.

He gave her a lopsided grin as he stepped up to the log round used as a chopping block, and turned to plop the chicken down on the block, neck extended. "I hope you plan on changing before tonight." He held out his hand. "Do you want to do the honors?"

"Uh...I..." She bit her lower lip and took a deep breath. "Yes. I should. I am a cook. In all its disturbing definition."

He chuckled, snatched the ax from her hands, and just as quickly decapitated the chicken for her.

She squealed and stepped back as the head rolled past her shoes.

"You can do it next time. Ease into it." He set the limp body on the block, adjusted two logs near it, and motioned for her to sit. "You can start today with plucking."

Still stunned from the rapid murder of the helpless chicken, she slumped down onto the makeshift seat. She wasn't mad at him for doing what needed to be done. More stunned at the rapid way it had all transpired.

"Don't tell me you've never plucked a chicken." He snatched the lifeless body from the log and dangled it by the feet.

"No. I haven't. I grew up eating chicken, but I've never butchered one."

"It's simple. All you do is hold it steady, and start yanking."

She took a deep breath to boost her determination, grabbed the chicken, and started plucking. After a few pathetic yanks, she glanced up at a smug Simon. "You're enjoying torturing me this way."

He stretched his legs out next to the chopping block and held out his hands in surrender. "I admit. I enjoy watching you bask in all your newfound squalor. It gives me some sick sense of satisfaction. Justice, maybe?"

"You, sir, are the backside of the chute monkey's horse."

"Such an eloquent way to insult me. I'll take it."

She yanked again at the chicken feathers. "What a mood you're in today. Almost the man I knew last year."

At that, his smile turned to a scowl.

She frowned with him. "And then I had to ruin it by saying something."

He kept silent, but his sour look lasted only a few moments before his expression grew blank. "I'll leave you to your bird, but if I were you, I'd clean up before tonight. Chicken droppings on a cook are not appealing."

"I'll clean myself up before supper. I am a woman after all."

"I don't care about how you look at supper. It's after you're done with your evening chores that I'm talking about."

She tilted her head. "Why?"

"Don't tell me you don't remember my promise?" He pursed his lips as if holding back a wolfish smile. "Never mind."

She mentally fumbled through every excuse she could think of to avoid what he no doubt referred to. She could fake an illness, disappear, or flat-out tell him to leave her alone. Then again, a part of her wanted to feel the experienced touch of Simon Sanders. The part of her that erred on the side of wickedness. No. A secret moment with Simon could never happen. She turned the chicken over in her hand and frowned. "You got blood on the feathers."

Simon laughed as if he could read her thoughts. "Just pick the bloody ones out before you put them in the bag."

Without another word, he disappeared around the cabin, leaving her to pluck the chicken alone. He had to be joking, right? He wouldn't make good on his ill-made promise. Would he?

Chapter 6

"Miz Carrie." Thomas handed her his plate. "Would it be all right with you if I were to come visit tonight? We'd stay near Aunt June, of course. Wouldn't want anyone thinking anything untoward of you."

Oh, good Lord. This was all Aunt June's doing, no doubt. "I came up here to get away from that for a bit."

"I won't take no for an answer. Even a woman as hardworking as you needs to have fun once in a while." He winked.

Carrie smiled at the easy way he spoke, but that didn't mean she wanted a beau. "I'm afraid you're going to have to take no for an answer."

"Well, I'll have to come back tomorrow and see if you've changed your mind." His eyes twinkled with mischief and challenge.

Carrie was about to respond when Elizabeth's voice sounded behind her. "Everything is ready for you. Garrett is filling it now."

"For what?" Carrie slid the last of the dishes in the crate. What on earth was Beth talking about?

"If you'll excuse me, ladies. I need to speak with those gentlemen over there." Thomas bowed and turned toward a group of loggers huddled around the fire.

Carrie waited for him to leave before turning back to Beth. "What is ready?"

"Your bath. Simon said you wanted to bathe and asked if you could borrow the tub in our caboose."

"He did?" She crossed her arms over her chest. Who was Simon to set up such an intimate affair for her? Of course, a bath in Beth's giant tub sounded divine. She could have arranged it herself. The damned man planned to tempt her tonight. She narrowed her eyes and leaned over so she could better view the group of men ten feet away, by the fire. "Thomas, if you want to meet me by the fire in an hour, Aunt June plans to bring out her knitting. I think she'd love to sit with us."

A grin stretched across the young logger's face. "I'll be here."

"Splendid." Carrie stood straight and faced Beth. "I'll take that bath. Thank you."

"What's going on?" Beth asked.

"I suppose your brother is being a good friend by setting a bath up for me, but I didn't request one. I was caught off guard, is all."

Beth turned toward the railcar. "Don't let him push you around. He can be a bully at times."

"Don't worry about me. I can handle your brother." Carrie smelled the arm of her still soiled dress. "But he is right. I do need to clean up."

"Leave your clothes outside the bath chamber and I'll wash them for you. You can wear some of mine. I'm about to do some wash anyway."

"I still can't believe Garrett bought you such an extravagant railcar."

"It was a wedding present from him. He said if we were going to live on the mountain as a couple, then at least we could do it in style." Beth opened the door to their locomotive home. "It's an improvement from the bath I had last year in Seeley Lake."

"If it wasn't for you, my life would be boring." Carrie followed and tried not to sigh in satisfaction. A sitting area took up half the space within the railcar. Candles sat on sconces lining the walls, leading to a door halfway through the car.

"The bath is back there to the right of the bedroom. You can wear any of my clothes while I wash yours, or I can go fetch your spare dress. I wear trousers when I'm working on the mountain so I have little use for my wardrobe." Beth walked into the backroom and returned with a wicker basket full of mud-caked clothes. She set it along the wall near the door. "I'll leave you to your bath, but put your dirty clothes in here and I'll be back in a few minutes for the wash."

"I think I'll borrow one of your dresses. Thank you."

Beth headed toward the door. "If you need anything, let me know."

Alone, Carrie walked into the small but comforting bathroom and eased the door shut. The tub stood near the wall, filling the room with steam. Last year, she'd sponge-bathed in Aunt June's cabin, but this was a far cry better than a rag and pot of warm water.

A towel and bar of soap had been laid out on a stand next to the washtub and she recognized Beth's favorite scent. Not that she hated the fragrance.

The main door to the railcar squeaked, and Carrie quickly undid her buttons down the front of her dress and stepped out of the top. Wrapping the towel around her, she grabbed the filthy dress.

"Beth, would you mind grabbing my soap from Aunt June's cabin?" She struggled to hold her towel closed as she opened the door, leaned out, and dropped the dress in the basket.

"If you wanted your lesson earlier, all you had to do was ask." Simon's voice sent shivers down her exposed skin. Her stomach flipped and she snapped her gaze to the man now taking up all the space in the car. A smug grin dimpled his cheeks, and his eyes shone with mischief and passion. A look she'd only seen him wear once. In his parlor the night she drugged him.

"Simon!" She popped her head back into the room and slammed the door. "What in the blazes do you think you're doing? Get out!"

His footsteps grew louder until he stopped next to the door. "You don't really want that, do you? For me to leave?"

"Yes, I do. Who in Hades let you in?"

"I apologize. I thought you were still helping Aunt June. I didn't know you were already in here. I have to do some darning tonight on my socks. I stopped by to get my sister's sewing supplies. May I have them? You'll find the kit on a shelf in the corner."

Carrie searched the room frantically and found the offending kit. She focused on the door knob. "Now. Go away before someone sees you in here with me."

"Oh, now. You know you want me to stay." She heard his jacket rub against the wood panel of the door as if he leaned onto it. "It's not like I won't see every inch of your body in a few hours."

"I want you to leave, and you will see nothing of my body. I know you set this bath up for me so you could try to seduce me later, but it won't work."

"Then why did you take the bath?"

"Because I am a woman."

"Every inch a woman…from what I saw."

"You're a pig."

"All men are."

"Fine." The rustle of his clothes against the wood sounded again as he stood. "I'll send Beth with your soap."

"No. Then she'll know you were in here."

"I don't want to smell my sister while I'm kissing you. I'll send the soap. Don't worry, I'll be discreet."

"Leave it be, Simon," she yelled, but knew it was fruitless. "Please? My reputation will be ruined."

"By the end of the season, that will happen anyway. You wanted me here; well, here I am. This *is* what you wanted, isn't it? Me in all my carnal arrogance. Pony up, Carrie, it's the law of the harvest. You reap what you sow."

"You reap it!" she exclaimed, but it was too late. His footsteps receded along with any hope that she would come out of this situation without struggle. The damned man planned to make good on his promise to seduce her. She was doomed.

* * * *

Night settled over the forest, leaving the trees menacing pillars of ink against the moonlit night sky. Carrie stepped tentatively from the railcar and surveyed the dark. Yards away the flicker of Aunt June's fire bounced off the low-hanging branches of the trees surrounding the camp. Men moved among the firelight doing whatever last-minute chores they needed to do before settling into their bunks for the night, their usual nighttime routine up here on the mountain. Some men sharpened their tools, some moved toward the bunkhouses no doubt to play cards or whatever nightly entertainment men were apt to do.

Carrie headed toward the fire as a shadowy figure stepped before her. She skidded to a stop and clasped at her racing heart at the abrupt intrusion.

"I thought you weren't entertaining beaus up here." Carrie recognized Jake's voice but couldn't see his face. Pinpricks tingled her hands as her heart continued its riotous speed.

"I'm not…that is…I've only agreed to sit with your friend next to the fire to talk."

"And the rest of them?"

"The rest of whom?"

"The men who said they are next to court you."

"I've no idea what you are speaking of, but I can assure you that I have made no promises to court anyone here."

"Shouldn't you be gettin' on to the Bonner camp, Jake?" Simon's voice boomed from the dark trees beside her. "If it gets too dark you may get lost up here. It would be a shame to find your dead body once the sun comes up."

The Bonner man gave a small growl and disappeared into the shadow of the trees. Simon's hand skimmed her back as he stepped around her to stand where the other logger had been. "Are you all right?"

"Yes. He gave me a scare is all." Carrie sucked in a deep breath to ease the knot in her stomach that had formed.

"If he bothers you again, tell me. I'll take care of him."

"I'll be fine. He may be a bit intense, but he's harmless."

"You give my sex too much credit, madam. No one here is harmless." The deep timbre of his voice sent goose bumps up her arms. "Promise you'll come to me if he harasses you again."

"If it will calm your conscience, I promise."

"Splendid." He stepped forward until the heat from his body replaced the gentle mountain breeze tickling the front of her body. "The man put a damper on our evening, didn't he? No matter. I've got ways to make you forget about him." Simon's warm hand grabbed her elbow and slid sensually up her arm, and back down.

Like times before, her body responded with wanton anticipation. Craving the gentle touch so many before her had experienced, she couldn't give in. "What makes you any better than Jake? At least he is blunt about his desires where you merely play games."

"Trust me, my love, any game I want to play with you is well worth the effort. I'm nothing like that man. One night with me, and your life will change forever."

"Why are you doing this?"

"To make you suffer, the way I do. You cannot command my life against my will and expect to not pay the price. The price of your control over me is your body."

"You can't have it. And I'll not give in to your silly rules."

"You set the tone of this game, not me."

"I have an engagement to be to."

"Yes. With me."

"No. With Thomas."

An almost inaudible chuckle reverberated from Simon's chest and made her want to growl.

"Well played, my love," he said.

"Stop calling me 'my love.' I am not your love, and the way you say it makes me think you've practiced that endearment on many women in your past."

"What would you prefer me to call you? Lover?"

"You're an infuriating man." This time she let out the growl pawing to get out and stepped around Simon, intending to stalk away. She'd taken a few steps when she heard his heavy feet behind her. She spun around. "Where are you going? Isn't your cabin the other way?"

"It is. But I plan to counter your move with one of my own."

"What move?"

He pressed his hand to her back, urging her to continue toward Aunt June's fire. "If I told you then it wouldn't be as effective. Please, proceed. Your weakling beau awaits."

"Go away," she commanded, and snapped her focus to the fire. Thomas sat near Aunt June, poking a stick in the flames. The poor young man. She wasn't interested in anything but one well-chaperoned conversation with him. And only agreed to it out of desperation. Half to ease his curiosity about courting her, and half to show Simon he didn't dictate where she went or who she went with. But the blasted man was hot on her heels, and sporting a smile similar to the one he had worn earlier in the day when he caught her with the chickens. One she hadn't seen on him since before his accident. Either he was starting to get better, or he'd been driven mad by their scheme. So which was it? Dear Lord, she hoped the former.

They entered the firelight, and Thomas stood from his position on the log. She settled next to him as Simon took a seat on her opposite side. Nearby Aunt June knitted, using the firelight to see her needles.

Carrie gave Thomas an apologetic smile and turned to Simon. "I thought you had some socks to darn."

"Oh, no, I don't. Turns out they're fine the way they are. Funny how things have a way of fixing themselves."

"What?" Carrie glared and whispered, "You're an ass."

"No. I'm a monster. Remember?"

She turned back to Thomas. "My apologies. Mr. Sanders here is a friend and has lost his manners."

"No apology necessary on your part, Miz Carrie," Thomas said. "I haven't known Mr. Sanders to practice manners since the first time I met him."

"You're both wrong." Aunt June dropped her knitting in her lap. "Simon has plenty of manners. I've even seen him use them a time or two. He simply chooses not to most days."

"I've always said Aunt June is an astute woman." Simon stretched one leg out in front of him but kept the other bent.

"Well, you're a cheeky fellow tonight." Aunt June grinned and picked up her knitting.

Carrie smiled at the easy way they bantered. It had been a long time since Aunt June and Simon had shared the good-natured ribbing they were known for giving each other in camp. And just as long since Simon had smiled. Yet he seemed to have done a lot of grinning that day. Carrie tried not to let her face show her confusion as she stared at the man in question. Why was he happy all of a sudden?

Thomas cleared his throat and turned slightly toward her. "Miz Carrie. What sort of interests do you have?"

"I'm afraid at the moment my only interests lie in cooking for a passel of lumberjacks."

"And in town?" Thomas shifted in his seat.

"Other than the usual social niceties, I don't do much."

"You have to have something that interests you outside the normal everyday hum."

"None that come to mind." Carrie glanced between Simon and Aunt June. She couldn't tell Thomas her last year had been spent obsessing over Simon's health, or her free time spent bringing him flowers. What sort of tattle would that cause? She really must refocus her attentions in town.

Simon snorted, and Carrie darted her gaze to him. She grabbed a fistful of her skirts to hold back her response to his sound.

"I beg your pardon?"

"You are being too modest." He sat up straighter and pulled his feet in closer to the log. "You always seem to be busy whenever I see you in town."

Carrie's skin heated, and she lifted her head, hoping the movement would loosen her clothing from her skin enough to let the cool night air circulate and cool her blush. The man was relentless in his quips and secret implications. If the Lord was on her side, Aunt June and Thomas would be oblivious to his real meaning. Being that the only time she'd ever seen him in town was in his home. At least once while he made a malicious attempt at seduction.

"And they are?" Thomas asked.

"Let's see. She likes to take in stray pets, especially small dogs. She's a very curious woman, adores botany and psychology, and she dabbles in anatomy." Simon gave a grin that made her want to forget all rules of propriety and punch him straight in the nose, followed by a well-placed kick to his shins, or higher.

Thomas jerked his head back in surprise. "You like the sciences?"

"I, uh, yes," she lied. The only truth behind Simon's reply was her love of small animals. Everything else was aimed at making her squirm. And it worked. She struggled to keep her body still so as not to give him the satisfaction of knowing he'd affected her. "But it goes no further than a curious mind."

"Nonsense," Aunt June joined in. "She has been educated quite soundly in the principle of causation. As in, if a man and a woman are meant to be, but they do not act on their affections, then they will live a lonely and miserable life. Even if they marry another."

"Really?" Thomas asked. His eyes creased at the corner, and a smile curved at the edges of his lips, as evident by the shadows playing in the firelight on his face.

Oh good Lord, Carrie thought. What was Aunt June doing? Giving the poor man hope while speaking, not so subtly, to Simon? Carrie turned her attention to Simon, who, by the scowl on his face, seemed oblivious to Aunt June's true intent. She needed a reprieve from what was shaping up to be quite an irritating evening. She covered her mouth and gave what she hoped was a realistic-looking yawn. "Oh, I apologize. It's been a long day."

"Tired?" Thomas asked. His shoulders and head dropped. "I'll walk you to your cabin. If that's all right with Aunt June?"

"Of course. It's not like I can't see you from here."

At that, Carrie stood and brushed off her skirts.

Thomas stood, followed by Simon.

"Oh, no you don't," Aunt June said, and leapt up to bustle over to him. "You leave those two alone. They don't need you getting in the way."

Simon held out his hands in surrender. "I wouldn't think of helping Carrie do a simple task like walk. I know all too well she's capable of doing that on her own."

Like she'd done when they were children, she shielded her face from all but him and stuck her tongue out, which caused Simon to chuckle under his breath and wink.

Holding back a growl, she turned back to Thomas. "Don't pay him any mind. He's just mad that we drugged and kidnapped him."

Thomas's brows pinched together in confusion. Carrie motioned for them to proceed, and they left Simon behind. Explaining the last few weeks, and her intentions, to Thomas was not on her list of things to do. Using one to get back at the other was, however. In a few breaths she stood before the door to the cabin she shared with Aunt June. She'd lied, and right straight through her teeth.

"I suppose I should say goodnight now," Thomas said. "I'll be back tomorrow evening. Hopefully Simon will have found something else to occupy his time."

"Tomorrow?" Where in the world had she found this Pandora's box? She should never have encouraged anyone's affections, let alone a young, amorous logger.

"After supper." He reached up and traced the side of her face with his thumb. His rough, callused hand grated on her sensitive cheek like sandpaper on a tabletop. Not something she wanted to feel for the rest of her life. He leaned down as if to take the liberty of a kiss, and she backed away—a smile hiding the sweat forming below her hairline. God was surely teaching her a lesson on the proper use of a man. And playing with one's affections to goad another was not on his list of approved applications. She should end this now and save the poor man a season of grief. "Unfortunately, I have a prior engagement with Beth tomorrow."

"Are you certain it's not Simon you are meeting up with tomorrow?" His voice was tinged with jealousy.

"I beg your pardon?"

"Nothing," he said, his voice calmer than before. "Sorry. But you two seem…familiar."

"We are dear friends, and nothing more."

"Are you certain?"

"He is Beth's brother, and I her best friend."

"Oh." He slid his hand down from her face to grasp her arm tight enough to cause her shoulders to rise and heartbeat to kick up. Whether the rough hold was supposed to be a show of passion or anger, she wasn't certain. The moment lasted only a second before he took a step back. "I'll let you to your evening. See you tomorrow."

At that, he pivoted and walked into the dark. Her heartbeat calmed, but not the niggling in the back of her mind. A cool breeze whisked across her heated face, but the reprieve wasn't near what she needed.

She searched the camp. In the firelight, Aunt June sat knitting, but Simon was nowhere to be seen. She stretched her senses to hear into the night. No sounds of men walking about in the dark. No one to intrude upon her time if she slipped down to the lake.

With one last glance at Aunt June, she snuck into the trees around the camp to skirt the firelight undetected. Any woman with common sense would forget all thoughts of traipsing about the forest alone at night, but she was Elizabeth's friend, after all. Common sense had left her friend long ago, and she was deftly afraid she'd been affected by the same affliction.

But then again, up here, instinct was more important than a sound mind. Now the question remained, did she trust her instinct?

Not really.

Her instincts told her to kidnap Simon and skirt him deep into a forest. All that had done was place a target right smack in the middle of her heart while a bunch of loggers forged their own bow and arrows. Well, she wasn't going to leave this summer with anything but her heart and innocence intact. No matter who tried to win her favor.

Chapter 7

Simon chewed on the apple he'd stolen from Aunt June's stash after leaving the fire and waited outside the camp. Far enough away to not be seen by Carrie or her new beau, but close enough to ensure the fool left her untouched at the door. He'd never had a bad experience with the fellow, but that didn't mean he trusted him. He didn't trust any man who showed an interest in Carrie, especially a logger. How many times in the past had he needed to run off some overenamored suitor not nearly good enough for his sister's best friend?

Too many times to count on one hand.

Carrie could never know.

Movement near Aunt June's door brought his mind to the present, and he stood upright as Thomas disappeared behind Aunt June's home, leaving Carrie standing alone outside. Simon tossed his apple into the brush and was about to head toward his bunk when, instead of slipping into the house like a proper woman should, Carrie turned and disappeared into the vegetation opposite where he stood.

"What in blazes is she up to now?" he muttered, and pushed himself up from his lounged position against the tree. The firelight caught a flicker of color as she stepped onto the trail leading to the lake. *The blasted woman.* She wasn't like Beth. She didn't go looking for trouble, but that didn't stop her from stumbling onto it.

He hid in the shadows of the trees as he followed her toward Seeley Lake, all the while keeping an eye out in case Thomas had doubled back. Instant pain pierced his stomach. What if she was skirting away for a tryst with the young logger? His neck grew hot and he undid the top button of his thick, flannel shirt. After seeing Carrie chase the chicken earlier, his mood had lightened, and all he could think about was making the difficult woman swoon beneath his lips as he showed her what a man truly was. That mood had carried over for the remainder of the day, shocking even him. It had been over a year since a whole day had gone by with no northern storm extinguishing the light in his soul. Perhaps Carrie was the key to remembering who he was.

He stepped out into the clearing until the flat, shimmering lake filled his view. Beside it on the bank, Carrie knelt down and splashed water over her face, then sat back on her heels. Thomas was thankfully absent.

"You're determined to kill yourself out here." He said the words more to startle her. While a small amount of danger existed between the cook camp and the lake, it wasn't like the Grove. Instant red didn't flash before his vision when he thought of her traipsing about the banks of the lake the way it did other parts of the forest.

"You frightened me." Carrie grasped the cloth to her dress between her breasts and drew his attention. He wasn't interested in winning her hand the way some of these fools were, but the thought of feeling her beneath him as he showed her the path to heaven—and while he reclaimed his soul with her body—appealed to him greatly. She needed to be taught that you couldn't mess with other people's lives the way she had his, but no one said he couldn't enjoy his time while he tutored her. And now was the perfect time to start.

"You frighten easy." He stepped toward her, bowing his head slightly and intentionally taking his time to make her feel the need to succumb to his wishes.

She stood tall, faced him, and met his hard stare with one of her own. *Good girl.* She challenged him. A move he loved in a game of cat and mouse. A woman who would test his skills. His heart started to pound, and he grew hard. "Where's your lover?"

"You well know he is not my lover."

"Ah, but you agreed to let him court you?"

She shuffled her feet. "I agreed to meet him by the fire to get to know him."

"Tell him to shin out."

"I will not tell him to run away."

"You will, my love." Without another word, Simon walked toward her, wrapped his arms around her back, and tugged her close. Lowering his mouth to within an inch of hers. "You're going to be too occupied with me this season to bother finding a husband."

"I don't want a husband." Her hot breath bounced off his mouth, and he closed the distance. Pressing his lips to hers. The words she muttered made him smile. If she didn't plan to marry, then maybe a little tryst this season could benefit them both. Her lips firmed and relaxed beneath his, evidence of her hesitation, so he squeezed her closer and deepened the kiss.

The rigid muscles beneath his palms relaxed, and she softened into him. He moved one hand toward her lower back and the other to the base of her skull to gently tug at her hair. Thankfully taking his urging, she eased her head back and bared her neck to him.

Her chest heaved with fast, passion-filled breaths. His inner beast roared with satisfaction. She was his. Even if she didn't know it yet and didn't realize the small movement of acceptance she gave meant something deeper.

He dipped his head and forged a trail of kisses down the sensitive lines of her neck to end at the dip above her clavicle. She clutched his shoulders, and her breath grew frantic, so he returned to her mouth. Devouring her breath as he gave her a taste of the future.

Not the now.

He stretched the moment until even he was about to lose all sense of control, then pulled back. Their chests heaved in unison as he stared into her perfect face. For years he'd fantasized about the feel of her lips beneath his, but never in his dreams had it been like this.

She reached up and traced her finger along his scar. He flinched to pull away, but she pressed her hand gently over the side of his face. "You mustn't do that again."

He tipped the corners of his lips back in a grin, but an ache began at the back of his throat at the thought of not kissing her again. He swallowed hard. "You're mistaken. You've crossed the point of no return. There's no going back."

"Please, Simon," she pleaded, her voice soft like the contours of her lips. "You can't do this to me. It's cruel."

He pulled her closer, but didn't kiss her. "The only thing cruel about this situation, my love, is that we've never given in to temptation before. Not that I haven't wanted to."

She pushed back against his chest enough to grow a few inches between them. "Then why haven't you said anything?"

"Because I'm not the man for you."

"Because of your scars? You know I don't care about that."

He dropped his hands and stepped back. Cold mountain air replaced her blessed heat. "Even before that. I've never been a man deserving of your affection."

"Don't you think I'm the one to decide that?"

"No."

"No?" She lengthened the distance between them with a few steps. "You must be joking."

"Women make decisions with their emotions, men with their heads. I do believe I have a better sense of who is right for a woman like you. And I am not, my love."

"Don't call me that, and don't fret. I wouldn't choose you even if you weren't my best friend's brother."

She'd intended to wound him with her words, and it worked. Much to his irritation. He didn't want to curse her with his reputation in town, not to mention his appearance, so why did her rejection hurt? What a ninny Carrie made him. A man he didn't recognize.

"If you'll excuse me." She stepped past him. "I need to get to bed."

She left him standing like the fool he'd turned into ever since his parents' deaths. He was a bounder not fit to have the only woman he truly wanted, and a man not strong enough to resist the temptation. Despite the potential hazard to her reputation and livelihood. The real reason he was the monster everyone believed him to be.

* * * *

"Beth," Carrie called out when her friend appeared in the line of men filing toward the wash bin to dispose of their dirty tin plates. Ever since she'd lied to Thomas the night before about having an appointment with her friend, she'd all but picked her apron to threads. Her friend moved down the line toward her and slid her utensils into the water. Carrie looped one arm with Beth's and guided her off to the side of the crowd. "You aren't busy this evening, are you?"

"Garrett and I were going to take the wannigan out across the lake." Beth lowered her chin. "Why?"

Carrie took a quick survey of the crowd to ensure Thomas hadn't appeared out of nowhere. "I may have lied to a man about why I wasn't available to sit with him by the fire today. I said you and I had planned to do something."

Her friend feigned surprise with a dramatic gasp and clasped a hand to her chest. "Beating the devil around the stump are we? Avoiding your responsibilities as Missoula's most sought-after wifely prospect? How dare you?"

"Please," she begged. "I'm desperate enough to swim out to the boat and join you and your husband if you leave me with no choice."

Beth chuckled. "No need. I'll tell Garrett he'll have to join the men in the bunkhouse for cards."

"You will?" To say she spoke the word with poise and dignity would be incorrect. With those two words, she begged. Pleaded for her friend to keep good on her word, and made promises to the most mischievous woman in Missoula. Promises she knew would get her in trouble later.

"You've certainly covered for me on several occasions. It's only right I return the favor."

Carrie once again looped arms with her bosom friend. "I knew we were kindred spirits for a reason."

Beth chuckled. "I'll wait for you to finish. Meet me by the water. Garrett wants to go right now and check out the raft. He swears he's happy working with the railroad loggers, but he misses being a riverman."

Carrie peered at the sun slanting low in the sky. "Give me thirty minutes."

She rushed to her wash bin and started scrubbing. At least she wasn't lying to anyone. If her mother—and Beth's many antics—had taught her anything in life, it was that a lie would always turn its ugly head and bite you in the bustle. This way her soul and conscience were clean.

In no time at all she stowed the box of tins and, with a quick excuse to her godmother, hurried toward the lake. As promised, Beth waited at the bank next to her husband. What she didn't expect was to see Simon with a peavey, adjusting a second bateau next to the first.

Carrie trotted up to her friend as prim as the uneven ground would allow her. Before she could speak, Beth waved toward her brother. "Change of plans. The river crew took the wannigan and left behind the bateaus when they went downstream. Simon suggested we all go across the lake together. He wanted to familiarize himself with the bateau again in case he has to stand in on the river crew later."

Carrie squinted at the man in question. The irritating, controlling, wounded man. "I wasn't aware Simon was a riverman."

Simon pulled the boat higher on the bank to stabilize it from the flowing water, and then walked up to stand beside her. "You never know when you might need to help out a Devil May Care. They are a needy bunch of debutants. Always demanding we timber beasts give them more logs to take down the river."

"One of these days you're going to be a Devil May Care. If you're not careful with your words now you'll be walking the banks with the river rats."

"I suppose women much prefer a man who can stay on for more than a few minutes." Simon winked.

Beth gasped and swatted her brother's chest with the back of her hand. He flinched, but smiled as Garrett chuckled. Beth smacked him again. "Carrie may be my friend, but she's still a lady."

"My apologies," he said. "I forgot you aren't as brazen and uncivilized as my sister."

"It's fine," she said, and motioned toward the bateau. "I suppose Beth can take me in one, and the men in the other."

"Nope." Simon stalked past her, his head bowed so they made eye contact as he walked past. She followed his movement as he took a stance next to the boat. "You're with me."

Carrie stiffened. Alone in a boat with the one man on earth who made her feel like she was a riverman riding a log down an uncontrollable river. She'd traded a chance to be uncomfortable next to a fire with Aunt June's hawk-like control for one on a boat with Simon. Her mouth watered as the image of his kiss the night before replayed through her memories.

She'd been kissed before, but never like the one she had experienced last night. Never had a man stolen the breath from her lungs and masked the wicked sensation with the hazy need for the feel of his mouth. His hot tongue had traced her lips and urged her to open for him. She'd wanted to. In that moment some primal seductress, chained to the post of chastity within her, fought to break free and let her best friend's brother take her to a place no proper woman should ever visit. Last night, for the barest of seconds, he'd persuaded her to question the need for propriety. Would anyone have known if she'd given in to Simon? He'd been with many women in need of discretion. Surely he could show her how to give in to temptation without so much as a watchful owl knowing she'd given herself to him.

No.

Riding in a boat, alone, with Simon Sanders was dangerous.

She shifted her stance, forced her breath to remain even, and feigned curiosity with her expression—or at least she hoped that's how her face read. "Doesn't he need to be tutored by Garrett?"

Garrett chuckled and climbed into the boat next to Beth.

Simon held the boat steady and motioned for her to sit on the seat closest to where he stood. "Sorry to disappoint you, but I've already learned the ways of the riverman. I just need some practice."

"Oh." Carrie stepped tentatively toward him. Some would say he would not bite, but she knew different. If given the chance, the man before her would bite, lick, lave…whatever he needed to do to make her feel something other than complete control and comfort.

With care to avoid brushing shoulders with him, she climbed in and sat on the seat he'd indicated. She adjusted her skirts and sat, spine straight, folding her hands on her lap.

Simon tossed her a humored smile and launched the boat into the water following Garrett and Beth's.

She'd expected the ride to tick by with uneasy looks and a few awkward words, but before long the gentle pitch and roll of the small boat calmed her enough to slouch. Off in the distance an eagle screeched, and closer still the gentle lap of the water against the hull brought her mind to nothing but the sensation of the moment.

"See, my love, I'm not such a bad captain." Simon's voice broke through the silence.

She rolled her eyes at his newfound nickname for her. To argue, at this point, was naught but a waste of breath. "Have you commanded many ships at sea?"

"I can traverse any difficult water and bypass any obstacle before me."

"Will you be speaking to me with double implications all evening?"

"That depends."

"On?"

"On whether or not I get a chance to teach you the next lesson."

"Lesson in what?" she asked, despite knowing exactly what he was going to say.

"Seduction, but for now I'll settle with teaching you how to row." He yanked the oars in and tossed them at her feet. "Here, have a go. Just dip and pull the way you saw me do it."

"Dip and pull?" she asked, hesitantly. "And you're a madman if you think I'm going to let that happen again."

"Oh, I don't expect that to happen again."

"Good," she huffed, and struggled to get the hang of rowing. They seemed, instead, to float in circles. Which, by the look on Simon's face, amused him immensely. Perhaps she was wrong, and he meant something else, but she doubted it. He had a way of blacksmithing words to fit his iron-clad intent.

"I expect more."

"You won't get it." She dipped the oars in deep and pulled them at the same time. Sending the boat forward with force. She gave a smug smile, not bothering to hide her pride. It wasn't like Simon ever disguised his accomplishments behind an expression of humility.

"Haven't you realized by now that I love a good challenge? And besides working I have nothing else to do up here."

"So you aim to torture me into submission for the remainder of the season?"

"Yes. The way you tortured my life by bringing me up here."

"For your own good," she defended.

"And this will be for your own good."

"How is promising to ruin me out of spite going to help me in life?"

"Because at least once in your life you will experience true passion at the hands of a master."

"Such modesty. You're that confident in your abilities?" Heaven above, why was she being so brazen with her words?

"I've no complaints to date. Only satisfied moans." Simon waved toward the oars. "I'll take over now."

She handed him the oars and turned her gaze to the far-off mountains to hide the flicker of desire sparked by the banter. If Simon's kiss last night was a catalyst for what it was like to be loved by him, then his claim to passion wasn't in jest. Deep inside she wanted to feel the way he'd made her feel last night. Perhaps whatever husband she married would give her such pleasure. But what if she chose another path? What if she took Aunt June's position as confirmed spinster and Missoula camp cook? Then the one moment she'd shared with Simon last night would have to hold her over for the remainder of her days. Could she live with that?

She must.

Giving into Simon's spell again was out of the question. "You won't hear those moans from me."

"You're mistaken," he answered, simply. He maneuvered toward where Beth and Garrett floated. With a few deep strokes, they pulled near the other couple's boat. Simon inclined his head toward Garrett. "I'm gonna pull her into the cove over there. My shoulder scars are pulling something fierce."

Beth perked her head up. "Are you all right?"

He waved off her concern. "Yes, yes. I just need a break. Don't wait for us. I'll be back in when I've worked out the pain."

"Should we come in with you?" Beth asked.

"No." After a silent moment, he continued, "Don't worry about Carrie. I'll ensure she gets back safe. Tell Aunt June not to send a search party."

"Okay, but be careful coming back. It'll be dark soon."

"I can navigate in the dark, Lizbe," Simon replied, and then eased the boat in the direction of the nearby shore.

Carrie glanced behind to see Garrett and Beth turning toward the lumber camp. She faced Simon again. "How bad does it hurt?"

To her surprise, he answered with a simple, sensual smile.

Chapter 8

Carrie's white-knuckled grip on the seat beneath her rivaled that of a Gospel Sharp's clutch to his Bible come Judgment Day. With a single look, Simon had told all. Somewhere between the stinging nettle and marigolds, he planned to seduce her.

The boat jostled as it came to a rest on the bank. Simon leapt from his seat, secured the boat, and extended his hand to help her out.

She shook her head and tightened her grip on the wood. "Nope."

The blasted man gave a lopsided grin. "Scared?"

"No. Terrified."

He threw back his head and gave a deep, belly-rumble kind of laugh. Once he thankfully came to a stopping point with his boisterous chuckle, he dropped his hand. "Terrified of innocent ol' me?"

"You, sir, are anything but innocent."

He shrugged, grabbed the peavey and oars, and pivoted. In another breath, he pitched the line to the bateau inside the boat, successfully freeing it from the banks. "Suit yourself, but if you float out to open water you're on your own."

"And you'll be stranded here."

"Perhaps for the night, but I can find my way home in the morning." At that, he disappeared into the brush, leaving her to rock gently in the boat as it inched into open water with each ebb of a gentle wave.

Her face grew flush, and every creak of the trees in the forest and croak of the local frogs screamed in her ears. She scrambled to snatch up the line and jump from the boat. Water drenched the hem of her skirt as she secured the line. She searched the brush where he'd disappeared. "Wait!"

Carrie ran through the opening, following Simon's spiked boot prints. What in Hades was he thinking, leaving her stranded like that, and with predators behind every tree? Well, not every tree, but there were bears and cougars. Simon had proved that last year. And he was one of the strongest, most fearsome men she knew. Now he forced her to make a choice between giving into his wishes, or floating away to take on the predators of the lake. Were there predators in the lake? Did that story in the *Missoulian* last year about the man who saw a water monster take place in this lake, or one in some far-off country? Either way, it didn't matter. He'd tricked her into obedience. Okay, it was little more than she had done to him when she had lured him to Aunt June's house so they could chloroform him and skirted him away to camp. But still.

In a few steps, she saw Simon, and the rapid beat of her heart—along with the image of the water monster from the *Missoulian*—dissipated. He lounged against the trunk of a half-dead pine, the oars on the ground at his feet, as if he hadn't just left her for dead. The blasted man smirked. "I knew you'd see things my way."

She stopped in front of him and fought to catch her breath from the exertion of the small hike. "Don't start taking your boots off. I simply didn't want you to have to stay the night here is all. Feel free to return to the boat once you've rested your shoulder."

The sparkle in his eye deepened to a smolder, and his jaw firmed. The fading light from the sun shadowed the lines of his face and enhanced the scar across his cheek. Her fingers itched to run along the smooth lines of the healed wound. To take the pain of last year away with one swipe of her finger. If only she could ease his burdens like he had many times in her life. Then he'd be whole enough to find the man he once was meant to be.

The warm scent of his sweat, mixed with whatever soap he'd used to shave that morning, filled the space between them and calmed her. Although he spun her up like a cowboy's lasso with each display of masculine stupidity, he also had an uncanny way of making her feel at ease with nothing more than being near him. It was an internal battle that made her dizzy.

She threw her shoulders back and lifted her head to break the spell. "Whenever you're ready."

In one fell swoop, he stood straight and wrapped his arms around her waist, tugging her close. Her head fell back with the quick tug, and her breath stopped short of leaving her chest. She struggled to gain control of her breath enough to whisper, "Simon, please."

"You asked," he rasped, and covered his mouth with hers. That's not what she'd meant, but her body responded the way he no doubt wanted.

She wrapped her arms around his neck and pulled him closer. Lord above, the man would be the ruination of her in every way possible. Did she really need to keep herself pure if she planned to remain a spinster here at camp for the rest of her life? She'd never let her life be ruined by a husband. This was just passion and lust. Not love. Love was dangerous.

Yes.

The oath to her parents was only as solid as her resolve.

She pulled away from his kiss and let her head drop back. "Simon, please?"

He must have taken her plea for release as an invitation, for he ducked his head lower and forged hot, wet kisses down the side of her face and neck, leaving her breathless. Her senses played tricks on her she couldn't fight as they focused solely on the movement of his lips. The way her heart seemed to shine inside her chest, lending light and warmth to every inch of her core.

His tongue played with the lace on the collar of her dress while his hands slid naughtily down her back to cup her bottom. Her lungs demanded more air, and her vision blurred until all she could see was the top of his head as he popped the top button loose on her bodice.

With a quick tug, Simon lifted her enough to spin them both around and press her to the base of the tree without her feet even touching the ground. Her most private of places ached with a need she didn't fully understand, but the press of his leg between her thighs seemed to speak of promises that would satiate the throbbing need.

Carrie tried again to plead her case, to get Simon to leave her be, but this time the words went as far as her mind and no further. She couldn't speak. Could do nothing more than moan as he stood straight and, with one hand, unbuttoned the rest of her bodice, freeing her undergarments to the cool, dusky air.

"Beautiful," he purred, and slipped his hand beneath her chemise to cup her bare breast.

This time the air wouldn't flow through her lungs, through her blood. Her mind swirled around the feel of his hot, experienced hand on the sensitive peak of her breast. At that moment, she knew she was lost to a man so wounded he didn't even know how perfect he was to her. Flawless in every way. The perfect logger, man, and—she suspected—the perfect lover. She'd yet to experience the entirety of his loving, but she knew it too would stay with her forever.

She arched her back to press her breast even further into his palm. "I can't fight the way you make me feel, Simon."

"Then don't." He gave her a few quick kisses on her mouth. "What you'll have with me is something you won't regret." He kissed her again, and drew back. He lifted her higher against the trunk and pressed his body tighter against hers. With one free hand, he untied the ribbon to the collar of her chemise until her breasts sprang free.

She gasped at the sensation of being completely free to the world.

Simon growled in appreciation. "I'll show you what it's like to be the vixen you desperately want to be."

All she could do was answer with a shake of her head, which only made him dip his head and suck one extended nipple in his hot mouth.

Carrie gasped for air, but arched her back again. Her vision failed to allow her to see anything but the sparks of light from her charged core. She tangled both hands into his hair and held on, grounding her to the earth as he sucked and laved her nipples. She panted. He moaned and adjusted his grip to pin her to the tree with his body. One hand held her back, and the other explored one lonely breast while he teased the other.

She opened her mouth to take in a much-needed deep breath when Simon dropped her to the ground and stepped back.

Jostled, she struggled to bring her focus on the man before her. Illuminated by what remained of the light, he stood rigid and stared hard at something over her shoulder. She yanked her chemise over her breasts and buttoned her bodice. "What is it?"

"Sshh." He moved his head in inch.

She let her hearing stretch and realized the forest had gone quiet. No noise but the occasional creak of a tree lent to the night.

"Let's go," he commanded, and snatched up the oar and peavey in one hand and clasped her palm with the other.

She all but ran after him, his stride long and fast. Not quite running, but with a sense of urgency that made her heart beat hard in fear rather than lust.

Before she made full sense of what was happening, he lifted her onto the seat of the bateau, yanked the line free, pushed the boat into open water, and leapt in. Water from the leg of his pants splashed into the bottom of the boat, and he dug the oar deep into the lake.

She glanced back at the receding shore as her mind struggled to make sense of the moment. "Is something wrong?"

"Something felt off back there. Like it did the morning I got attacked. I didn't want to chance you getting hurt." He maneuvered the boat to head toward Aunt June's campfire, visible between the darkened trees.

"Oh," she managed to say through the range of emotions coursing through her body. The moonlight glittered off the lake where they traveled, but farther down the body of water the last breath of daylight reflected off the glassy surface. She'd never been out this late before in the wild, but the view lent a serene and calming effect. She could stay out here forever basking in the beautiful tranquility of the mountain night. The feeling interrupted only by the ebbing sensation of Simon's hands on her body and the tense moment following. What in the world had happened? She'd let herself go. Given in to the enchantment of the moment and forgotten who she was supposed to be. She couldn't let that happen again.

Chapter 9

"Garrett," Simon called out as his friend, and new brother-in-law, exited the railcar. Garrett stopped. Simon waited until he was close enough they wouldn't be overheard. "Do you have a spare pistol I can borrow for the season?"

His friend narrowed his eyes. "I do, but I thought you didn't like to carry a gun while working."

"I've changed my mind." Simon kept his face blank. The men in camp couldn't find out that ever since his accident he'd been deathly afraid of running into another cougar. Although rarely seen, the beasts did exist in these woods. And if his accident, and last night with Carrie, proved anything it was that he had to be ready for the unexpected. He'd only experienced the quick silence of the woodland creatures and thick atmosphere change once. On that fateful morning when his world had changed forever. He couldn't let that happen to anyone else in his life, especially Carrie.

Garrett nodded. The look in his eyes proved he understood. "It's under the mattress."

If there was one thing Simon could count on, it was Garrett's discretion. He didn't need to look like a scared debutant in front of his men and Carrie. While most loggers carried a knife on their belts, few toted around a gun. Then again, most stayed within the confines of their work zone and didn't wander into wild territory alone.

That's exactly what Simon planned to do. He needed to know what sort of predator had stalked them the night before, hiding out of sight as he and Carrie had their moment of passion. A moment he'd never forget.

"Are you going up to the Grove?" he asked, hoping the answer would work to his benefit.

"I hadn't planned on it. We're having some issues with the new machine. Haven't gotten a log onboard the train in two days, but I can swing by if you need me."

Simon shook his head. "No need to take an extra trip, but if you happen up there within the next hour or two, can you tell the Bull that I've gone to check out an area along the lake for our next clear-cut?"

"I'll catch him before he heads up there. He usually stops by the train first."

"Thanks," Simon said. "When I get back I'll stop by the Railroad Grove before I head up the hill."

"I could use a good hand. The machinist who helped Wall build the piece of tin has moved on to California. I'll need all the eyes I can get to fix the issue." Garrett nodded his goodbye as he brushed past on his way to the Railroad Grove, and Simon all but jumped onto the train to grab the gun hidden underneath his sister and Garrett's mattress. This whole blasted season was one for the books. They were supposed to be producing twice the amount of logs but had yet to get anything to the mill. Nothing was going as smooth as it had in years past. Except for last year when they'd had a small handful of saboteurs in their crew, they'd never experienced a season with so many blunders.

Once he secured the pistol, holster and all, to his belt, he left. If he was going to make it back in time for noon chow, he needed to get going. He wouldn't leave Carrie alone for the ever-present human wolves of the camp. She was finding her place as cook, but that didn't mean she belonged there. A woman like her, with her golden hair and steal-a-man's-soul desserts, seemed to attract every man she came across, and they needed to know she wasn't on the menu.

One of the two bateaus that the river crew left behind dipped with each small wave. He lengthened his gait. The other boat was noticeably absent from where he'd tied it up last night. Simon yanked the line free, leapt onboard, and started to row toward the bank where he'd tried to seduce Carrie the night before.

It took less than a quarter of an hour to traverse the waters to the bank and secure the boat. Once in the little patch of heaven where he'd finally been able to feel the soft skin of Carrie's bare breasts, he searched the ground and underbrush. Something had been out here last night stalking them. He'd felt it in the air. Smelled the dank scent of moldy vegetation mixed with an earthy smell he recognized but couldn't quite pinpoint.

Simon circled the tree where they'd stood, arcing out toward the direction the smell had originated. There on the ground, day-old bear droppings lay half-hidden beneath the grass. Unsure whether the bear had come through earlier in the day, Simon searched for clues.

He adjusted the gun and holster on his hip as he followed the telltale signs of the bear. Dipping down, he surveyed some disturbed ground under brush yards away from his new favorite tree. He'd expected sharp, clawed indentations; instead he found the hole-riddled footprint of a logger spiked boot too small to be his own. The broken grass beneath the brush gave the perfect outline of a man lying prone, watching the tree where he and Carrie had been.

Who the hell else had been out here? And when? Simon's neck heated, and he pinched his lips together. A few feet away a hand-rolled cigarette made with some sort of printed paper lay burnt almost to the end. Simon bent down and plucked it off the ground to study the hand-rolled cigarette. He growled. Had whoever lain here watched him undress Carrie? Had they seen her perfect body exposed to the night air? He threw down the smoke. If caught up with whoever had watched, the man would wish he'd met with a sheriff's hoosegow first. Simon might be injured, but that didn't mean he'd lost his strength. And with the rage boiling the blood through his veins, no man stood a chance. Especially a mudsill like a man who would lie beneath a bush to spy on another man seducing a woman.

Simon's stomach burned, mimicking the emptiness in his heart. He set his teeth until his jaw began to ache. Whoever it was, and whatever they had seen, he couldn't let this happen to Carrie again. He had to be more careful with her. And he certainly couldn't let her know that they'd been spied on.

A branch in the tree above cracked and a bird took flight. Simon moved toward the boat, and work. Whether the feeling he'd gotten the night before was from the bear or mudsill didn't matter. What did matter was Carrie. He couldn't let her be compromised while he punished her for bringing him to the increasing nightmare of a season. The mountain might have called to him in his youth, but did he feel the same about the Great Mountain Lumber Mill and his work as he had before? This season proved his life had changed forever. And not for the better. The only light he had in his life was Carrie. He couldn't lose her to some four-flusher logger—or the mountain.

* * * *

Carrie juggled the half-filled basket of huckleberries in her arms and searched the ground for more. Although a bit early in the season for such a delicacy, she'd stumbled upon a patch ripe enough to pick. One thing she'd gotten good at since last year was making huckleberry flap-jacks. The men devoured the sweet breakfast like the hungry loggers they were. She'd grown fond of her position here among the men. Most treated her like a sister or friend. On the other hand, a few chose to torture her with romantic requests and nonsense proposals. As if she'd come to a logging camp to find a husband.

Simon she excluded from the throng of suitors filling her days with angst. He was simply attempting to make her life difficult by any means necessary. And it had somewhat worked last night. Although now she had to avoid him for a day or two so she could set her runaway emotions right. The moment he'd kissed her, she'd lost all semblance of sanity. She'd become one of his harlots, basking in the way he made her feel with the skillful touch of his hands on her body.

Her breasts ached at the memory of his palm, warm against her nipples. At that moment, she'd forgotten why she had come to the camp and wanted more. In a forest full of predators, he was the most dangerous of all. And the one she needed to be around the most. The force behind Simon's touch fractured her resolve to remain strong. Somewhere deep inside, she wanted to give in to him, but she was a practical creature by nature. She needed to remember who she was in the face of Simon Sanders.

"Fancy meeting you out here." The high-pitched male voice broke through her reverie. She spun on her heels as Thomas's friend Jake stalked toward her with a strange glint in his eye.

"Oh, it's you." She grasped the base of her neck, then bent down to pluck a few from the bushel at her feet. "You startled me."

"Wouldn't want to do that." He stopped before her and simply stared. "It's been a few days since I asked you to marry me. So how's about it?"

"Marriage?" He couldn't be serious. A proposal in the teasing moments during chow was vastly different from one made in a grove. God, she hoped he didn't ruin berries for her. "Still no. Sorry."

"Ah, no matter." He grabbed her by the shoulders, causing the basket to topple from her fingers and berries to scatter along the ground.

"What are you doing? Let me go!" she demanded.

"I heard you don't mind being kissed. Maybe this will change your mind." At that, he pressed his dry lips to hers.

She choked back the vomit stuck in the base of her throat as he moved his mouth over hers and pressed to urge her to open up to him. Struggling against his grasp, she tried to step back.

Her mouth ran dry, and the ache in her arm grew as he tightened his grip even more. She yanked her head back to end the kiss. "Stop."

"I thought you liked to be kissed in the woods."

"Who told you that?" There was no way Simon would have gone bragging about their moment. Was there?

"Someone who was there." He bent down and forced another kiss on her lips. This time, he let go of one arm to paw at her breast.

With all the strength she could muster, she lurched her knee up in hopes of connecting with a place that would leave him in pain for the remainder of the day. The rest of his life—if she could put enough force behind it. Her aim was perfect.

Jake lurched down, doubled over, and howled in pain.

Not one to waste a good escape, she ran. Faster than she'd ever before with no care for the basket now crushed beneath the curly, liberty-taking wolf. She glanced back to ensure he didn't follow.

As expected, he remained doubled over in pain. Carrie let the smug smile tugging at her lips go. The man deserved more than what he got. And who the hell was Simon to go bragging to others of her indiscretions? Perhaps she could teach him the same lesson she had taught Jake? Simon might be a surly grumpard of a man, but she certainly wasn't afraid of him. Now all she had to do was find the blasted fool.

She made a quick stop at the Railroad Grove to look for Simon, but he wasn't there. She didn't dare climb the hill to the other Grove, so she made her way to camp. She'd have to tell Aunt June the loggers would go without flapjacks in the morning because she wasn't about to go traipsing back to the berry patch alone. It seemed every time she ventured out of the safety of Aunt June's mothering gaze, she found herself in a compromising position.

This season was turning out to be the opposite of what she'd envisioned. Vastly different from the year before when all she had to worry about was keeping Beth from trouble and nursing Simon back to health. Then again, last year she hadn't gone anywhere alone. She had been too frightened to do such a brazen thing.

Since then she'd grown comfortable with her surroundings. She wasn't about to be a wilting miss anymore out here. A bit more like Beth, and less the needy socialite the men believed her to be. But her brazenness always seemed to get her into trouble.

Around the bend in the trail ahead, the cook camp would come into view. Perhaps Aunt June knew where Simon worked. The woman seemed to keep tabs on the man like she was a mother hen and he her chick.

Footsteps ahead caused her to slow her gait, and she studied the trail until Simon came into view. Her ire returned. As soon as he approached, she reared her foot back and kicked the blasted man in the shin.

He yelped like a wounded puppy and jumped back to rub his leg. "What was that for?"

"You're lucky I don't castrate you." She glared and stalked past, leaving him to bask in his newfound fear of her. Bully the man she left behind. He could stay there wallowing in pain until another logger found him for all she cared. She picked up speed to make it to camp before he caught up with her.

Inside she fought the urge to cry. If she showed up in camp with tears, Aunt June would demand an answer and eventually learn the truth behind her tardy appearance to bed last night. Not only would she demand Simon marry her right then, she'd spread the news.

While Aunt June didn't mean to gossip, she couldn't seem to find a balance for the space between her brain and her mouth. In the past, Carrie had found that trait about her godmother endearing. Today she found it downright annoying. She needed someone to talk over her emotions with. She couldn't go to Beth. God only knew what her friend would say when she learned Carrie had given in to her brother's skillful seduction, even if only a little.

Hell, Beth might even demand marriage. But Carrie didn't want to marry Simon. Didn't want to marry anyone. She wanted to be like Aunt June—a rich old spinster, hiding away in the mountains. A place where one could simply be themselves.

Not Carrie. Here, even the trees seemed to think she needed a husband— as evidenced by the pine that had held her upright last night as Simon tortured her. Okay, she'd let him tease her sensually. But the pine didn't know that.

She rounded the bend, expecting to see Aunt June in her usual position over the fire, but she was nowhere to be seen. Liquid in a pot above the flames bubbled over, and Carrie hurried to lift the contents from the grate and set the pot on a large stone next to the cook pit.

"Carrie!" She recognized Simon's voice before she saw him rush toward her from the trail where she'd left him behind.

"What?" She stood square to him, and plopped her hands on her hips like Aunt June did all too often during the day.

Simon surveyed the camp before lowering his head closer to hers. His warmth immediately ensconced her like an embrace. She needed to step back, but her feet wouldn't move. *Deadbeat feet.*

"You're angry with me?" He traced the back of her hand with one finger. Her skin tingled wherever he touched. She yanked her hand away from his. He must have known the effect he had on her, because his eyes fired with lust, no doubt aimed to remind her of her indiscretion. "You didn't seem to mind my touch last night."

"A mistake I will not make twice, but that's not why I'm going to kick you again."

Simon stepped back, but a wicked smile stretched across his face. "Then why the violence all of a sudden? If you wish to play that way, I can accommodate. It's not usually my style, but I aim to please. In more ways than one."

She took what she hoped was a menacing step forward and glared. "If you think I'm going to let you touch me again just so you can go bragging to the crew about your conquest, you've another think coming. I won't let you ruin my reputation to accommodate your game of revenge."

"What are you talking about? I haven't told a soul." The arrogant gleam in his eye disappeared, and he squinted in concentration. He took a step closer and grabbed her shoulders like Jake had, only with Simon the touch was soft and more protective. "What happened?"

Could she trust Simon's denial? He'd never betrayed her before, but he was not the same as he had been through years past. "You're telling me you didn't brag to that river rat Jake about kissing me last night?"

The muscle in Simon's jaw flexed before he answered. "No. What happened?"

"He knew what we did across the lake and felt as though I was free game to any who wishes to destroy me. Or claim me, apparently." Tears filled her eyes, and she no longer tried to hold them back. She shook her head. "I won't compromise myself for anyone in this camp. Anyone."

She hoped he got the point.

His face went red and he widened his stance. "Where? What did he do to you?"

She shuddered. With a voice to match her tears, she answered, "I was picking huckleberries. He kissed me and pawed at me as if I was his for the taking. Sort of like what you did last night."

"I would never do anything to you that you don't want me to. But I will kill Jake for touching you."

"You'll do no such thing." She folded her arms over her chest. Partly to block the feel of Jake's hands violating her, partly to show Simon she was serious. "I didn't drag you all the way up here so you can go and commit murder and go to jail."

"Accidents happen all the time in a logging camp."

"That man better not end up dead."

Simon didn't answer, but stared at something behind her with a far-off look in his eyes. He took a moment of silence before stepping back and turning his gaze to her. "Don't leave the camp. Don't go anywhere. And do not let anyone come visit you. Not even your beau Thomas."

"Don't do anything that is going to get yourself arrested."

Simon's hard stare didn't falter. Whatever was going through his head dominated his thoughts. "Even if I do, it won't be the first time someone threatened me with the hoosegow. I'll be fine."

"Simon." She said his name in warning, but he ignored her and ran up the trail. Leaving her to stare at his retreating back. She bit the tip of her thumb while she stared at the now empty trail where he had disappeared. Where was he going? She wanted to follow, to try to talk him out of whatever he had planned, but in all honesty, she didn't want to leave the safety of the camp even if Simon hadn't forbade it.

Carrie hugged herself around her stomach and viewed the empty camp. Where had Aunt June gone, and what was Simon going to do once he found Jake? The tears she had suppressed changed course and formed a lump in her throat. This whole season was a disaster as big as the mountain they lived on.

Chapter 10

The gentle ding of bells, ringing in tune to the thump of off-balance wagon wheels, filled the camp. Carrie searched the men, now settling in for their usual after-supper rituals. Simon wasn't among them. The need to chew on her now ragged thumbnail itched her finger. She bit her lip against the urge.

Aunt June emerged from her cabin, yanked her apron over her head, and hung the apron on the peg. She kept her head turned in the direction of the noise. Carrie followed her stare as a colorful wagon bedecked in trinkets and pictures of scantily dressed women rolled into view.

At the sight of the wagon, some of the men whooped, leapt to their feet, and ran toward the end of the path leading down the mountain, while others ran toward the Bonner camp. In the midst of the chaos, the five Devil May Cares who had gone down the river the week before leapt from the wagon and disappeared into the crowd.

Carrie caught Aunt June's gaze and ran toward her. "Who's that?"

"Bud McGill, and it looks like he brought back Wall and the boys. Garrett said the train hasn't been able to take a load down since the pulley stopped working. They probably hitched up with Bud to get back up here." Aunt June ran a hand over her frayed tendrils of hair and straightened her shoulders. "Bud is a traveling merchant who comes up here whenever he's in town. He always brings me fresh produce from the Bonner market and only charges me the same price he bought it for."

"Aunt June. Such shameful behavior. Getting a man to deliver your goods for free. Why, you're no better than Beth bamboozling her way up here last year," Carrie teased.

"Well, she got her man, didn't she." Aunt June looped her arm through Carrie's and tugged her toward the newcomer. "Now, come help me carry the potatoes."

Carrie searched the men for Simon, but as before he wasn't among them. Her heart sank. Had he done something brash? He'd left in a worrisome state earlier. If it were last year before his accident, she would have waved off his threat as nothing but a manly outburst. With him at this point in his life, however, there was no telling what he was capable of doing.

Carrie approached the wagon with her godmother as the man set the brake and leapt from his seat. He yanked his hat from his head and bowed. "Miz June. I think you'll be happy with today's find."

"Oh?" Aunt June waggled her shoulders and dropped Carrie's arm. "We missed you last year."

The man clutched his heart. "Had I been able to make it out this far, I would have been here for you. But alas, I was stuck in Oregon."

Carrie let the smile stretch on her face. She'd never seen her godmother act like such a giddy schoolgirl before. Not even when Simon charmed her did she react with such childish glee.

"So what have you got for me?" Aunt June's hungry eyes roamed first the man and then the wagon. Carrie stifled a giggle with the back of her hand.

"Peaches." Bud smiled as if the word was a precious secret he had kept for Aunt June. He undid a latch on the side of the wagon and opened it to reveal a plethora of trinkets and treasures. The men already near the wagon began to crowd.

Bud's secret must have been quite a doozy, because Aunt June answered with an equally enthusiastic nod and smile. She rubbed her hands together and peeked over the man's shoulder as if searching for her treasure. "I knew you'd be back this summer *and* bring me something delightful."

"Don't I always?" The man dropped the back gate to his wagon, reached in, and pulled out a crate overflowing with the promised fruit.

"You can give it to my assistant cook and goddaughter, Carrie." Aunt June pointed right at her. She stepped forward with arms extended.

"No, no." Bud shook his head. "This one's a bit heavy. Why don't you grab that sack o'taters in there, and I'll help Miz June with this load?"

"What about the men and your trinkets?" Carrie thought the question a practical one, but by the looks on Bud's and Aunt June's faces, she was alone in her thoughts.

"I trust this lot of men not to steal from me." Bud smiled—his eyes transfixed on Aunt June—and followed as she headed toward the cook fire. Carrie made short work of grabbing the potatoes. She didn't want to miss the exchange between the two smitten souls.

If nothing else, at least she could have something to razz Aunt June about for the remainder of the season. By the time she reached the cook fire, the pair were already returning to the wagon. Depositing the potatoes next to the crate of peaches, she ran back to the now thick group of loggers around the new visitor.

She muscled her way through the crowd of men, as much as a woman of her stature could, and stopped to peer into the wagon. To the right, rows of beautifully arranged jewels shimmered in the sun, but the men mostly ignored those. All but the occasional man who no doubt planned to send a trinket back to his sweetheart at home.

On a shelf above, vials of medicine took some attention, while further down a cache of knives and weapons were plucked one by one from their position, only to be set down and picked up again by another hand.

As Carrie perused the goods, a hand floated before her sight, clutching one of the bejeweled pieces. She looked up into Thomas's face. "A beautiful piece for a beautiful woman."

"Oh, I couldn't." She shook her head.

"I bought it for you."

"I don't know where I would wear such finery up here."

"You could wear it when you come for a walk with me this evening."

She didn't want to hurt the man's feelings, but this was too much. Too intimate. "I can't take that. It's not proper of me."

"I bought it because it matched your eyes." Without stopping to ask, he stepped behind her and looped it around her neck to fasten it. "I also saw you admiring it a few minutes ago."

He stepped around to face her and smiled.

She mentally stumbled through a list of excuses to return the personal gift. A gift that made her uncomfortable, to say the least.

"The color brings out the sparkle in your eyes," he said with pride. "I won't tell you how much I spent on the little piece of beauty, but I couldn't bear to see it on any other woman."

She opened her mouth again but snapped it shut when he placed his clammy fingers over her lips. "You are too modest, my dear. It suits you. I will not hear another argument."

"Carrie!" She heard the feminine call above the dull rumble of the men's voices, and she all but cried out in relief. She looked past Thomas to find Beth waving at her from outside the crowd.

Thomas too must have noticed Beth's call, for he turned a quick eye to her, and then faced Carrie. She caught a scowl before he masked it with indifference.

"If you'll excuse me. I've needed to speak with Beth all day."

"Of course." Thomas gave a quick bow with his head, but his neck remained stiff with the movement. "I'll see you after supper."

She smiled her response, ducked low to avoid the jagged elbows thrown haphazardly in every direction, and picked her way back out of the group. Every fiber of her muscles seemed to ease the farther away she grew from Thomas. Why couldn't she tell the amorous logger once and for all she wasn't interested? Why wouldn't he take her rejection for what it was? In all her life she'd hated to disappoint others, and she'd let her amorous suitors be shuffled off by her father and, she suspected, Simon. But Thomas was different. She needed to take care of her own problems. Needed to let him down personally before he started to believe they had something more than they did.

Why had she ever let him think she was interested in him?

"This is quite a sight," she said as she reached Beth. Carrie ran another eye over the mayhem.

"Garrett says Bud doesn't come every year, but when he does it's a good time for the loggers to stock up on supplies and whatever else they feel the need to buy." Beth motioned with her head toward something behind Carrie.

Carrie frowned as Simon handed money to Bud and pocketed a bottle of amber liquid. Her face grew hot. She didn't want to be upset about his drinking, but she couldn't help but be disappointed. His debauchery was what had brought him to this place in his life. She didn't care if he drank, but could he do it without spiraling back down the same path he'd taken in Missoula?

"Sometimes the men send people to get them things when they are too busy to show up themselves. Maybe it's not his," Beth supplied.

"Perhaps. I think I'll go ask him."

Beth gave a pathetic smile, and Carrie started toward the wayward man in question. Ready to give him an earful if needed.

To her irritation, he rounded the other side of the wagon following Bud. She followed. The voices of the men behind her seemed to fade as she slipped around the corner of the wagon.

"Carrie!" Simon exclaimed with a toothy smile on his face.

She narrowed her eyes. What was he so happy about?

She opened her mouth to ask him the question burning in her mind when the soft bark of a puppy sounded.

"Perfect timing. Pick one." Simon motioned toward the inside of the wagon.

Carrie peeked in to see the wiggling bodies of four small puppies. Small enough to fit in a saddlebag, and fluffy enough to sleep with on a cold night. "They are darling! Where'd they come from?"

"From a butcher's wife over near Bozeman. Had four too many, so I took them off her hands. They're a hungry little bunch. Can't stop eating to save their lives. Which one do you fancy, young lady?" Bud stood tall and watched the little pups.

"Oh, I couldn't."

"You gotta. This young man's already paid me. I'm afraid in my line of business, there are no returns. Pick one." Bud glanced behind where she and Simon stood. "If you'll excuse me. I need to attend to my other customers."

She locked eyes with Simon. Her heart soared. He knew she loved animals. Although he'd acted like an uncouth ruffian the last few months, she knew that somewhere deep inside was the same considerate man she had known from before. This only proved as much.

"Are you certain you wouldn't like to find something else on the wagon to purchase?"

"I could get you a necklace, but I see some other poor soul has tried to woo you with finery. Was it Thomas?" Simon clicked his tongue to the roof of his mouth and shook his head. "Shame he doesn't know the woman he's trying to romance."

"I like fine things as much as the next woman." Carrie tugged the necklace away from the back of her neck. Its delicate chain hung heavy against her skin. As heavy as the guilt in her heart allowed it to be.

As Simon tilted his head, his expression softened. "Take a pup, Carrie. He's not a fine jewel to mark you as mine. It's a gift from a friend. And if it's feeding him you're worried about, I can give him half my meal. Aunt June would probably bop me over the head, but I'd risk her wrath so you could finally get that dog you've always wanted."

Carrie heard his words, but her mind was only half-listening. The other half concentrated on the animals. Searching for the perfect match. "What will my parents say when I come home with a dog? They were the ones who forbade me to have one in the first place."

"Well, he could stay at my place when we're in town. My grandmother won't care. She's already written the home over to me."

"Really? You'd do that for me?"

Simon stepped closer and bowed his head near hers. His voice lowered as he spoke. "Not just for you. If you have a puppy, then I look a bit manlier when I come and play with him. My men will never know I'm visiting you to pet your pup."

Carrie moved her head back to look into his eyes. "What do you mean by that?"

Simon chuckled and held his hands out in surrender. "Only what it sounds like. I love dogs. In fact, my love has been the downfall of my family."

"Nonsense. Your parents' deaths were an accident. Your grandmother has always been in good standing, and Beth is now a Jones. The whole of Missoula believes they are now her most intimate of friends." Carrie plucked the biggest puppy from the box and snuggled her face into the fur. She tried not to giggle as the little creature licked her face. She pulled her head away from the excited pup, placed him in the box, and faced Simon. "You know what your problem is?"

"That you won't make your mind up about the dog?"

She picked up a small, whimpering female from the corner, and held her still by caressing her head. "No. You cannot forget about the past and focus instead on your future. You blame yourself for things that are not your fault."

"Like my parents?" He lifted his head.

"Yes. And last year. You were wounded in a horrid accident, but you are alive. Why can't that be enough for you?"

"I am alive only in body. My soul did not make it past the end of the season." Simon plucked the small animal from her hands, tucked her into the crook of his arms, and ran his strong fingers over the small animal's delicate fur.

Carrie too caressed the dog, in tune with Simon's movements. "Why? Because a few insolent reprobates and backstabbing madams have slighted you in town? You yearn to be accepted again but don't realize that those who love you have never turned their backs on you."

Bud peeked around the corner, interrupting the moment. Carrie took a step away from Simon as though they'd been caught in a delicate position.

Bud smiled. "Made up your mind, Miss?"

Simon handed her the pup. "I think this conversation is for another time. Have you made a decision?"

Carrie snuggled the little female pup. "She's perfect."

"Splendid choice," Bud said, and disappeared behind the wagon.

Simon motioned toward the trail to the lake. "We've a few minutes before you're needed for supper. Let's show your new friend where to find water."

Carrie nodded, and followed in Simon's wake until the noise from the wagon at their backs dissipated. Simon slowed as she drew next to him. His shoulder brushed hers, and memories of the night before flooded her senses. She was as ninny-headed as the rest of the ewes down in Missoula. Why did she let his charm affect her? At this point she wasn't certain who was more dangerous to her—Thomas and his determined attentions or Simon's sensual pull.

He jumped off a rock in the path, and the side of his coat holding the flask fell heavy. Carrie didn't miss the movement, but she didn't want to break the serenity of the evening by mentioning the whiskey. Instead, she let him help her down from the rock. "You didn't hurt Jake, did you?"

Simon shook his head. "I couldn't find the little blowhard, but I did bring back your basket. I'll expect your now famous huckleberry flapjacks in the morning."

"You like those?" She blushed. "I have perfected that particular dish, haven't I?"

Simon chuckled. "I suspect you're a much better cook than you let people see. Be honest."

"I've no intention of being humble. Aunt June has taught me most of the recipes. I've made the entirety of the suppers for the last few days." She exaggerated her proud smile.

"I thought something was a bit off with the brisket last night." He winked, and Carrie giggled. This was the man she'd wanted back for over a year. He might argue the mountain had no effect on him, but her and Aunt June's plan proved a good one.

She wanted to say as much. Shake him, and argue until he saw the truth behind his happiness up here. Force him to remain happy, but she didn't want to ruin his newfound mood. The pup wiggled in her arms, and she let her go.

"What are you going to call her?" Simon asked, keeping his gaze on the small dog now ahead of them on the trail.

"I don't know. I've never had a pet long enough to name one. Mother always scurried them off to the cook, and the cook would dispose of them. I'm certain half of the time I would have cried at whatever method she used."

"Since most of your desired pets were purchased to be your dinner, I have to agree. I wouldn't want to know what the cook did with them either."

"What do you think I should call her?"

Simon gave her a sideways grin, then stared at the treetops as they walked. After a moment of his not-so-subtle show of thought, he nodded. "Nots."

Dawn Luedecke

"Knots?" Carrie raised an eyebrow. What sort of name was Knots? Unless you were a sea captain with a canine stowaway. Captain Simon was not, and Carrie had never even seen the ocean. "You're joking."

He stopped and faced her with hands extended as if to stay her judgement. She stopped, and after a breath, he reached out and moved her hair off her shoulder. The tenor in his voice grew low and sensual when he said, "Her full name will be Forget-me-not. Nots for short. Or have you forgotten?"

The man could melt snow when he spoke in such a tone. She swallowed hard and shuddered at the tingle running down her spine from Simon's caress. With a deep swallow to bring moisture to her dry mouth, she continued down the path. "Because I brought you the flowers when we first got here?"

"You still have it?" Carrie didn't bother to hide her smile. The fact that Simon had kept the small token meant more to her than any show of appreciation she'd ever received for her cooking.

"You gave it to me. It's mine." He tucked it back in his pocket and patted the fabric where it was secured.

"Is this how you seduce all of your women?"

"Only the difficult ones. Usually I only need to wiggle my eyebrows at them." He demonstrated the comical movement.

"The woman who falls for that will end up working in the Grizzly Bear Saloon. That's the most ridiculous seduction technique I've ever seen."

"By the way you responded to me last night, you've been wasting your life away with all of those fools, waiting for me and my techniques."

"You flatter yourself too much. It was a slip in judgement is all. It won't happen again."

"Says the woman who hasn't even realized the fancy jewels from her foolish beau are now missing."

Carrie clutched the base of her neck where the necklace had been, but as Simon promised, they were gone. "What did you do?"

"Do you care?" Simon shoved his hands in his pockets and followed Nots to the edge of the lake. "They don't suit you anyway."

"They were a gift, and Thomas is expecting me to wear them tonight when he comes to visit."

"You mean to court you."

"No...yes." She hung her head and kicked a pebble into the water. Simon knew her almost as well as she knew herself. There was no use lying to him.

"Tell him to go away. Stop dangling hope in front of the boy or it's going to come back to bite you in that perfect little backside of yours."

"It's not that easy."

"Yes it is. You say, 'Thomas, I'm sorry, but Simon has my flower, so I can't be with you.'"

Carrie's face heated, and she blinked several times. By now she'd honestly believed Simon could no longer shock her with his words, but he continued to prove otherwise. "I'll say no such thing! Not only is it ludicrous to commit social suicide with such a retort, but you and I together in such a way will never happen."

"It will." His eyes slid over her body, sending tingles wherever they roamed. "Eventually you'll see what it's like to be mine in every way."

"Even in marriage?" Hah. *I got him there.* She stared at him in triumph. The man had vowed on many occasions never to marry. A confirmed bachelor with enough pain on his hands with a sister to watch over.

"Perhaps one day I will marry you. When you're so old you can no longer see." He stopped before her, towering, as he was apt to do when aiming to browbeat her. It wasn't going to work.

"I'm sorry to disappoint you, but women in my family do not grow senile. You're going to have to keep your hands to yourself. Or do as Aunt June says and marry me first."

"Don't temp me, Carrie. If you play coy, I may take you to the preacher, just to show you who is right, and who is satisfied."

She gave a playful glare. His words were games. She wasn't intimidated. "And which do you claim?"

"Right."

"So that would make me satisfied?"

"Mmm," he moaned his agreement and stared at her lips. The sounds sent heat to her core and made her stomach flip. She took a deep breath to help boost her confidence, but it didn't work. To her relief, Nots chose that moment to wiggle her way between their feet.

Carrie gave him a victorious stare and stepped back. She'd won the battle by pup. Unfortunately, she had a feeling the war was far from over. At least she had a few hours to gain her wits before being forced to battle Thomas and his game of passion. Somehow, that battle didn't sound as fun.

Chapter 11

Like nights before, Carrie finished her dishes as the men gathered around the fire to settle in for the evening. Except tonight their new friend Bud sat at Aunt June's serving table as he watched her godmother's every move like one of the dogs in his wagon eyeing a treat.

Thankfully Thomas had chosen to eat in his own camp, giving Carrie a necessary respite from ardent men. The only males she encountered tonight, besides Simon of course, were the ones who regarded her only for her food.

Simon hung back, keeping his distance, but he watched her. She'd locked eyes with him several times over the meal, and he'd stolen her breath with the memory of more lustful promises.

He wouldn't dominate her thoughts tonight.

Tonight she would concentrate on getting Thomas to turn his attention elsewhere. Which would be a lot easier if she wasn't the only eligible woman in camp. It would appear that to be a successful spinster cook, you must first be a spinster.

Thomas appeared on the other side of the fire and smiled. His hair had been slicked back as though he'd made a valiant attempt to clean up after a hard day's work.

Carrie gave a questioning glance to Aunt June, who waved her off distractedly. It appeared her godmother would be no good to her tonight.

Carrie walked to Thomas and motioned toward a seat by the fire, but he shook his head. "I thought we could go for a stroll tonight. Don't worry, we'll stay where we can be seen."

She tried her best to give a genuine smile as she followed, but the strain in her cheeks made her doubt her own sincerity. Thomas maneuvered her to walk near the chicken coop, and Carrie stifled a sardonic chuckle. What a romantic stroll, right through a giant pile of poo.

"I'm glad to finally get to speak with you alone." He turned a thin-lipped grin on her, but immediately frowned. "Where's your necklace?"

"I'm sorry. I must have forgotten it when I bathed earlier," she lied. Her hand flew to her empty neck, then back down to her side.

He gripped her palm in a painful hold and laced it through his arm. Her heartbeat sped up, but not in the same way it did when Simon touched her. This was different. More visceral. "When a man gets you a gift, you cherish it. My mother has never received a gift from my father that she hasn't kept a close eye on. One would think you didn't appreciate the present."

"About that." She stopped and faced him. "I shouldn't—"

"Carrie!" Simon shouted behind her. She pivoted as he jogged up to them. "You forgot this at the lake."

The blasted man turned to Thomas and winked before leaving Carrie to wallow in embarrassment.

Thomas's face grew red, but all he did was clear his throat. Carrie clasped the necklace and placed it around her neck, then focused back to their walk. "You have to forgive Simon. He's a little uncouth."

Thomas scratched the back of his neck. After a few moments of tense silence, he finally spoke. "I apologize for my odd behavior. We can't seem to find my friend. The Bonner camp is a little frazzled."

"Which friend?" *Lord, please don't let him say Jake.*

"Jake. He went missing sometime today. Hasn't been seen all afternoon."

"How terrible." Her ribcage felt fit to break with each hard thump of her heart. There was no way Simon had caught up with the reprobate and beaten him to death. Was there? Although he had shown signs of the easygoing Simon she once knew, he was fiercely protective of what was his. And for some reason he'd taken to protecting her ever since she and Beth had grown close. "You should be out searching for him instead of here with me."

"Jake would have wanted me to keep my word with a woman."

"You talk as if he's already dead. Did you find him?"

"Oh, no ma'am. He's still missing, but this is wild country. There's no telling what happened to him. He more than likely went down to a saloon somewhere."

"With any luck he will waltz into your camp later this evening with not even a scratch."

"God willing," Thomas said.

The moment grew tense. She didn't know what else to say. The way he spoke, as if not concerned about his friend. She supposed it could be as he said—Jake went down for a drink and a good time.

Thomas tugged her closer to his side by her arm. "You have a way of making a man feel special, Miz Carrie. Like I can take on the world, and everything would go my way. As long as you are by my side."

She smiled. What else could she do? This wasn't the first time a man had said something similar to her. It didn't make it any easier to believe, though. A man should be able to take on the world by himself. A woman should only have to help make him stronger, not be the strength for him. A man should know himself before seeking a wife.

Perhaps it was a good thing Simon chose not to marry. With the way he wandered through life, he'd never be in a position to accommodate a woman. *For the best,* she thought. If she was going to be an old spinster, at least he was going to wither away, unattached, right alongside her. Now all she had to do was get the courage to persuade Thomas to turn his focus somewhere else, without allowing him to talk his way out of rejection.

* * * *

Simon sat next to Aunt June and her traveling beau. Unlike the couple who were focused on no one but each other, his attention stretched across the meadow to where Carrie strolled alongside Thomas. He'd used the necklace to warn Thomas off, but it hadn't seemed to work. The blasted man kept mooning over Carrie like she was a prize he'd already won and had no intention of letting go.

She wasn't Thomas's prize, and he planned to let him know as much. First he'd let the little vixen dig her pit deeper. She needed to struggle every once in a while with the consequences of her actions. And letting her find her own way out of a sticky situation with a beau was as best an example as any.

"Simon." He heard his name being called. He peered over his shoulder to see Garrett and Wall waving him over. *Blast*! He'd been so wrapped up in Carrie's affairs, he'd forgotten the Devil May Cares had caught a ride up on the wagon.

Simon stopped next to the men, far enough away from the camp to talk in private. He raised his head in greeting. "How's the river?"

"Low," Wall answered. "We're only going to get one drive down before we run out of river. We had to block some forks and unblock others in order to get a direct route. The boys and I are going to have to take the drive down in no more than two days or else the raft will have to stay here until next spring. By then the logs will be no good to the mill."

"That's where we have a problem," Garrett said. "The steam pulley you designed over the winter is busted, and we have no idea how to fix it. If we're gonna get a load down the mountain, we need to get it repaired."

Wall kicked something on the ground and shook his head. "If I stay behind to fix it then the boys will only have four on our team, two who know the waters and what they're doing. My two greenhorns did a run over in Wisconsin, but this is their first experience with Montana white water. I'm going to need someone experienced to go down."

"I'd go, but I have to stay with the train," Garrett said.

"What about Beth?" Wall asked, his voice dripping with hope.

Simon was about to respond when Garrett shook his head first. "No one tells Beth. She'd go whether I wanted her to or not, and I'd go mad up here wondering if she's gone and gotten herself killed."

"I second Garrett," Simon said. "Beth stays behind, and no one says anything to her."

"Well, then, that leaves you." Wall stared at Simon with a look on his face of half pleading, half order.

As much as he hated to leave Carrie, his friends needed him. And Wall was right, the Devil May Cares needed one more experienced person if they were going to get the logs down the rivers. Especially since they were so low. Lower rivers meant more log jams. This drive wasn't going to be like the rest. This was going to be fast, difficult, and dangerous. Not a drive for Beth, and barely a drive for the two experienced loggers turned greenhorn river men. If Wall couldn't go, then Simon was up. "I'll go."

"You're one to ride the river with," Wall said, and slapped his shoulder in thanks.

"I'll remember you said that next time you need me to take your place. Can't ride the river with me if you're staying behind." Simon gave a crooked smile to his friend, who chuckled.

Wall craned his neck and studied the top of the hill where the chute sat lifeless after a long, hard day's work. "I think the big bugs at the mill will be happy with the drive. Happier if we can get two down before the river runs low."

"Or get the train to start running loads." Garrett's forehead wrinkled, and Simon knew his concern was deep. His new brother-in-law, and friend, had put everything he owned into this venture. His future as partner in the railroad logging rested on the new system doubling what they brought down the mountain. If he couldn't get shipments going, he'd lose his contract and new business, which would leave Beth with less security in her life. Simon couldn't afford to worry about his married sister's future when he barely kept control over his own.

"I'll go talk to Aunt June and get the men ready to head out in two days." Wall rushed past, leaving Garrett and Simon alone.

"Don't let my sister go," Simon said.

Garrett held his hands out in surrender. "I agree. The rivers are way too dangerous this year. The only safe place would be in Aunt June's wannigan, but it's still down at the mill. Aunt June's going to have to make do with a bateau to carry the cooking supplies and food."

Simon locked his hands together to keep from revealing too much of his emotions with gesture. "Could you also keep an eye on Carrie? Especially around Thomas. I don't trust him, and he seems a little too eager to court her. Desperate even."

Garrett chuckled under his breath. "Beth mentioned something about him earlier at the wagon. I'll have her stay by Carrie's side the whole time you're gone. Wouldn't want something to happen to your woman."

"Thanks. And she's not my woman."

"Of course. Why worry about someone you don't care for?" Garrett studied his palms and gave a smile that irritated the heck out of Simon. Not that what his friend said wasn't true, but it meant too many people knew about his newfound infatuation. He hated people poking sticks at his personal business.

"I'm simply concerned for my sister's friend is all." Simon clenched his teeth until his jaw ached, hoping Garrett would take the hint and change the subject.

"Right." Garrett nodded, and started toward the Railroad Grove. He motioned for Simon to follow as he continued. "At least it will help keep Beth occupied while I get this train fixed. I know you must realize this already, but your sister is one hell of a bullheaded woman. She wants to help, and no one's going to tell her she can't."

"Carrie is a bit more manageable than my sister. She gets into trouble, but most of the time she sees her wrongdoing and will respond as a woman should."

"Are you certain there's not something between the two of you?" Garrett gave him a sideways glance. "I mean besides the fact that she is your sister's bosom friend."

"No." Simon knew Garrett would ask the question eventually. They spent a great deal of time together, and she had risked her future to bring him up here. And for what? So he could discover what he'd known back in town? That he was no longer built to be a logger. No longer had the passion he once did for the job and the mountain. He knew the question about he and Carrie burned in everyone's mind, but he still didn't know how to respond.

Carrie was a dream. A waif a man like him could never fully catch. A distraction to keep him occupied while on the mountain, but once they returned home she would disappear like all ghosts were supposed to do. Unless, of course, she chose to stay behind and haunt him for the remainder of his lonely years. In which case he would have to marry her once she was senile enough to see past his scars. Despite her claims otherwise, he'd seen her cringe a time or two when she'd nursed him back to health. She'd noticed. What woman wouldn't?

There were more than his looks. She was pure and good, where he'd lived his life searching for those few moments of happiness in the arms of any woman willing to crawl into bed with him. On more than one occasion he'd regretted his actions, but he had a name to keep for himself. Scoundrel. A flannel-mouthed mudsill to the lonely women of Missoula. What woman didn't love a good chase? And everyone knew a predator always got his prey.

But Carrie wasn't prey. At least not in the visceral sense. Seducing her was the only thing he found up here on the mountain that gave him happiness. The moment he'd seen her chasing that damned chicken he knew he needed her. The choice he made then and there to make her his, at least in the carnal way, eased the ache in his chest. As if someone had lifted an entire pine tree off his ribs. The decision brought him to a level of life where he could function once again. Well, mostly. When at the Grove he hated life, and all he could think about was the next time he could be with her. What she felt like beneath his palms. Even the thought of watching her tiny hands serve the loggers food calmed him enough to bring a smile to his face. People thought her balled-up plan had worked, but the only thing keeping his soul at ease was Carrie.

He felt like a scallywag, but he needed to have her—body and soul— maybe not for the rest of her life, but at least for now. She was the only way to get through this season. What was he going to do once he didn't see her face for the next few weeks? Wallow in self-pity and bourbon?

Simon patted the pocket of his jacket where the flask full of whiskey lay tucked away. He'd bought it in case a moment ever arose where he needed a huge swig, but he didn't intend to drink it otherwise. He always refrained from drinking when at camp, and this year was no different. He needed to get back to a place where a level head and hard day's work weren't simply visions of a past life but who he was as a man. He wanted to find his way back. If not for himself, then for Carrie and those he loved.

* * * *

Carrie arranged a few pans in the wooden crate that would carry what little supplies Aunt June would take with her in the small boat, while Nots played at her feet and chewed on the hem of her dress. Unlike last year, when they had had a whole kitchen in their raft, this year Aunt June would have to make do with the bare minimum supplies needed to feed the men.

"I need you to go get me a bushel full of huckleberries for the drive." Aunt June tightened the lid down on a canister of flower and placed it in the box of food. "If I can't give those boys big hearty meals for the next few weeks, at least I can give them something that tastes good."

Carrie tipped half her mouth up in a smile to the older woman, but inside her stomach hollowed even more. Aunt June was leaving and Carrie would be the sole cook for dozens of men. This would be the biggest test of her womanly skills. She was destined to either drown or swim in this river she'd chosen to take in her life. Too bad she hadn't purchased the three-piece bathing costume she'd found at the Missoula Mercantile last summer. She was destined to at least float through the next couple of weeks. "I'll get the basket and go."

"Nope." Aunt June dusted the loose flour off her hands and adjusted the crate. "I've done picked all the berries in our patch. You're going to have to go higher up the mountain. I'll go get a man to take you up past the Grove. Mind you don't go getting yourself ruined. Your mother swore to lock you in the attic if I returned you a soiled dove, and your father threatened to pass you off to the first man to show interest."

"I've no intention of ruining anything about me. I'll get the basket ready." Carrie smiled, but her stomach flipped. The last time she'd been up past the Grove was when she'd gotten lost. The memory still fresh and frightening in her mind, she swallowed back the lump forming in her throat. At least Aunt June was kind enough to send her with an escort, and she had one guess as to who the older woman wanted to fetch.

"Better hurry." Aunt June studied the sky. "Looks like the clouds can't decide whether they want to storm or not. If you're not back before the storm, I will send a search party. I swear it."

At that, Aunt June pivoted and headed out of camp, leaving Carrie to gather her supplies. A few minutes later her fears were confirmed as Simon sauntered into camp. Nots bounded toward him with tail wagging.

As soon as the pup reached his feet, he scooped the little scamp up and stopped before Carrie, plucking the basket from her hands as Nots sniffed the wicker handle. "Aunt June says you're too scared and vulnerable to go berry picking alone. You need a guide. Of course, I volunteered."

"I've also heard her say you were a prize of a man. She's senile."

The blasted man chuckled and led the way up the hill while carrying Nots in one hand and a dainty basket in his other. "Senile or not, she's usually right. And if she's not, then we pretend she is so she keeps feeding us."

"Where'd she go?" Carrie asked, peering over her shoulder to the spot where Simon had appeared alone. "I thought she was going to return with you."

"Ran over to talk to Blue and the boys. I think she's putting them to work to get her set up for the drive."

"Oh," she answered, and hiked silently as she enjoyed the quiet serenity of the mountain and physical strain on her legs.

Carrie let the time tick by in happy quiet until after they passed by the graveyard of widowmakers that marked last year's Grove. "I'm a little nervous about this whole situation."

"Why? Because you don't trust me to be alone with you?" Simon teased, and juggled Nots as she wiggled in his arms. "Well, you shouldn't."

"No, you blowhard." More to herself, she said, "Bully me to try to talk my feelings out with a logger."

"I'm not any logger. I'm the man you can't stop thinking about."

"You certainly are a confident one." She leapt over a large tree root jutting out of the damp earth. She looked up. Her stomach rolled when she realized they had walked past the spot where she'd strayed from the path weeks ago. She moved closer to Simon's side, as if his mere presence could change what had happened in the past.

"Fact is, you *do* think about me." Simon smiled down at her. Humor shone in his eyes. "Otherwise you would never have concocted this sideways plan to fix me, or snuggle up next to me whenever you feel threatened."

"I do no such thing," she lied. "And for your information, Mr. Sanders, the plan was Aunt June's. I simply went along with it."

"And took credit." He sent her a dimpled grin. A smile that made her want to slap it off his face and caress the indentation on his cheek at the same time. He was infuriating.

"I've done no such thing."

"You've let me believe all this time you cared enough to kidnap me."

"If you remember, no one coerced you into putting on the chloroform mask." The air grew thinner, and Carrie struggled to climb over a particularly large boulder in the path. "You did that all on your own so you could escape into oblivion without a care to the rest of the world around you."

"You're right. I should never have trusted you. I should have known you planned to drug me so you could have your way with me." He wiggled his eyebrows up and down, which made her want to growl.

Instinct told her to snarl at him, but she was a lady and fought the urge. Although why she would care to act like a lady in front of Simon, she had no clue. It wasn't like he acted like a gentleman—she gave a sideways glance to the dainty basket he'd toted up the mountain for her—well, most of the time.

He could be chivalrous on occasion.

She moved to the opposite side of him so she could see the evidence of his fight with the cougar. The jagged, but fading, wound across his face wasn't as bad as he believed. To her the scar proved only one thing. Simon Sanders could take on a hungry predator and escape with his life. No man she knew had ever been able to claim such bravery. Such strength. Why couldn't he see that and be proud of his courage? "You're a frustrating man."

"Then we are at an impasse, because I enjoy finding every chance I can to tease you. It's utterly delightful." He said the last like a chattering, overzealous socialite.

Carrie rolled her eyes, but a giggle fought to burst free from deep within her chest. She enjoyed the easy banter she shared with Simon when he wasn't engrossed in his misery. Almost as if he were the same man he had been before the accident.

He caught her stare and moved away from her, blocking the view of his scar.

Almost.

Her heart grew heavy as she crested the top of the mountain to reveal a large, flower-speckled field. The peaceful sight around them lightened her mood. In the center, a crude cabin commanded the attention of all who entered the meadow. Behind the small abode and field of trees beyond, the jagged peaks of the Mission mountain range sat high against the azure sky. Gray clouds floated by like filthy puffs of cotton on their way to whatever storm cloud in which they wished to collect. Aunt June was right. If they didn't hurry they could be caught in a storm. Alone on the mountain with a reprobate like Simon. Her reputation would be ruined for certain.

"The huckleberry patch is over behind the cabin." Simon set down Nots, who scampered off to bound in the flowers. "If it hasn't been picked off by the local animals."

"Like deer?" Carrie asked while keeping an eye on Nots. She giggled at the way her little dog's head bobbed up every once in a while in the tall grass.

She chanced a look at Simon, whose expression mimicked her own—one of contentment and happiness. He motioned toward the berry bushes. "And rodents and bears."

"Bears?" Her stomach flipped. Instinct told her to fetch Nots, and she took a step toward the grass where her pup played.

He must have heard the concern in her voice, because he pressed his hand on her back reassuringly. "Don't worry. You can usually smell them before you see them. And I have Garrett's gun. You're safe."

Her riotous body leaned toward his warmth, but not for fear of bears. She knew he'd protect her from any threat, and she'd yet to see a ferocious animal in this wild forest. Not that they didn't exist.

No.

She sought the freedom she'd felt the other day when he'd held her against the tree and gave her the lesson in seduction she didn't really want. Or did she? Would letting him bring her to a plane of happiness be so bad? She didn't plan to marry. Why not feel the skilled touch of a man one time in her life? Or twice.

Because you are a lady and made a promise to yourself and your parents, she mentally chided. Deeper inside her mind, Simon's mischievous voice whispered, *What mother doesn't know can't be held against you.* The damned devil in her conscience always sounded like the man walking silently by her side as he watched her pup play in the grass.

She needed to get these berries and down the mountain before the storm, and Simon, decided to keep her occupied otherwise.

Chapter 12

Why is she suddenly in a hurry?

Simon placed a handful of huckleberries in the basket next to Carrie and moved to the edge of the bushes so he could watch her. She knelt on the damp ground with no care to her dress as she furiously plucked berries and tossed them toward the growing pile, almost missing the basket in her haste. As if she wanted to get away from him as soon as possible. Or was it that she feared being this high in the forest? Either way, she'd changed from the prim husband-hunter she'd been since coming of age. One who wouldn't dare be seen with a dusty hem, let alone the stains she'd have mid-skirts upon standing.

The lumber camp had a way of changing people. Most of the time for the better. With Carrie it gave her a freedom she reveled in. One that dusted her once pale, flawless skin with a pink tinge. Broke her tight, perfectly arranged hair into a mane hastily tied back with a ribbon, which allowed wispy blond tendrils to frame her face and take his breath away with her waif-like beauty.

His stomach dropped at the thought of not having her there each morning to center him with nothing more than the sight of her cooking over a fire. He dreaded the drive. The last few years he'd been a timber beast. Not a riverman. Although he'd learned the trade over the years, he had never wanted to be a riverman.

Carrie ducked her head underneath the bush and stretched her arms to get to a hidden berry. He clenched his hands against the desire to touch her, and his mouth grew moist at the memory of her sweet lips against his. She was a drug more powerful than the chloroform she'd given him. More powerful than the booze burning a hole in his pocket.

Thunder boomed overhead and made her jump. He would have laughed if the sound hadn't caught him off guard as well.

"What was that?" She searched the skies as a raindrop hit the back of his hand.

"Just a little rain." In two steps he stood over her and helped her stand. He plucked the basket off the ground and handed it to her. "Go inside the cabin. I'll fetch Nots."

Instead of doing as he bid, she studied the trail across the meadow. "Shouldn't we go back to camp? I think we can make it before the rain gets too hard."

He shook his head as the rain began to drizzle, wetting her wisps against her forehead. "No time. We'll have to wait it out."

He'd never seen her bite her nails before, but she did as she glanced between the cabin and trail. He raised his voice enough to let her see the urgency in his command. "Get into the cabin."

Lightning struck miles away, causing a thunderous boom to echo through the trees around them. Carrie ran toward the front of the small abode. Simon searched the field for the dog, but luckily didn't have to search long. The scamp came bounding toward them, shivering as another flash of lightning filled the sky. He scooped up the pup and ran as rain poured out of the skies.

Simon thanked the crying heavens above Carrie had the good sense to leave the door open for him as he rushed through. He kicked it closed and let the soaked dog down onto the dirt floor. In no time at all mud would take up every inch of the animal's fur. Then who was going to carry him down the mountain?

He would, of course. He might be unwilling to participate in social niceties in town, but he wasn't going to make Carrie tote a mud ball down the trail. No matter how much he wanted to see her bask in the reality of life in a logging camp. It was quite enchanting to see her rough it in this world. Like a dirt-speckled sprite frolicking around in the forest.

Carrie shivered on the other side of the one-room cabin with the basket set securely in the center of the table closer to him. Opposite the table, a makeshift bed he'd built years ago lay a mere foot off the ground with the bedding rolled up to maintain some semblance of cleanliness. A trick he and Garrett had insisted upon when they built the cabin. After all, no one wanted to hike all the way up here only to have to wash and hang the bedding before using it. At least this way it was somewhat clean enough for use.

He glanced between Carrie and the bed, and a vision of her sprawled out naked—her skin flushed with passion and body writhing in need—flashed across his mind. He grew instantly hard at the thought. Dear Lord, he'd take on another cougar if he could have that happen.

When he had first threatened to seduce her, it was in jest. But the more time he spent with her, the more he weighed the benefits and consequences of such an occasion, the more he needed to feel her naked body against his. The woman dominated his every thought.

"What now?" Carrie asked, huddled against the cold stove he and Garrett had put in years ago for cool days such as this one. Luckily he'd stocked firewood and kindling next to the door when he stayed up here the first night back on the mountain, and from the looks of things, he'd been the only one to visit this season.

"We can both take off our clothes and I can keep you warm in bed, or I can make you a fire in the stove." Heaven above, he hoped the former.

She glared.

Well, that answers it. He'd have to make her a fire.

In a few minutes, the flames roared inside the stove and warmth began to fill the small chill inside the little cabin. And if nothing else, at least they could dry their rain-soaked clothes by the heat, before he took them off of her.

Without waiting for her to object—which she most certainly would—he grabbed her hand and towed her next to the heat. She resisted only a moment before she must have realized his intent and thankfully obeyed. Of course, he wouldn't mind tossing her over his shoulder and depositing her on the bed to keep warm.

Simon stood behind Carrie, close enough to warm her backside and satisfy the burning need to touch her. He wouldn't. Not yet. Not until the right moment.

Nots had already curled up beneath the legs of the stove and drifted off to sleep. Simon smiled at the little scamp. When Bud had taken him to the other side of the wagon to show him his secret stash of home brew, he'd spotted the pups and known he had to get Carrie one instead. She'd always wanted a pet, but her parents were sticklers when it came to animals within their home.

Carrie's head fell back and brushed against his chest as she basked in the warmth. The touch caressed the sensitive skin of the large scars across his heart. Instead of his usual defensive reaction to being touched on his horrid wounds, the sensation of her against him—anywhere against him—made him ache to have more.

"Are you warm?" He said the words to distract her from his touch as he reached up and caressed her shoulders and tops of her arms. He slid his palms up and down to aid in staving off the tremble in her body.

"Mmm," she answered. His breath hitched at the moan in her reply.

"I'm getting there."

Blast, so was he!

He'd had dozens of women throughout his adult life. Many more skilled at the game of lust than he was, but Carrie turned him into a giddy, confused greenhorn with no more than a husky noise. If he took her now, he wasn't confident he could last any longer than a few seconds. And he knew their relationship—however friendly-foe it was lately—would only last until they walked out the cabin door.

Blast the woman!

After a few breaths—in a failed attempt to gain control of his desire— he tugged her back against him. He held his breath and only released it once she fell against his body and relaxed. They didn't need the damned fire. Not with the way she heated him with a simple touch. Drove him to madness with a simple noise. The woman didn't need to be seduced. She was already well versed in ways in which to drive a man to pure madness.

He placed his hand over the exposed skin of her neck, his palm cupping her small throat as he slid up to her chin and back down to the edge of the valley of her breasts. What was she doing? She didn't fight him the way she should.

"Do you remember the time I tried to kiss you behind the schoolhouse?"

She nodded; her head rubbed against his scars and somehow made him harder than he'd ever been before. He dipped his gaze to where his hand rested at the top of her breast, just above the collar to her cotton shirt.

She took a deep breath. "I slapped you and ran away."

"Yes." He moved his hand until the buttons to her bodice teased his fingertips. "You should do that now."

She swallowed hard. "Why?"

Dear Lord above, she was going to punish him the way he wanted to do with her. He dipped his head low until his lips caressed the curve of her neck. He let his breath tickle the base of her neck as he spoke. "Because I don't think I can stop myself."

At that he kissed her neck. The blasted woman ignored his request and tipped her head to the side. He responded as any red-blooded man would, by yanking the buttons to her blouse free and cupping her breast. Somewhere in the back of his mind he thought he heard the ting of a button bounce off the stove, but he didn't care to look.

He had warned her.

Now it was too late. He was at the point of no return, and she spun around in his arms. The sprite rushed toward the abyss with him, and somewhere deep within his soul a flame flickered to life.

"What do you want from me?" he asked, his confidence shattered.

She shook her head. "I don't know what to ask of you."

"Ask me to leave."

Again, she shook her head.

"Then ask me to kiss you."

The rise and fall of her chest stopped. She nodded slowly and licked her sunset-pink lips. Heaven above, she was beautiful.

Not wasting time, he cupped her face and lowered his lips to hers. Heaven above, she tasted as sweet as he remembered. Like a fruit-filled elixir made just for him. He moved one palm behind her head to hold her steady as he plundered her mouth.

Showing a bravery he didn't feel, he slipped her blouse off her shoulders. Her breasts sprang free as the shirt dropped to the floor, leaving her standing in nothing but her skirt.

Had she been in her usual fashionable attire—like what she wore in town—this would be a lot more difficult. But up here she was free to dress in nothing more than a blouse and skirt. Now there was nothing between him and the entirety of her naked body but that blasted skirt.

He teased her lips with his, not quite kissing her, as he moved his mouth over hers. A distraction to keep her mind off his hands as he unbuttoned the last offensive clothing she wore. The fabric pooled at her feet, and he stood back, tipping his head to the side as he admired Carrie's flawless beauty.

He'd seen many women in nothing but what the Lord gave them, but none as beautiful as she was. Even with the strawberry birthmark on her hip above her curls, she was God's greatest design. Perfection.

She shivered and hugged herself, shielding her breasts from view. His chest tightened. Was she going to deny him now? Take away the one thing on earth he needed. Would she be so cruel?

"Don't do that," he rasped, his mouth dry. He took a hard swallow. "Don't ever cover up your body from me."

She licked her lips again and dropped her hands, once again revealing herself to him. The ache in his chest eased, and his mouth flooded with moisture.

In one step, he pressed his body against hers. His clothes were the only things stopping him from taking her against the wall right where they stood. She needed time. Needed to be shown what it was like to be his lover. Taking her fast and hard would not be the way to win her over.

He cupped her buttocks in his palms and lifted her. She wrapped her hot thighs around his hips and bent down to kiss him as he carried her to the bed. A bed too small and low to be of any justice to the woman before him now. He should stop. Not because he wanted to, but because she deserved to be taken on a large down bed with forget-me-nots tossed about the sheets.

It was too late. He couldn't stop, but he would bed her the way she deserved or die dreaming of her blond hair spread over the flowers she had given him and on his sheets at home. Come hell or high water, he would have Carrie on the bed of his fantasy. One day.

* * * *

Carrie swallowed hard as Simon stopped at the foot of the makeshift bed. Her womanhood throbbed with the need for something, but she didn't know exactly what she wanted. Simon dropped her gently to her feet. The rough fabric of his thick shirt and denim trousers were coarse against the sensitive skin of her thighs.

Simon was right. She should have slapped him and run away like she had years ago, before she was friends with Beth. Back when they were in school and he'd kissed her. She'd known what his intentions were and gladly let it happen. But social protocol called for a slap, so she'd supplied it. Today she had no desire to run away. Today, up here alone on the mountain, she wanted to forget about what others expected of her and to simply be what she wished.

With Simon, what she wished was to be his lover. At least for today. Tomorrow she would deal with the consequences of her actions, but this moment was too perfect to squander.

She was tall enough that her line of sight came to his shirt front. She reached up and opened the buttons in the most brazen of ways. One by one the shirt loosened to reveal the angry scars across his chest.

She knew the sight of them. Had been the one to wash and tend to said wounds after the attack. They were healing better than she'd hoped.

As she undid the last button, she yanked the hem from where it was tucked into his waistband, and he sucked in a deep breath between his teeth. She dropped her hands. "I'm sorry. Did I hurt you?"

He gave an almost inaudible growl and clutched her wrists in his large hands. "The opposite, my love."

"Don't call me that unless you mean it, and I know you don't."

He bent and kissed her lips. She reached down and undid his pants, tugging them off his hips.

He helped ease the drawers down until his manhood sprang free.

She swallowed hard at the sight of how large he was. Good Lord, what had she gotten herself into?

His eyes twinkled in the firelight, and he gave a smile that made her want to take another hard swallow. He watched her as he unfolded the bedroll and laid it out over the straw mattress. He stood upright, and his manhood once again caught her attention.

"I…I…" She stopped talking, because frankly she had no idea what she was trying to say.

"You don't have to do anything, my love." He encircled her in his embrace and eased her down on the bed. He kissed her hard and long. His tongue darted in and out. Each movement made her mind swirl. She wanted more. When she grew dizzy with the need for air, he lifted his head back and peered down at her. "Except feel. Just feel me. All of me."

She licked her lips and ran her fingers down over his scars. The marks that tortured his soul, but ones she loved because they were a part of him. He quivered at her touch but didn't pull back like she'd honestly thought he would. With another brazen move, she reached down and wrapped her hands around his manhood. His quiver turned fierce, and his breath came in short bursts.

He groaned, reached down to grab her wrist to tug it above her head, and brought the other to lay over the first. He adjusted on his elbow to pin her hands to the bed with the arm he braced on. With his free hand, he caressed her. Each touch, each stroke sent sharp heat to the place beneath her curls. She arched her hips upward, begging for something.

"Ah, my love, you want me inside you?" His voice was huskier than she'd ever heard from him, but it mimicked the sultry voice inside her head whenever she tried to talk herself out of his arms. Of course, she didn't want to leave his embrace.

She nodded, but in truth, she was scared.

"I'll give you what you want, but it will hurt. Only for a moment. After that you'll feel nothing but pure rapture." He ran kisses down her neck and back up to her chin. Then placed a passionate one on her lips. "Do you still want me inside you?"

She nodded again but focused on keeping her breath steady.

"Ask me," he said.

"What?"

"What do you ask of me?"

"All I ask of you," she said, no longer able to deny the need to feel the sensual promise he'd made come to fruition, "is to love me."

Simon sucked in another breath through his teeth and kissed her harder than he ever had before. His tongue violent against her mouth, but welcome. He moved his body over hers and, with his knees, spread open her legs.

Almost as soon as she'd opened to him, he gently pressed his manhood into her. She clenched her thighs instinctively when a piercing ache shot through her core.

"Easy, love," he whispered, and kissed her hair. "Give it a moment."

"You've done this before?" she didn't know why she asked the question. Maybe to fill the awkward silence her weakness had caused.

He shook his head. "Not like this."

The throbbing continued for what seemed like forever, but was probably only a few seconds. Soon, Simon flexed as if to move, and she clenched her legs, waiting for the pain.

"It won't happen again. Trust me." He covered her mouth with his and ran his hand down her side, to cup one buttock with his hand. He pressed his scarred cheek to hers, and she closed her eyes, focusing on the connection. How the one simple action spoke more than he would dare say. She nodded against his face and kissed the scar.

She eased the hold her legs had on his hips, and he moved. She gasped. Not out of pain, but of the need for air.

Simon withdrew and pressed into her again, and she fought the urge to cry out. He repeated the motion, and each time she needed extra breath until she grew dizzy. The need to release the pressure building within her dominated her every thought. She fought the urge until Simon leaned his head against hers as he took her. "Let it go, my love."

She obeyed, unable to do anything else. The wave of relief hit her like one of the lightning bolts thundering outside the cabin. She shuddered beneath him mere seconds before he did the same on top of her.

"I shouldn't have done that inside of you. I'm sorry."

All she could do was shake her head. She had no idea what he was talking about, but she didn't care. He'd told her to trust in him, and at that moment, that's all she could do. Trust.

Chapter 13

Simon tangled his fingers in Carrie's hair and leaned forward to smell the sweet scent of her soap. She was more beautiful than he'd imagined, lying next to him with nothing but him and the thin blanket he'd pulled over them to keep her warm from the slight chill.

What he wanted to do was pull back the covers and follow his hands' progression as he ran them over every inch of her skin. He wanted to study the contours of her body. Imprint the memory of her on his mind for all eternity.

Her words rang in his memory like a chapel bell. *"Love me."*

He knew her words were meant for a moment of passion. Perhaps prompted by the nickname he'd given her in order to irritate her. A nickname he now knew fit her to perfection. He did love her. Always had. Only Carrie could center him on this earth. He was only home whenever she was with him. All of those times she visited his house. All of the moments he saw her smiling face in camp and felt grounded. It was all because of her. She was what made him a better man. He had to make her love him. He couldn't live without Carrie Kerr.

He toyed with her hair for a moment longer, then kissed her passion-plumped lips. The image of her beside him for the rest of his life flickered the flame she'd ignited into a roaring fire. He ran a thumb over her mouth. "We should get to camp before Aunt June sends a search party."

Carrie sat upright, holding the blankets over her chest. He frowned at the sudden bout of modesty. Instead he tugged the blanket down for one last view of her bounty. She snatched the cover back up and glowered. "We need to dress now. Aunt June *will* send a search party. She swore to me she would. And we all know she keeps her word."

Simon would have chuckled at Carrie's wide-eyed stare if he hadn't felt the same. The last thing he needed in his newfound quest to make Carrie fall in love with him was Aunt June sticking her nose where it shouldn't be. A gift the woman had in barrels.

It took a few minutes to dress, but luckily their clothes had dried, despite being hastily deposited around the small room. If he were a better man, he would have hung them near the stove to dry.

Carrie buttoned the top of her blouse and tucked it in as Nots woke suddenly and ran to the door to bark.

"Either we have a visitor, or she needs to use the bushes." Simon slipped on his jacket—the last of his wardrobe—and quickly tidied up the bedding.

"Or there's a bear." Carrie tilted her head and wrinkled her nose as she wrapped her wool shawl around her small shoulders. "I don't hear anything."

Simon stood from rolling up the blankets and stared at the door. "I'll check it out."

Carrie scooped Nots into her arms as Simon slipped outside. The air was thick with moisture, but the sky had already cried out all of the rain in the clouds.

It didn't take long before a flicker of crimson caught his eyes from the outside corner of the cabin. The red flannel shirt he'd seen Thomas wearing earlier flashed through his memory.

"Oy, Thomas," he called. "What are you doing here?"

Like the louse he was, he popped out from his hidden position. "Aunt June sent me up here to fetch Carrie. There's been some talk down there. We're a bit worried she came up here alone with you and never returned." He slid a telling glance to the cabin door. "And now I see our fears were for real-play."

"You've no idea what you're talking about, and don't go spoutin' off scuttlebutt down there or I'll beat you until your mother doesn't even recognize who you are." Simon shoved the young logger's concerns away, but deep inside he cursed himself for not taking better care with Carrie's reputation. It seemed every moment they were alone, his time ended with regret. Never for what he did with the woman he'd desired all his life, but for what strife he might cause her in the future. Next time he would make certain she was protected from everything. And there would be a next time. He couldn't imagine a life where he never touched her again. She was his.

"Carrie is a lady, and nothing untoward happened up here, do you understand me?" He took a menacing step toward the mudsill lowlife. "If I hear otherwise, I'll knock your galley west."

"Threatening me won't get you nowhere. I know you've been in the cabin alone with a single woman for quite some time. And you with the most reprehensible reputation in town. You've ruined her." Thomas's nostrils flared. "She was a decent woman, but now she's nothing more than a dime whore."

Simon ground his teeth. Heat flashed over his body. Even if Carrie had given herself to him, there was no woman on earth as flawless and deserving as she. "She is still a decent woman."

Thomas's eyes bulged from his head. "If she's loose enough to sneak away with a cut-up swine like you, then she should have no problem hitchin' herself to me. I'll look past the fact I didn't get her first. As long as she pleases me good enough when I'm on top of her."

Simon flexed his jaw, clenched his fists tight, and growled. The man had no idea how close he was to a broken rib or two. "Stay away from her."

"That's up to her." Thomas gave a malicious chuckle. "And she ain't gonna choose a deadbeat like you over me. Hell, at least I won't scare her every time I bed her."

Unable to hold back his demons any longer, Simon slammed his fist into the man's stomach, sending him sprawling to the ground. Simon panted as he stepped over Thomas, his fists clenched so tight his knuckles had surely turned white. "I'll say this only one more time: stay away from her."

Thomas answered with a laugh as he rolled to the side, clutching his stomach.

"Test me again and I will kill you."

Thomas struggled to his feet and ran toward the trailhead.

Simon flexed his neck to ease the tension at the base of his skull, and opened the door but stood shielding Carrie from the outside. He gave her a quick perusal from head to toe. "It's Thomas. The rain's let up, but it'll be back. Best get down the hill before we're all stuck in this little cabin for the night."

"What?" Carrie tucked Nots beneath her wool shawl and curled the other end around her arm. She stood on her tiptoes to peer past him at Thomas and then back at him. She narrowed her eyes. "Why would Aunt June send Thomas?"

The blasted woman! If she'd stopped this whole mess from spiraling out of control in the first place they'd be left alone. Instead she'd placated the persistent logger. And let Aunt June run roughshod over the whole situation. "If *you* had told him to shin out already, she wouldn't have sent him up. Tell him now so she can't play any more games."

Carrie pursed her plump lips. "Why don't you do it for me?"

Simon glowered. He'd tried, for God's sake, and all that did was encourage the man to try harder. No. "You and Aunt June dug this hole, you have to fill it in yourselves. Any decision you make is going to have to come from you, and you will have to take action. For the first time in your life, you're going to have to choose, and act on your choice."

Simon shielded the emotion he couldn't keep from flashing in his eye by lowering his gaze to the floor. If she cared for him at all, she would toss the deadbeat timber beast down the chute. Whatever choice she made next would determine the fate of not only her life, but his.

Please, God, let her choose me.

* * * *

Carrie mimicked Simon's scowl, snatched up the basket of huckleberries, and followed as he left the little building, shutting the door behind. Of course he wasn't going to help her out with Thomas. He'd already gotten what he wanted from her. Punished her for deceiving him—although what they did in there had little to do with punishment. Unless you take into account that she could never marry now—not that she wanted to anyway—and she would have to hide her indiscretion from her parents, which was the difficult part of this whole situation. She was the worst liar this side of the continental divide—although she did have a cousin over in California who was by far the worst liar in America. Her particular shortcoming was the one reason she'd never learned to play poker with Beth and Simon on the many occasions they'd tried to get her to learn. Her parents would see right through her to the truth.

Why should Simon care about her future if he'd already claimed his prize? She couldn't fault him for not wanting to get involved with her decision to let Thomas down. Still, she didn't like his answer. It would be much easier if he would do it for her.

Thomas paced back and forth, halfway to the path leading down the mountain. One arm crossed over his chest like a half hug, while he tapped on his teeth with the index finger of his free hand. Carrie frowned. Whatever grated on his mind deeply affected his mood. As soon as she drew near enough to join him down the mountain, he stopped. A deep frown followed his perusal of her—one long enough to make her shuffle her feet and tug her wrap tighter.

Did he know what had happened in the cabin?

There was no way he could. Was there? She surveyed her clothes to make certain her skirts were on straight when she noticed a button missing from her blouse. She yanked her wrap around her chest and lifted her head as Thomas moved toward the trail.

Simon motioned for her to follow the angry logger and—much to her relief—stayed beside her on the trek off the mountain. All the while, Simon glared at Thomas's back while the latter made no attempt at conversation.

The whole experience was tense enough that even Nots hid in the folds of her wrap and didn't dare peek her head out. Why couldn't men feign friendship the way women did? At least then they wouldn't have to hike off the mountain in uncomfortable silence.

Carrie let the silence take them all the way to camp, which seemed to take a lot longer than when she and Simon had climbed to the cabin. Odd since they were descending the mountain instead of climbing.

They reached the Grove as a long whistle sounded through the trees. Simon clutched her arm and stopped. Carrie stilled as Thomas searched the trees around them. Throughout last year she'd heard the noise on a few occasions, and the outcome was never good. Something had happened.

Men bounded through the trees from their posts, appearing as suddenly as if they were ghosts from a graveyard on All Hallows' Eve.

In the first positive moment Carrie had ever seen the two men before her give, Simon exchanged a worrisome glance with Thomas. Simon inclined his head. "Listen, it may be one of my men. They've been working this way for the last few weeks. Can you go down and tell Aunt June to prep her cabin?"

Thomas nodded and left, his mood altered from mere moments ago when he'd glared over his shoulder.

"Let's go." Simon grabbed Carrie's hand and towed her behind him through the trees.

Carrie clutched Nots tight enough to keep her safe through the flight as she leapt over trees and waded through vegetation, all while keeping an eye on the widowmakers above.

Simon emerged onto a trail and gently eased her to walk next to him as he moved toward the sound of the whistle, now blasting for a third time.

"What's happened?" she asked as loud as her breathless voice would allow.

"Most likely an accident." Simon stopped before a large downed tree across the path and lifted her over the obstacle as if she weighed no more than Nots. "When we get there, you stay back. Do not look at what we find. I don't want you seeing those images in your head for the rest of your life."

A few minutes later she saw the crowd of men. Simon turned to her as she approached him. "Stay here."

Carrie gagged at the smell permeating the air.

She nodded numbly and clutched Nots to her chest as Simon waded into the group of loggers. She covered her nose and mouth with her shawl to stave off the stench surrounding the group. Simon's height let her see his progress through the crowd, and it wasn't until he stopped and ducked down that she lost sight of him.

Carrie took a lungful of breath-heated air from within her shawl. What had happened? And who? *Dear Lord, don't let it be Beth or Garrett.* She froze at the thought. She wasn't like Beth. Her friend was adventurous and afraid of nothing, but Carrie had no desire to see the mangled body of another logger. And what if it *was* her best friend? She'd never get over the image. The one time she'd seen a dead man on the path was enough to haunt her dreams for the remainder of her days. If she was forced to look upon her dearest friend's lifeless body, she might spiral down into a darkness right next to Simon.

Nots squirmed and barked as Carrie struggled to keep ahold of the only comfort she had at the moment. If Beth wasn't the injured logger, she'd go down right now and beg her to never venture out of camp again. This whole experience up here was a lot more dangerous than she'd ever imagined. More than she'd experienced the year before.

Simon appeared before her as he tucked something into the inside breast pocket of his jacket. The muscles in his jaw flexed and eased several times.

Tears formed in her eyes at his silence. Why would he remain speechless if it wasn't someone they held dear? "Who is it?"

Simon's chest rose with a deep breath. "Jake. Looks like he's been there a while, judging by the way his body looks."

The fear twisting her heart into knots eased, but a hole dug in the deepest pit of her stomach. He'd been missing ever since she had told Simon he'd assaulted her. She didn't respond, but stared at Simon, her eyes going dry from the forest air.

He lifted a single eyebrow and widened his stance. "I had nothing to do with this. The boy was gone when I got to the berry patch."

She took a step toward him. She should believe him. Trust in him, but he was possibly the last one to see him alive. She glanced around to ensure no one overheard her and whispered, "You said you were going to kill him."

"A figure of speech," he hissed. "I could never kill someone out of cold blood. Honestly, I thought you'd have a better opinion of me by now."

"Then what happened?"

Simon surveyed the crowd, then directed Carrie to start down the path toward camp. He pulled something out of his inside pocket and held it out for her to see. "I found this."

Carrie leaned over his cupped palm and wrinkled her forehead. "A smoke?"

"Hand rolled using printed paper to hold in the tobacco."

"What does it mean?"

Simon replaced the evidence in his pocket, then dropped his hand to his side and led the way down the hill. "Don't know yet. Jake clutched the smoke, but the end was burned into his palm. I don't think it was his. I think he grabbed it from whoever beat him. Keep this between you and me. Do not tell anyone." He caught her eye, his shining with desperation. "Do you hear me?"

"Yes."

"Good girl." He tugged her by the hand, forcing her to walk closer to him.

She looked over her shoulder, but the group of men were too far away to see. They were alone once more. She pulled her hand free, which garnered a long, pained look from Simon.

"I don't want others talking," she stuttered. "Thomas no doubt already knows something happened in the cabin. I don't want to risk others knowing."

Simon's cheek twitched below his scar, and he faced forward. He paused, and then responded, "Just make certain you take care while I'm gone."

"I can hold my own in camp," she promised.

"You'll be alone." He rolled his shoulders back as if to work out a kink in his muscles. "You won't even have Aunt June. She may be a horrid gossip, and meddler, but she is damned good at protecting you."

"I'll be fine."

"Maybe I should see if we can make room for you in the bateau," he said. Although she suspected he spoke more to himself than to her.

"No. I'm needed here." She stopped walking to try to prove her point, but when he continued down the trail, she followed. "I can do this job as well as Aunt June."

"No doubt you can, but you're still a target to at least one person who will be left behind."

"You're talking about Thomas?"

"Of course I am."

"I'll be fine."

The trail before them opened up at the bottom of the hill to the Railroad Grove. Simon gave her a sideways glance. "Can you honestly say you trust Thomas with your life?"

"There are few people in the world to whom I would entrust my life." In all honesty, there were three. Aunt June, Garrett, and Simon. She'd love to trust Beth, but the woman had a bad habit of getting into trouble. "But I'll not shirk my duty because of a little danger. If I let that dictate my decisions, I never would have come up here in the first place. I'd have let you drown in a cask of whiskey in your parlor."

"Then you will talk to Thomas before I leave. And I need proof you've done it, otherwise I'll kidnap you and force you to take a trip you don't want to make. Then when we're at the mill I'll send you on the first train to Missoula."

"You wouldn't do that." When he didn't respond to her accusation, she continued. "Fine. Tonight I will let him know I am not interested in his advances any further."

"Good girl," Simon said mere seconds before he tromped into Aunt June's camp.

The only reason she gave in was because he'd made sense. Best deal with this mess before she no longer had Aunt June to watch over her every move. In all honesty, she was a bit afraid of what might happen while she was alone at camp. She knew she could handle the chores, but the thought of being left behind to fend for herself amongst a group of loggers was daunting at best. Maybe she'd talk to Beth. Get her to stay with her during the days instead of traipsing around in the dangerous trees. A request that would work in both of their favors.

Chapter 14

Carrie paced in the little cabin she shared with Aunt June. Supper was over, and Jake's body had been brought down and cleaned up for transport to the mill once the train started running again. Against Simon's advice, she'd seen the body—bruised and battered from a beating, but that's not what had killed him. No. He'd been killed by a bullet. Simon carried a gun.

Part of her knew he hadn't murdered the young logger, but the more logical side of her put the facts together. Simon was beastly. Not in appearance—in that aspect he was perfect. No, he was beastly in temperament. Could he be capable of such atrocity? He had said accidents happen all of the time in the forest and sworn to kill the man. But this was no accident.

Regardless, Jake's death was a result of the attack by the berry patch. She was certain. The timing of his death could not be a coincidence. This whole plan was turning out to be one disaster after another.

Starting with the moment she gave in to temptation with Simon.

The moment was one she wanted to regret. She needed to cast blame on Simon, or on Thomas for discovering them in a compromising place, but all she could do was blame herself for not being stronger. The problem was, every time Simon drew close, touched her, all she could do was melt in his embrace. She was weak. Too weak to fight him when he spoke to her in low, sensual tones. Years ago she'd been enamored with him, but she thought that had come to an end when he withdrew into himself and all of his selfish desires.

Apparently not.

She needed to find Beth. Ask her what to do. Plead for her to stay in the camp with her—at least during the days. But first she needed to talk to Thomas.

Carrie checked to ensure Nots slept hard on her bed near the fire, then eased the door open to take stock of her surroundings in the dark. Simon sat by the fire and perked up when he saw her but thankfully didn't move from his seat. She didn't know what to say to him. Didn't know how she felt about the whole situation. Were it last year, she'd work to keep him enamored with her. Hope he meant more than a romp in the hay—or in her case cabin. She'd gone into the season hoping to forge a new path for her future. One without a man to run her life.

Across the meadow, Aunt June's shadowy form supervised some loggers carrying the last of her supplies to the lake. Before sunrise tomorrow Carrie would be left to man the fire alone. For the first time in her life she'd be the only one dictating her daily activities.

The crisp night air cooled her heated face as she shut the door behind her and searched the meadow for Thomas. Seeing no one but Simon, she headed toward the railcar. At least she'd find Beth there so she could plead for her company.

She'd gotten halfway to the train and studied the ground. Wheel tracks where the traveling merchant's wagon rolled out the day before gave way to a path down the mountain—as if a sign from above. Perhaps she wasn't meant to be up here muddling up her life even more than she'd already done. She should steal a horse and follow the wagon down. After all, her main reason behind coming up here would float down the river once the sun rose.

She took a step toward the corral, then stopped and scrunched her nose. She'd never stolen anything before. She'd get caught before she even rode past the chickens. Those clucking, troublemaking tattletales would give her away. The loggers would tie her to a tree and force her to stay just to make more huckleberry flapjacks. Although soon it would be huckleberry that made their mouths water. Who else was going to keep them well-fed while Aunt June was gone?

The heavy thump of shoes on the ground alerted her to a man's presence, and she turned as Thomas slid from the shadows of the trees.

"I thought you'd never come out." His voice was more accusatory than she'd anticipated. Why? Because she hadn't come out earlier? The more time she spent with the man, the more she realized the mistake she'd made in using him as a way to get back at Simon. And Simon was right, she should have never played Aunt June's games.

"I've a lot to do before the men leave in the morning."

Through the moonlight, she saw him nod. "Ah, yes. You'll be left unsupervised to do as you wish."

She didn't miss the lustful hope in his words. Her stomach dropped, and a sour taste formed in the back of her throat. It was now or never. She should do it before she lost her nerve. "Thomas, I'm afraid I can't entertain you anymore. I'm not the woman for you, and I shouldn't have encouraged your affections."

She'd expected a quiet acceptance. Pleading for her to reconsider. Perhaps even anger, but the man gave nothing but a half-chuckle. "I'm afraid we're beyond that, my dear."

"Pardon?" she asked, and grasped the necklace. If she could take back the day by the wagon, she'd have stayed in the cabin. Away from amorous men and their gifts. Although, she did love Nots something fierce.

"I know you were compromised by that fiend," he spit the words toward Simon's shadowed figure near the fire. "But don't worry. I'm willing to look past your indiscretion and marry you anyway."

"Again I ask, beg your pardon?" Who in Hades's fire did he think he spoke to in such a way? She'd met some reprehensible men in her time, but never one so presumptuous as to assume bullying and blackmail would win her hand.

"You'll never find a decent husband after your indiscretion is known, but don't worry. I'll still be here. I'm not one to shirk because of a little wickedness on your part." Did Thomas wiggle his eyebrows on the last words? She couldn't be certain in the darkness, but one thing she was certain of—her blood boiled like a witch's brew.

"I wouldn't do you the disservice of gracing your life with my *wickedness*. I thank you for your gracious concern for my reputation, but I can assure you I have no intention of marrying you simply because you will look past my indiscretions. I am perfectly content with becoming an old maid. Now if you'll excuse me, I have somewhere to be." She pivoted and stomped off toward the railcar, but her chest quivered with suppressed emotion, and tears formed in the bottom of her eyes.

At least she'd gotten rid of the overzealous, wife-hunting logger once and for all.

* * * *

Hidden in the dense shadows of the pines, Simon waited for Carrie. He'd watched her stomp off after talking to Thomas, then kept an eye on the man as he headed toward the Bonner camp. From the looks of their stiff postures while they spoke, she'd let him down. Hard. The knot around Simon's chest eased a bit at the event. Now all he had to do was convince her to fall in love with him—a scared, imperfect shell of a man. But a man who needed her desperately.

Thomas was not good enough for Carrie. Frankly, neither was he, but he was a helluva lot better than a young, two-bit timber beast. If only Aunt June hadn't started this whole mess. He needed to speak with the meddlesome cook about her intrusions. Maybe even beg her to keep her nose out of his future affairs, especially those pertaining to Carrie. He didn't need Aunt June ruining any chance he had at making Carrie fall in love with him. Which after their time at Mother Goose's Cottage was his sole intent. He couldn't live without her, and he'd spend the rest of his life making her love him as much as he did her.

Carrie had stayed in Beth's railcar until the fire had long since burned out, and he'd waited patiently. He needed sleep for the coming drive, but even more, he needed to see her one last time. Maybe even steal a kiss to carry him through until he returned.

His chest hollowed at the thought of leaving her. Especially now. He'd found peace with the intimacy they'd shared. The moment she'd let him slip her clothes from her luscious body, he knew they were destined for one another. All those years he'd teased her, fantasized about bedding her like one of his conquests, he'd never imagined she'd end up stealing his soul and mending it with hers. With one simple glance, one compromise she'd made for him, she had reached into his heart and stolen it forever. A heart he didn't think he had anymore.

He couldn't lose her.

The squeal of a door needing grease echoed through the night. Simon waited in silence as Carrie left the flickering light of the candle within his sister's railcar and hopped down the steps. It was too dark to see her expression, but the speed at which she moved through the night let him know she was in a hurry.

He listened for her footsteps to grow near. "A little late to be traipsing around the forest, isn't it?"

Carrie let out a squeal and stopped quickly. "Good Lord, Simon. You startled me. You're no better than a bear out here."

He stepped close to her and wrapped his arm around her waist to tug her until their bodies melded together. He didn't bother to ask. Didn't want to risk resistance to his touch. "Promise me you won't leave the cabin after dark while I'm gone."

"I promise," she said, breathlessly. "I've no intention of getting killed out here in the dark."

"Promise me you won't be alone with Thomas."

"Simon," she chided, and pushed against his chest.

He held her tight. "Please, Carrie. That's all I ask of you."

He used the words she'd seared into his soul to plead his case. Would she remember what she'd asked of him? Did she remember? He did.

The pressure against his chest eased, and she leaned into his body. "All right. I promise. I won't leave after dark, and I will not be with Thomas alone."

He knew where her mouth was by the feel of her body in his arms. During their time together, every inch of her printed onto his memory. He could move his hand over her birthmark without so much as stripping a single piece of clothing from her body.

He nestled his nose in her hair above her ear and smelled the sweet honeyed scent of her, and then moved down to kiss her as he had before. He lifted her slightly to allow him better access to plunder her mouth. He wanted her to remember him when he left. Wanted every thought in her mind to center on him. Leaving her breathless for his kisses was the only way he knew how to leave her dreaming of his return.

He pulled back from her mouth. Her chest against his fell in rapid breaths, and she clutched his jacket as if he grounded her to earth, to him. "Don't do anything to endanger yourself while I'm gone. I can't lose you."

"I won't." Her voice sounded husky with passion, and in the darkness, she cleared her throat and stepped gingerly out of his embrace. This time he let her go. He envisioned her smoothing her hair as women were wont to do after a good, hard kiss. To his delight, Carrie reached out and touched his arm. "As long as you take care on the river. Garrett mentioned it was dangerous this year."

"It is." He nodded, although he knew she couldn't see him through the night. "But don't worry about me, my love, it's nothing I haven't done before. I've run with the Devils a time or two, but I've never been one of them before."

"Still, take care," she said.

"Did you tell Thomas to leave you alone?"

"Yes. I told him the truth. I do not plan to wed anyone anytime soon. Having been paraded before every wealthy bachelor in Montana, I'd like a chance to discover who I am. Without a husband."

"I'm glad you finally addressed Thomas." He said the encouraging words, but a knot grew in his stomach and slid to his throat. Her words bored a hole in his heart, but at the same time caused the tightening in his chest to ease at the thought that she would not entertain anyone's affections. At least he could leave knowing Thomas wouldn't find a way into Carrie's marriage bed, and Simon could always come back and convince her otherwise.

Simon wanted to ask her to wait for him, but her words echoed in his mind. Her nonchalance after having given herself to the skilled caress of his hands, the hard decision to avoid marriage altogether, maybe even the way she hadn't spoken a word about the moment they'd shared had all combined to give him pause. She was a woman, and in his experience, they wanted to chatter nonstop after having experienced his lovemaking. Carrie hadn't said so much as a word about it, which caused his heart to palpitate whenever he thought about her response, or rather lack thereof.

He'd have to explore the issue later. Take more time to convince her he was a man worth having. Tonight, he needed to get her back to the cabin before Aunt June took a spoon to him like she would a wayward child. She'd do it, too. He'd seen many large-statured loggers whither under Aunt June's spoon. "Come, my love, we need to get you back to the cabin."

"Don't call me your 'love,'" she said, but her voice lacked the strength behind her words.

He didn't respond. What she didn't know, and what he'd only just discovered himself, was that he was in love with her. The hard kind of love that grips the bitterness from your soul and replaces it with her light. And he'd live the rest of his life proving it true. Even if he had to wait until she was old and senile, he would.

Chapter 15

Carrie stood on the banks of Seeley Lake and watched Simon float away behind the logs joined together to make what the rivermen called the Raft. She wanted to cry. Had fought the urge ever since the night before when Simon kissed her. She didn't resist the moment. Didn't want to. At that instant, all she'd wanted was to be with him. Let him into her soul like Garrett and Beth had done with each other. She wanted what they had discovered together. A lifetime of struggles, love, and passion.

She wanted Simon.

Forget about his accident. His torrid past. She wanted the man she knew he was deep inside, and she wanted him to finally realize who he was meant to be. If she couldn't have him the way he was meant to be—a man passionate about life and happy in love—then she wouldn't have anyone. Life as Aunt June's protégé looked more realistic now than it had when she'd first made the decision to die an old maid.

Simon made love to her, then continued to seduce her the way he had many women. She wasn't fool enough to believe she was any different from the tainted women he'd previously seduced. Before long he would grow tired of her and move on to another conquest. That's how he worked. How he always treated his women. Weeks, sometimes months, of seduction followed by a lifetime of tears for the ladies he left behind. How many times had she gone about town and had to console the distraught women as they tried hard to hide their broken affair? She didn't dare even try to count.

Now she was one of them.

A chattel in his collection of hearts.

She'd brought it on herself, she supposed. If only she'd been stronger. After all, she'd known what he was before he'd even had the accident. If only she'd battled him harder. Maybe then she could have kept her heart from shattering like the glass in a looking glass tossed across a room.

When Simon stood close, though, she lost the ability for rational thought. Only the sensation of what she felt when he touched her dictated her next move. More like impaired her judgment. When he dipped his head low, she could think of nothing but him.

"Where do we start?" Beth asked from behind her.

Carrie swiped at the tears with the back of her hand and faced her dearest friend. At least Beth had given no qualms about staying with her in camp. Carrie really wasn't like her friend, but she supposed they balanced each other. Beth with her brazen, adventurous spirit and Carrie with her more conservative and logical approach to things. They often prevented one another from entering into horrible situations. Simon was one mistake she couldn't let Beth know she'd made. Not yet, anyway. "The noon meal, I suppose."

Beth lead the way to camp. "Are you all right? Did Simon do something to you again? I swear, he never acted like such a blowhard before his accident. Now he's all insults and outbursts. I can talk to him when he gets back if you want. Tell him to get over what we did to him already, and leave you be."

"No." Carrie sniffled. Beth, involved in building a new life with her husband, left Simon to wallow in his own misery. Even today she remained oblivious to what had happened in her brother's life, let alone Carrie's. For the best, she supposed. Her dearest friend was newly wed and completely troublesome. She didn't need Beth making her life any more complicated than Aunt June had already done. "No. It's not Simon. Must be the air up here, or change in season."

"It is a bit dry for having just rained." Beth all but skipped down the trail. "I thought we'd have enough weather to wet the mountain, but it didn't last. With the low snowfall and dry spring, we'll be sitting in a tinderbox and striking matches with the chute. Glad we don't have to run it anymore."

"It's a good thing they took the river load down," Carrie said, leaping over a stone-laden patch in the trail. "Spring is over. Now the men can focus on the Railroad Grove and still meet the contract."

"Sure, if we ever get the steam loader running again. We can't get the loads down if we don't get the logs on the train." Beth strolled into camp and leaned against Aunt June's serving table, her pants such an odd look on a woman about to prepare meals, but one Beth loved to wear.

Carrie followed, but with a less enthusiastic approach to being left behind to brew and bubble about her moral spiral. She wanted to blame Simon, but she'd made a conscious decision to let her heart think for her, and now her brain had to pay the price. She could blame no one but herself. Would she give into temptation again? Did she even want to tempt fate? "Since Simon took the position on the drive, I expect Wall will be able to focus solely on mending whatever needs to be fixed. With luck, the train will run soon. Then perhaps we can get Aunt June and the rivermen back up here."

And hopefully by then she'd have a better idea as to what she wanted to do about Simon. She walked to the cook cabin and let Nots out. Maybe she should stop stewing about what had happened in the past and start planning for what was to come upon his return. If she were the woman she planned to be, she'd let logic and reason make her decisions. She would walk away and not let him tear out her heart the way he'd done before.

"God willing, they'll be back up within a few weeks. Earlier if they push hard." Beth slapped the table in a most unladylike way. "So, what did you plan to do for the noon meal?"

"I have an idea to help the men get more work done. And with them close by, it'll be a lot easier than when they were at two separate Groves." Carrie smiled. She refused to let her heart dictate her path. It always seemed to get her into trouble. From now on, she'd let her reasonable side decide her fate. And it started with food.

* * * *

Simon ran this thumb down the scar on his face and watched the men leap from log to log. One of the new rivermen wobbled precariously while he poked his peavey into the center of the nest in a weak attempt to dislodge the obstruction. Only a few hours on the drive and already they'd encountered difficulties. Wall had said his men were all experienced, but this greenhorn jabbed his peavey at the log like a stuffed child to his vegetables. He didn't look fit to ride the bateau, let alone the logs. The man wobbled on one leg as he struggled to gain his balance with flailing hands. In a mere breath he could roll right into the white water beneath the growing nest and be gone forever.

Simon couldn't lose a riverman while leading the Devil May Cares. Victoria would have his head mounted in her new doily-filled office at the Mill. The tree under Simon's feet wobbled as it smacked into the nest and lodged. Like a mountain goat on a cliff, he leapt across the rolling logs until he reached the young logger. "Get to the bank!" he shouted, and pointed toward the safety of the riverbank a quarter of the way across the river.

The young man shook his head.

Simon's face heated at being disobeyed. Who in Hades's name did this *boy* think he was? Simon jumped onto the log next to the boy and leaned close so as not to be mistaken. "Get to the bank! Now!"

His fingers tingled with the need to toss the young man toward the shoreline, but he resisted. To do so would only send the logger tumbling into the water. He needed to get his plow cleaned, though. Maybe a good beating would teach him to obey a command the first time.

The young logger nodded and jumped like a mouse following a frog across a lily pad field. Not that he'd ever seen such a sight, but the way the man carried himself—shaky and uneasy—brought the image to mind.

Simon shoved hard at a log in the center of the nest, and the wood beneath his feet shuddered. He searched the water around him for the bateau, but it was nowhere in sight. Who the hell was manning the safety boat? Without another option, Simon shoved hard at the key log and felt, more than heard, the crack of the nest breaking free. His heart pounded against his ribs as he ran over the shifting logs toward the bank.

If he didn't get there in time, he'd be sucked down into the water. Tossed about with the violent force of the logs as they shot down the river, propelled by the pressure of Mother Nature and the logs behind.

Each time he lifted a foot, water immediately replaced the wood beneath him. In a few hard heartbeats, he leapt across the last piece of timber to land with a thud on the bank.

Water splashed up his back as the last log broke free and cascaded down the river rapid. Simon leaned over and rested his hands on his knees as he caught his breath and stilled his runaway heart. He stood tall and searched the river. Where was the blasted bateau?

"Damn, boss. That was quite a show you put on." The young logger approached him with a ridiculous grin plastered on his face.

Simon glared at the boy.

"You're walking the bank with the Bonner boys." Without waiting for a response, he followed the river downstream. On instinct, he reached in his breast pocket to feel for Carrie's forget-me-nots. The night she'd given him the flowers, he'd pressed them in a book he'd borrowed from Aunt June. The older woman had thought he wanted to improve his mind. Huh! No good there. All he'd wanted was to preserve the flowers Carrie so obviously hadn't realized had meaning behind them.

He'd found it funny when she brought him a small bouquet of remembrance and undying love. She didn't know the loggers at Great Mountain paid a particular respect for this flower. Choosing not to destroy the beauty of the flower unless taken for a wife or loved one back home. Although those bouquets were usually taken toward the end of the season when the men returned home. Many timber beasts downed their trees so that they missed the small flowers that grew beneath the forest giants.

These were his. Given to him by the woman who at the time had been nothing more than a friend, and woman he dearly loved to tease. One who now held a light in his soul with one hand and a bouquet of little blue flowers in the other. She had to know how he felt. He'd tried to show her last night as he said goodbye.

Two logs slammed together and brought his mind back to the present. Downstream, somewhere near the start of the logs, the old salts on the Devil May Care team worked their logs. Farther upstream, Aunt June steered her little boat at a safe distance from the rest of the crew. Near nightfall they'd corral the logs in a slow-moving pool to rest for the night. Although if he had his way, they'd ride through the dark. Every night, in fact, until they reached the boom at the mill.

But where was the bateau? Simon searched the river farther upstream with no luck. He waited at the water's edge as the logs rushed past him, and for the perfect opportunity to climb on the hump of a passing tree.

A large grandfather timber eased toward him. Simon tucked his peavey under his armpit and caught the log, jumping on the back to balance as it floated downstream. He adjusted the peavey in his hands and used it to stay on the hump and maneuver around the rocks and obstructions.

He floated, steering the log and leaping across others until he grew even with the men at the beginning of the drive. The sun dipped low in the western sky as he brought his log toward the bank where the Devil May Cares wrangled the boom logs to hold the Raft together.

Behind him the bateau floated lazily toward him and the banks, carrying both greenhorns. Simon faced the Devil May Cares. "Oy, Blue. How long have these two been rivermen?"

Blue watched the men move down the river for a second, then turned back. "They're both river rats. Said they were on a crew out Wisconsin way last year."

"I thought you were a selective lot. This is the first time I've heard of you taking on a river rat or two."

Blue yanked on the line to check the tightness of the boom logs. "With the new logging system, and most of the Bonner river crew being moved to the Railroad, we had to take on a few new guys. Didn't have a chance to be picky. Tried to get you to be in the brotherhood, but Wall insisted he needed you at camp."

"He's been an odd case this year," Simon wondered aloud, although he spoke mostly to himself. First the push from Victoria to put Wall in charge of virtually everything in camp, and then this new information. Why had Wall not wanted him on the team? Not that he'd wanted to even be at the lumber camp, let alone ride the river. Seems fate didn't want him to have any control over his life this season.

"Wall's been talking to the big bugs at the mill," Blue said. "Don't know why, but I get the feeling he's into something big. Maybe a little too into it. When we came down the river the first time, he went into Victoria's office the morning we got to the mill and didn't come out until after dark."

"Maybe he's chiselin' his way into her skirts," Simon suggested, but somehow he doubted the prim new boss would allow Wall—a rough winter cowboy turned summertime logger—to kiss her. Let alone do anything else.

"Whatever he was doing, it took a long time." Blue moved his gaze to the bank behind him. Simon turned to see Aunt June slide her boat onto the bank.

"You should have hired the chickens to be rivermen. They'd have done a better job of rowin' the bateau," Aunt June shouted as she steered toward the overnight camp. Like the rough woman she was, she leapt onto a large rock and yanked the entire flat-bottomed boat halfway onto the land. She stood tall and placed her hands on her hips. "And if they didn't, at least you could have eaten them for supper."

"Maybe you should have brought one with you," Simon said. "I could go for some roasted chicken."

"Welp." Aunt June heaved a large pot out of the boat and dunked it in the water. "If you have any brains in that handsome head of yours, you'll take that pistol you've done shoved in my boat and go shoot us a pheasant. Otherwise it's day-old biscuits and huckleberries for supper."

"I'll see what I can do." Simon hurried over to the boat and plucked the gun he'd borrowed from Garrett from where he'd stashed it earlier. He couldn't wear the thing while riding the hump, but he wasn't about to traipse about the forest alone without a weapon. Call him yellow-bellied, but he wasn't about to get caught unaware again.

"Good," Aunt June said, then turned to Blue and the rest of the Devil May Cares. "Now one of you boys make me a fire. Once those two greenhorns finally get that boat in, tell them to catch us some fish in case Simon comes back with all of his bullets."

Simon didn't wait to hear the rest of Aunt June's orders. He had his direction, and he was damned glad to finally get a few minutes alone. What he needed was a solid plan for his life. Carrie needed someone who could support her in comfort, not leave her every spring and summer, only to return in the winter and do nothing more than waste money.

Hell even Wall had a job punching cows on his father's ranch when not riding the river, not to mention a stake in the new railroad logging system. And Garrett owned the biggest railroad company in Montana. What did

Simon have to offer Carrie besides lonely days and cold winters? To be fair to himself, he would have a hefty inheritance once his grandmother died, but he loved the senile old lady. And did he plan on forcing Carrie to live with his grandmother?

No. He needed a plan.

Unfortunately, his work skills centered on the logging business. He could always hire on as a permanent logger. Work both winter and summer. But he didn't want to force Carrie to leave the safety of a town where everyone vied for her attention and she lived under a feathered blanket of safety and love. He refused to condemn her to a life of misery on the cold mountain. If she'd even have him at all. Chances were her parents didn't approve of him anyway.

Off in the distance the forest opened up to a crisp, dried meadow. The hoarse call of a pheasant hidden in the woodland undergrowth sounded through the trees. He slid his gun from the holster and cocked it. Killing a bird with a pistol was difficult, but good practice for any large animal he might come across.

He tightened his grip on the weapon and searched as far into the trees as possible for any sign of a cougar. The year before he'd have thought a grizzly the most fearsome creature in the forest. Until he experienced the undetectable strike of the cat. He hadn't even heard the murderous beast until it was too late. At least a bear you can smell, and a lot of times hear. With a cougar you didn't know you were dead until St. Pete met you at the gate.

Simon slowed down the closer he got to where he'd heard the bird. He stepped over a large fern as a pheasant squawked and took flight. With quick reflexes, he lifted the gun and fired. He frowned as the bird flew away, leaving him one bullet short.

In three steps, Simon crouched low over the brush where the female bird had been and moved the leaves aside. He smiled at the six eggs hidden beneath the brush. If he couldn't have Carrie cook him breakfast, at least he could get Aunt June to make him eggs with the biscuits and gravy she'd planned for supper. A meal that used to be his favorite before Carrie came into his life with her wooden spoon and cast-iron pan. Now all he wanted was to wake up to huckleberry flapjacks.

Simon gathered the eggs and smiled. If things went as planned, in a few weeks he'd see Carrie again. He'd spend the rest of the season convincing her to marry him or he'd die trying.

Chapter 16

Carrie snatched the steaming pot of burnt pea soup out of the fierce flames that licked the air around her. The blasted fire! The bane of her existence since her godmother had left her in charge. Sometimes it wasn't hard to believe that the forest, and everything within it, simply bent to Aunt June's will, while trying desperately to sabotage her every move. The blasted trees, and the wood rounds they gave out!

"Ouch!" She yelped as the side of the hot cast-iron pot seared the inside of her arm. She dropped the pan, barely missing her toes, and clutched her wound. What remained of the blackened contents spread across the dirt. The urge to let out a well-placed curse tickled her tongue, and her chest vibrated with the need to let out a cry. But she refused to show such foolish weakness. It had been a few weeks since Aunt June had left, and already she'd ruined at least four meals. Frankly, she was running out of salt pork, which she'd used with potatoes and gravy on more than one occasion as a stand-in for whatever disaster she'd attempted. Today it happened to be split pea soup. A recipe she'd gotten from her mother's cook, and one of her favorites.

Not anymore. To Hades with the difficult meal.

Nots dipped her head low as if to lap up the dirt-filled puddle of once-green mush.

"No!" Carrie yanked her back by the scruff of her neck, but the determined little pup fought hard to get to the meal. Carrie plucked her off the ground. "It's too hot. You'll burn your mouth!"

"Poor girl." Beth brought out a crate of dishes from the cabin and set them down.

"I know." Carrie ran her fingers over the pup's soft head. "She's hungry. I swear if I don't feed her every few hours, she goes primal for the smallest of bits."

"I was talking about you." Beth grabbed a shovel from the side of the cabin, scooped up the soiled dinner from where it had fallen on the path, and tossed it into the brush behind the long supper tables. "You're a mess lately. I've never seen you unorganized. My proper friend has turned into a chattering wretch."

"I beg your pardon?" Carrie feigned offense. "I have never chattered my entire life."

"Except every time you've ruined supper." Beth waved toward the grate on the fire, which had once held the soup. "I've heard you scold the fire before."

"When?"

"The great beef pie debacle three days ago." Beth replaced the shovel and smiled. "Don't worry. I shall tell no one you've become touched in the head. Downright crazy."

"You are pure humor and kindness." Carrie pursed her lips and shook her head, but more at herself. Beth was right. She was a mess. She'd honestly believed she could handle the job alone, but these few weeks proved she wasn't ready. She had Beth, of course, but her friend was closer to a logger than a cook. Still, it was good to have her by her side while she burned things like the split pea soup. By God, Carrie was going to figure it all out before Aunt June returned or work herself until nothing remained but bones on her fingertips.

"Feel at ease, my friend, I only extend my humor and kindness to the dearest of people." Beth smiled like a child who had stolen a chunk of cheese from the icebox.

"How kind of you," Carrie replied, but a movement across the meadow caught her attention as Thomas trudged toward her. "Blast! He's back again. I've told him to leave me alone every day since Simon left."

Beth followed her gaze and frowned. "Why would it matter if Simon left? If the man plans to court you, why wait?"

"What?" Carrie snapped her gaze to Beth. Did she know?

"Is my brother chasing off your suitors again?"

"He's done that in the past?" She had always suspected he'd done such a thing, but only now was it proven to be truth. The base of Carrie's neck where her collar met her skin grew hot. Was that why none of the men she'd found amiable failed to show interest beyond a dance or two? Had Simon been the reason she had made the decision to become an old spinster cook?

"I thought you knew," Beth replied. "He's always been meddlesome. It came as no surprise when I overheard him warning off the Army colonel from Fort Missoula a few years back."

"The one I thought was going to propose and finally take me away from the humdrum of Missoula?"

"That's the one."

Carrie turned her head slightly as Thomas approached. The man would not leave her alone. Why in Hades would Simon frighten off a perfectly good officer but leave her to fend for herself where Thomas was concerned? Men and the stubborn teamster bulls out in the barn maintained the same level of common sense. Absolutely none.

"Ah, there you are, my dear," Thomas said as he drew near. "Looking vibrant today, as usual. Can I help you with anything?"

"No. There's not much you can do. Thank you." She tried to let the man down as easy as she could, but he made it difficult.

"If you need me, I'll be behind the cabin chopping wood."

"That isn't necessary. I think you've chopped enough wood already to last me until the end of the season, let alone when Aunt June returns." Every day since Aunt June had left, Thomas had showed up to chop wood for her. Perhaps that was why her flames seemed to be out of control. One too many logs in the fire.

Carrie looked at Beth, who lounged against the supper table with one leg resting over the other as if she enjoyed the show more than she should. Carrie glared at her, and Beth gave a stupid grin. By the look on her dearest friend's face, Carrie was on her own.

"I'll replenish the stack you used today." Thomas pivoted and disappeared behind the cabin.

"What do you think he's doing back there?" Beth asked.

"Chopping wood?" Carrie answered.

"Are you certain? Have you ever gone back to check on him while he works?"

"Why would I? I'm trying my hardest to avoid the determined man. I've let him down four times already." She motioned toward the stack of logs near the fire. "Every day he replenishes my pile. I've no need to go back and get any more. For all I know the whole forest has been cut and stacked neatly between the cabin and chicken coop."

"Aren't you curious?"

The question didn't deserve an answer, so she simply stared at her friend with an are-you-joshing-me glare. She'd much rather avoid the man than spy on his work. He had obviously chopped firewood throughout the last few weeks, as evident by her overflowing pile next to her cook fire.

After a moment, Beth gave an exaggerated frown. "Don't be surprised if he shows up with a risqué wooden sculpture of you."

"Why? Is he an artist in the winter and logger in the summer?" Carrie tried to lighten the mood, and it somewhat worked.

"Right up there with Rembrandt, I'm told." The grin on her friend's face gave a humored edge to the words.

"Rembrandt was a painter," Carrie reminded her friend.

"Either way, you'll end up with a picture of you without a stitch on. I'd go back and check if I were you. Set it on fire if you must." Beth's eyes twinkled the way they always did when she planned a scheme. "I'll help you burn it."

"You're a horrid tease." Carrie picked the now cooled cast-iron pot off the ground, dunked it in the nearby wash bin, and began to scrub. The blasted pan and devilish soup!

Through the trees the piercing blare of a train horn shrilled and caused Carrie to jump. She followed Beth's stare at the trees in the direction of the sound. Not that they could see the train from where they stood.

"Did they fix the steam pulley?" Carrie returned to her work once her runaway heart settled from the shock.

Beth shook her head. "No. Wall needs a part. He sent down a rider with a note for Victoria. That must be a second engine with the order. I've got to get over there. Will you be all right alone with Thomas?"

Carrie tossed a glance to the cabin, but she could see nothing. The rhythmic sound of chopping had stopped, so perhaps he'd slipped down the back trail. "Yes. I think he's gone to the train."

Beth stepped hesitantly toward the trail leading to the Railroad Grove. "Ring the dinner bell if you need anything. I'll come right away."

Carrie nodded and turned back to her wash bin. She made short work of cleaning the pot, filled it with fresh water, and placed it over the fire to heat. Once finished, she prepared the salt pork and potatoes. What she wouldn't give to have fresh vegetables to serve the men. Perhaps tomorrow she could convince Beth and Garrett to go with her to search for asparagus. It was a little late in the season for such a delicacy, but there was a chance she could serve something different. Asparagus pie might be good.

She searched the area for signs of the tall plant needed for the next day's meal, but stopped when she spotted a log that had tumbled from its perch on the pile behind the cabin. Her stomach hollowed at Beth's suggestion of something nefarious happening right under her nose.

With another quick glance to ensure no one was watching, she ran to the back of the cabin. The stump where Simon had murdered the chicken for her sat in the middle of the scene, with an ax laying haphazardly next to it. Neat piles of logs ready for a fire were stacked on one side, and on the other larger rounds needing to be cut lay in a dwindled pile. The man had done quite a bit of work. The year before, Beth and a young boy had worked together to keep the pile down and wood stacked for Aunt June. This year the job was left for Carrie, and apparently now, Thomas.

Carrie studied the scene, but nothing untoward could be seen. Except, of course, the crimson-stained stump where Simon had prepared the chicken for dinner.

Simon, with his ability to woo her with a simple smile, a touch, a perfect gift.

For Hades's sake, she'd been charmed with a dog. And now she had to replace Aunt June's good apron after Nots had chewed the strings off. Not to mention the piles of poo she cleaned from the cabin every morning. Perfect indeed. Although the cuddles and kisses were well worth the trouble the little pup caused.

As if called by her thoughts, the dog galloped around the corner of the cabin and rolled around in a large patch of grass. Carrie smiled. She wouldn't give up her pup for all the aprons in Missoula.

With Nots running through her legs, Carrie returned to the cook fire and plopped the potatoes in the water to boil. At least she could spoil the men with huckleberry flapjacks in the mornings. The one thing they loved best was the one meal she could get right.

The salt pork began to sizzle in the large pan as a movement near the path from the Railroad Grove caught her attention. She lifted her gaze as Victoria walked into the cook camp flanked by Wall and a group of men she'd never seen before.

"Working alone?" Victoria asked as she approached. "If I remember correctly, even Aunt June has an assistant cook."

"Beth helps."

"Hmm" was all Victoria responded. Why was she here? And what in Hades did "hmm" mean coming from her? The regal new owner of Great Mountain Lumber Mill simply stood and watched, offering no other words in response to her unnerving, yet slightly accusing, noise.

"Can I offer you some coffee?" Carrie always kept a fresh pot on the fire for the men. Especially on Sundays when the men were free from work and able to come and go as they pleased.

"Yes. With milk." Victoria walked to where they kept the tin cups.

Carrie checked the milk pitcher, but found nothing but a few drops. "I'm fresh out of milk, but I can give you a bit of sugar to sweeten."

"Hmm," Victoria muttered again, set the cup she'd lifted back down, and turned to Wall. She beckoned him closer, and he dipped his head next to her mouth to listen, then nodded.

"Gentlemen," Wall said, and motioned toward the lake. "If you'll follow me, the river operation is this way."

The men stumbled as they followed like sheep behind the leader of the Devil May Care boys, leaving her alone with the boss.

Carrie shuffled her feet. "I was about to go milk the cow once Beth returned from the train." Why was she so nervous around the woman? It wasn't like she was of lesser breed than Victoria. In town, before Victoria had become ensconced in running her father's company, they had often run in the same circles. They had attended the same teas, parties, even dances. Victoria had never made her nervous. Until now.

Carrie plucked a cup up and checked it for dirt. Using her apron for protection from the heat, she poured coffee for her new boss, then set it before her with a spoon and small tin of sugar.

Victoria stirred two spoonfuls of sugar in her drink and took a small sip. Carrie's stomach twisted as she waited for the woman's response. Why did she care? Heavens above, how many times had she conversed with the woman? Usually about drab, unimportant topics women often chatter on about, but the topic was neither here nor there.

"I hear you're hoping to stay on as cook after Aunt June gives up her post," Victoria said.

Carrie nodded, not inclined to hide the truth. "I have thought about it, yes."

"Then I'm afraid I need to tell you now that you are wasting your time. I cannot in good conscience hire on a lady." She took another small sip but stared at Carrie over the top of her cup.

"I beg your pardon?" Carrie stepped one foot forward and shifted her stance. "You employ plenty of women at the mill, and even up here."

"Up here as cooks," Victoria corrected. "God willing, Aunt June will be with us for quite a while yet as she seems to be the glue that holds this whole operation together. I will not have a position for you. And by the time I do, you will more than likely already be married off with a handful of children."

Carrie glared. "You're a strong, determined woman. As am I. Like you, I do not intend to wed."

"Who said I don't want to find a husband one day?" Victoria frowned.

"I...I just assumed because you broke off your and Garrett's engagement..."

"Garrett was in love with Elizabeth. I wasn't going to stand between him and true love." Victoria circled her finger around the rim of the cup. "I want to marry as much as the next woman does, but I will only do so with the right man."

"Well, I have no intention of marrying. The whole game seems to be nothing but man's ploy for control. If I don't have to depend on someone else to provide for me, then I have no one to blame but myself. And I'm determined. I do not want to be someone's cook and housekeeper unless I get paid. Why not do it in a place as serene as the mountains?"

"Because they are dangerous, and you're a lady of substance. Be honest with yourself. Your position in life will allow you to have people to do your work. You will not be a slave to any husband. Quite the opposite, in fact." Victoria finished her cup of coffee and held it out. Carrie slowly reached for it, and Victoria continued. "You will be better served somewhere else."

Water splashed onto the ground when she tossed the cup into the wash bin. "Did my father have something to do with this?"

"No," Victoria said. "Your mother did. And she's right. Stop playing lumber camp cook, and go find a husband to support you."

"And your father was right in selling you to Garrett's father?"

Victoria glared and stood. Carrie's heart beat fast. She hadn't meant to use such harsh words on the woman, but she couldn't help herself. "If you wish to fight for your independence, then do. But I cannot employ you here beyond this summer. You cannot have a job here."

"Then I will go to Garrett. I'll wager he knows another logging company who needs a cook."

"Fine." Victoria nodded. "I wish you luck. I know how hard of a fight you will have with your parents. Their generation is a tenacious bunch of etiquette hounds. They are set in their ways, and will continue to avoid progress."

Carrie inclined her head in agreement. The tears blocking her voice from forming prevented her from being able to give much more than a grunt, and she certainly wasn't going to grunt at Victoria, one of the wealthiest giants of the Missoula social circuit.

After all, if she lost the war with her parents, she was going to need Victoria's acceptance in town while Carrie withered away under the thumb of whatever man she married. Grunting like an animal would not help Carrie's cause.

Dawn Luedecke

Victoria was wrong about one thing, though. Her father's company struggled to keep their heads above water, not that her mother or father would let anyone get wind of their misfortune. As soon as the Missoula wolves heard such a thing they would run for the hills. She'd be in dire straits. She would not have people to keep her house. If she were to marry, her title would read: Carrie—whatever her husband's last name would be—cook, nanny, and maid; depending upon said husband's success. Perhaps she should throw in her lot with Thomas. At least then he'd do a lot of the work for her while she struggled to figure out how they could afford to keep their livelihood.

Chapter 17

Simon walked the bank of the river, searching for logs stuck along the edge. The hair on the nape of his neck stood on end, and he searched the trees behind him. He knew this area. Had been here several times during past drives, but most of all, this was where he and Garrett had pulled the bateau onto the bank to search for Beth the year before. Down the trail was where the cougar had changed his life forever.

Simon checked his belt for the gun, but having ridden a log down, he'd stashed it in the safety boat.

Across the water one of the greenhorns walked the banks like him, while the other manned the bateau. He whistled and beckoned the boat toward him. After weeks of strict instruction from Simon, the boy struggling with the boat had started to get the hang of the job. Now all Simon had to do was last one more week, and he could return to Carrie's loving arms. Or at least he hoped they'd still be open for him upon his return.

The boat floated close enough to the bank that the boy could hear. "I need my gun."

The young river rat eased the boat closer to the bank and leaned over to gently toss him the weapon and holster. "Everything all right?"

"Just taking precautions, is all," Simon answered. The boy saluted his understanding and eased the boat away. Simon turned his attention to his weapon. He strapped on the holster and checked to ensure the bullets were in place. Chances were a cougar wouldn't strike twice on the same path, especially since Garrett had killed the one the year before, but Simon felt more at ease having protection.

A splash of water downstream, different from the normal sounds of the river, penetrated his thoughts. Alert, he searched the water for any sign as to what had made the noise. He scanned the bank and the break in the river as a beaver heading upstream swam past him.

He let the tension ease from his shoulders and watched the animal struggle to yank and tug a long, leafy branch behind him as he swam against the current. Making little progress, but determined nonetheless. Further upriver, a log bounced off an underwater boulder and headed straight for the creature. Undeterred, the beaver darted as quick as he could out of the path of the large log while clutching the branch in his teeth. Once free of both the fierce stream of water and the log, the beaver disappeared around a bend, and likely toward his little wood-covered home.

The varmint had a good point.

No matter how difficult the task, or how long the journey, you couldn't give up. Life would throw logs in your path, she was a dime-night whore that way, but you couldn't let the logs take you down.

Carrie had tried to show him that during his whiskey-filled nights at home, but he wouldn't listen. Instead, he'd used her presence as an excuse to have another drink. Or two. Never a woman, though, not last year. Although he was known for his debauchery in town, that particular vice had gone along with his flawless appearance. Carrie was his first since before the season a year ago.

She'd seen him at his lowest. Covered in makeshift bandages. His face caked in mud and scarlet blood. When he'd laid in Aunt June's cabin recovering from the attack, Carrie had been the one to care for him. She had never left his side.

Her soft fingers had worked the bandages. Cleansed his wounds. Cared for him like a tender healer. Every time he woke, she'd smile down at him. No pity or judgment shining in her eyes, only love and concern. It was then that he saw her in another light. No longer as Beth's friend that he needed to protect like a sister, but as a woman.

And then he'd looked in the mirror.

The man who stared back at him—scarred and hideous—could never be the man a woman like Carrie needed. She was flawless. In both beauty and spirit. Would she go about town with a wretch like him? Her life would be thrown into shambles. She'd live in misery. In his mind she'd never have the man the cougar had made, so he had floated into a pool of self-loathing and booze.

And there he'd stayed until the same woman who haunted him drugged him and brought him back to face his demons. He undid the strap securing the weapon. He'd face them like a man, then get the hell off this part of the river.

Simon followed the same trail he'd taken that fateful morning. He rounded the bend and quickly faced the trees where the cat had attacked and dragged him into the brush to finish the job.

The sun had barely peeked over the horizon then, but today it blazed full on. He stepped off the logging path he followed and instead made his way past the bear grass and toward the meadow where he'd given up hope of life.

Unlike the year before, the meadow shone with beauty, speckled in little white tips and long lush grass. The pale blue sky above, void of all but a few clouds, lent a false calm to the day.

Simon swallowed hard and brushed at the cold sweat dripping down his forehead. He gulped down his breath to keep the noise he made to a minimum. Although the cougar was dead, they'd been chased off by a hungry grizzly looking for the cougar's remains. Grizzlies were territorial. If it hadn't died during the winter, it could still be around.

A bird twittering high in the trees rang like a warning whistle through his ears. A twig snapped somewhere deep in the brush and his senses heightened.

Simon stepped light as he walked to the spot where he'd lain when Garrett caught the attention of the cat and lured him away. Simon slid his gaze to where his friend had sliced the cat's jugular before picking Simon up off the ground and carrying him out of the field as the bear approached.

Curiously, the only thing left from the vicious attack was a single rib bone, void of meat and bleached from the sun. He searched the trees again for signs of the bear, but there were none. Without a second thought, he picked up the rib and headed back to the river.

Honestly, he had no idea why he'd taken the bone. Most people he knew would have let it be, but holding the smooth, weathered piece of the deadly cat made him feel at ease. A reminder that in the end he'd come out alive.

Simon snapped the safety strap on the holster shut, tugged to make certain the gun was secure, and ran toward the gently worn path next to the river. The trail—forged by years of rivermen walking the banks to search for logs, sometimes several times a year depending on the rivers and production—made it easy to find his way. Times were changing, though. Soon with the railroad logging, the river drives might become unnecessary.

Simon shoved at a log, dislodged it, and went to the next. He followed this same comfortable path until the quiet mumble of men talking reached his ears. Low in the sky, the sun began to dip behind the mountain.

He tucked his peavey under his arm and grasped the bone tight as he made his way toward the camp.

"Ah there you are." Aunt June stood and walked toward him. She slid her gaze from head to toe like a mother assessing a troublesome child before Sunday morning services. "I was afraid I'd have to send out a search party for you."

"I'm fine." He walked to the bateau and tossed in his peavey.

"Supper's been over for an hour, what'd you do, stop to nap?"

Simon smiled. "Something like that."

"Lucky I love you," the old cook said, and used her apron to ease a tin plate off a large rock arranged around the fire. "I've kept it heated for you. Otherwise it don't taste good."

Simon settled onto an empty cook crate next to the fire and slid the rib bone in his belt behind his back. The hard memory of his attack pressed against his skin, but not in a painful way.

"Got a jam up ahead," Blue said as he whittled the end of a stick. "The boys and I are going to go up ahead and see if it can wait till morning to free."

Simon nodded and shoved a forkful of potatoes in his mouth.

Blue stowed his knife and tossed the stick into the fire. With a motion to the rest of the Devil May Care boys, they headed out.

Aunt June stood watching him. She squinted in the firelight as she stared. He moved the food into his cheek like a squirrel. "What?"

"Where have you been?" She tapped her foot.

Simon swallowed hard. "I went to see the spot where Garrett killed the cougar."

"And?" she asked, pointedly.

He slipped the bone out from behind him. "And this is the only thing left of the bastard."

Aunt June frowned so hard he thought she'd spit just to accentuate her mood. "Good."

Simon searched the camp for anyone who might have overheard, then turned to Aunt June. Carrie's godmother. What would she think if Simon asked for Carrie's hand? She'd probably return from the drive with a preacher. But would Carrie's father approve? Simon didn't exactly have the best reputation in town. "What can you tell me about Carrie's parents?"

Aunt June's frown melted away, but not the crease in her brow. "Carrie's mother, Beatrice, was my best friend throughout school. She's a sweet woman, but she hasn't the fortitude for adventure. And Carrie's father, James, owns Kerr Leather Company. Fancy hats and shoes mostly, but they've had a few problems lately."

"What problems?"

"His usual supplier was a few mountain men up Lolo way. They either died off or moved on, 'cause they haven't brought in any furs for quite a while." Aunt June slouched in a manner normal to her, but not common for a socially conscious woman. "And the dandies out east who used to order the goods decided to switch companies."

Simon scowled. Why hadn't Carrie said anything to him? Why did she act like nothing was wrong at home? Didn't she trust him? "Carrie never said anything to me. And if she told Beth, I haven't heard."

"She wouldn't. James is struggling to keep his head above water, but they don't want others to know they're about to be ruined financially. So they hide it from everyone."

"Is that why Carrie has decided to throw in her lot with the spinster camp cooks?" Simon teased, but the passion wasn't behind his voice as much as he'd planned, and he suspected Aunt June knew.

"I'd venture to guess so, but she needn't worry. Once I go, she'll get all my money. She's the closest thing I got to a daughter."

"So why don't you buy out her father? Change up a few things and get the business on track again?"

"I tried, but James said he won't take no charity from a woman. He's a donkey's ass that way." A smile grew across the weathered woman's face as she stared at the flames. "But he might take on a strapping young lad like you as a partner."

"I'd do it, but I'm only a poor logger until my grandmother dies. And the sweet old bat is hanging on like a cat in a tree."

"I'll give you a loan until you can pay me back."

Simon sat back and extended his legs out in front of him, crossing them at the ankle. Pride told him to reject the offer, but common sense—and the desire to have Carrie's belly full with his little babes—urged him to accept. "Now why would I do that?"

"If you don't let me loan you the money, I'll give it to you. It'll be Carrie's in a few years anyway."

"Then I definitely couldn't take Carrie's money."

"It ain't hers yet." Aunt June gave him an easy nod. "Call it a wedding gift."

"Whose wedding?" Simon asked, surprised. There was no way Aunt June knew about him and Carrie. Was there?

"Young man," Aunt June started, and moved to sit on an empty crate next to him. "I've been on this world for longer than I care to admit. I know when two people are as in love as you and Carrie. I've known it since it happened over a year ago. Only problem was you needed to see for yourself. Since you came traipsing up here asking about my goddaughter's parents, I assume you've figured it out."

"What if I had wanted to know more about leather making?"

"Do you?" Aunt June smiled.

"No," he confessed, mimicking the old cook's grin. "Am I that transparent?"

"Only when we've been watching and waiting for you to come back to us. That was only going to happen once you got out of your own self-loathing mind and realized what I've known all along."

"I'm no good for her," he said, and picked up a pebble to toss in the fire. "She could do better than a wretch like me."

To Simon's dismay, Aunt June nodded. "True, but not for the reason you think."

She took his chin in her hand, again like he was her child. The woman did that a lot. Mothered him. She gently patted his scarred cheek. "You're as handsome as you were the first time I saw you. I knew then that I wanted you to meet my Carrie. I'm just relieved Beth made the introductions for me before I had the chance." Aunt June dropped her hands in her lap. "No. You're no good for her because you're a scoundrel. Always have been. But the thing about a woman is, if she's strong, then she makes her man even better than he deserves to be. You may not think you're good enough now, but that's only 'cause you need a good woman by your side to complete you."

Simon stared at the firelight as it flickered off the pebbled ground, and soaked in Aunt June's words. The only woman he wanted was Carrie. His whole life now needed to revolve around persuading her to give him a chance. Not what she'd given him at the cabin, but a real, for-all-eternity chance. "She's bound and determined to make it on her own. Without a husband."

"Oh, bosh." Aunt June waved off his words. "That's only because of her father. He's made Beatrice quite unhappy with this whole leather business. You take my loan and buy him out. Or at least buy part of his company. Bring her security and independence in one big romantic proposal, and she'll be yours."

"You make it sound simple."

Aunt June shook her head. "Ain't nothin' simple about love. It's as complicated as the stars, but those who figure it out will be nothing but happy for the rest of their lives."

"So why didn't you ever marry? If you don't mind me asking." He'd asked the question every logger in camp wanted to know. The woman they loved dearly. The one who took care of them, fed them, and mentored them had never so much as looked twice at a man. Except for the traveling merchant. "Because of Bud?"

"Oh, no. Bud and I enjoy a good banter, maybe a coy smile here and there, but we're friends. Nothing more." She sighed. "I did find love once. Real, tried-and-true love. But God had another plan for me. He took my man before we could ever make our vows."

She shook her head.

Simon didn't regret asking the question dear to her soul. She was like family to him, and he cared for the old cook dearly. She gave a confession he didn't think anyone had ever heard before tonight. At least no one in camp knew. "And you still love him?"

Aunt June swiped at a tear. "To this day. But now it's your turn. Come with me to town, and go get your life in order. When we come back up the mountain, you make that girl remember that she fell in love with you a long time ago. And why."

Simon's heart no longer pressed hard and immovable in his chest. Tonight, after talking with Aunt June, his soul fought to soar like an eagle above the treetops on a sunny day. He wouldn't disappoint Aunt June. He'd make Carrie fall in love with him as soon as he returned. But Aunt June was right: he needed to get his life in order first.

Chapter 18

Carrie held her breath until the grating echo of the metal wheels against the rails subsided. *Thank the Lord above!* Now that Victoria was gone, she was free to cry. She let the tears trail down her cheeks like rain over a petal and didn't care to hold back the shuddered breaths she'd forced into submission for the last few days. Victoria and her parade of big bugs had overstayed their welcome by about three days. As far as she was concerned, at least. This place, this haven, had been her backup plan. Her one chance at controlling the outcome of her life.

Victoria had ruined her chance at happiness.

To be honest, she could have been well married with a passel of children clinging to her legs by now, but if what Beth said was true, Simon had seen to it that she'd die an old maid. *For the better.* If it wasn't for him, she wouldn't have been home to see what happened when the husband could no longer provide and the mother spiraled into a pit of misery and desperation.

Her poor mother. Clinging to any hope that her father's business would pick up and she'd be able to see Carrie well married. Her mother, desperate to see her connected before news of their financial downfall hit the newspapers, had sent up the harpy of Missoula society to put Carrie in her place.

To hell with her parents. She would not give in to marriage simply because they manipulated those around her. At least Aunt June would see things her way. She would never allow others to force her into compliance, and neither would Carrie.

The gentle crunch of grass under feet sounded before her, and Beth all but bounced into camp. "Did you hear? The logs are expected to be at the mill this afternoon. After that the crew will come up with the trains."

Carrie sniffled. Her damned nose always grew cold and difficult when she cried. "Has Wall fixed the steam pulley?"

"Yep. Took him a few weeks, but the first train load should go down in the morning."

"I'm glad to see it all working out for everyone." Her voice shook, and she struggled to keep it steady.

"You seem down today. I mean, more than usual. What can I do to help?"

"I need to get dinner going. Now that Victoria's gone, maybe I can concentrate on my food."

"I'm sorry she won't let you stay on after this year." Beth pulled out the tin of coffee grounds and plopped it on the table. After pouring herself a cup, she smelled the contents, scrunched her nose, then promptly pushed it across the flat surface, leaving it to cool in the mountain air.

Carrie didn't know how to respond to her friend. She wanted to say she was all right with it, but she wasn't. Lying seemed like too much work. She kept quiet and walked over to stock the fire. She plucked the last log off the ground and tossed it in the fading flames. Sparks flew into the air and fizzled out. Where had the ever-growing stack of wood gone? She searched the camp. "Have you seen Thomas?"

"He left on Victoria's train. He took some time off for something. Said he'd be back day after tomorrow."

"Oh." It was about time she did her own chores anyway. "I wonder what he's gone to do?"

Beth shrugged, poured water into the pitcher, and placed it on the grate over the flames to heat. "No telling. Men usually take days off for personal reasons. Probably something to do with family." Beth grinned. "At least now you can take off the necklace for a bit. I've heard him ask you every day where it is. He's determined to have you wear the thing."

Carrie fingered the pretty but ill-given necklace, then reached back and unsnapped it. The usual heavy sensation of the trinket eased from around her neck.

She sat down on the bench along the table and slumped her shoulders. She'd been defeated the last few days, in more ways than one.

Nots nudged the necklace in her hand, and Carrie smiled down at the pale little pup. The jewels looked vibrant against her dog's white and gray fur. "This would look beautiful on you."

Nots nudged it again. Carrie wrapped it around her dog's neck like a collar and fastened it, then scooped up the happy animal to snuggle. She truly did appreciate every gift anyone gave her, but Nots was more than any piece of finery anyone could buy. She was someone to love when life chiseled at your emotions. She was happiness with fur, and she was Carrie's. Simon had given her the perfect gift.

"If you'd like," Beth interrupted her thoughts, "Garrett and I can ask around to see if anyone needs a cook. There's more than lumber companies around here. I mean, Wall's family has a cattle ranch. Those type of operations always need cooks."

"Thank you." Beth was right. This was not the end of her fight for independence. Great Mountain Lumber Mill was not the only company in this blasted forest. "Do you think Wall's family is hiring?"

Beth shrugged. "Doesn't hurt to ask."

"I'll do it as soon as he comes in for supper." That is why Carrie loved her friend dearly. With only a few words Beth brought reason to her life and a plan for her future. As friends they understood each other. As cohorts, they improved each other's plans. Carrie breathed easy as she poured the ingredients and mix the batter for crust. Tonight's dinner would not be made for the dogs.

For the rest of the day, Carrie prepared the meal for the loggers with a smile on her face and hope in her heart. She wasn't going to give up. Even if Wall couldn't find her a position at his ranch, chances were someone, somewhere, would hire her.

The light grew hazy with the impending onset of dusk when the men shuffled into camp. Beth caught her eye and motioned toward Wall as he stopped near the water bin to wash the day's worth of dirt and grease off his hands.

"I'll do the serving," Beth said, and motioned toward him again.

Carrie placed the large meat pie down on the serving table. A meal she'd made without problem. Finally. "I'll only be a minute."

On Beth's nod, Carrie started toward the man who, God willing, would soon be her boss.

He stood alone near the water, elbow deep in suds with his sleeves rolled up past his biceps. He glanced up as she neared. "Something over there smells like heaven."

"Chicken pie. First time I haven't burned the meal on the first go-round," she said with pride.

Wall chuckled. "I've loved every meal you've made, Miz Carrie."

"Don't lie to yourself." She smiled at the easy way Wall made her feel. Last year, Wall had vied for Beth's attention, but alas, Beth's heart belonged to Garrett. Carrie hoped dearly this man would find a woman for his own soon. He was as good a man as Simon and deserved as much happiness as any logger she'd ever known.

Carrie checked to ensure she wouldn't be overheard, then dipped her head closer to where Wall stood—not that the small distance would do much to shield their talk from curious ears. "Do you happen to know if there's a position at your parents' ranch for a cook?"

Wall tipped his head to the side as if curious. "Victoria told me what happened between the two of you. She's a good person. A bulldog when it comes to business, though, for certain."

Carrie sighed, took a quick look at the ground, and pursed her lips together. "So you don't have a job for me either?"

"I never said that." He dried off his hands and rolled his sleeves back down his arm. "Let me write my father and see. I know our cook is getting on in age. He may want to take on another to help her out."

"Really?" The tightness she hadn't realized twisted in her chest until that moment eased. "You'd do that for me?"

"With the way that food over there smells, my father would take a switch to me if I didn't let him know about you." Wall winked and strolled past her toward the chow line.

Carrie took a moment to compose herself and tamp back the smile tugging at the corner of her lips. Things were going to work out. If she was anything like Aunt June, nothing would stand in her way. Nothing.

* * * *

Simon dipped his hat down low over the side of his face with the scar and skirted the three clacking women who walked past. In a few more doorsteps, he'd stand before Carrie's father and outline his plan for not only the business but also a life with Carrie.

God he hoped everything would go smoothly with her parents.

He unlatched the gate to the front of the house as the door opened, and Thomas all but skipped down the front steps. Simon stepped back onto the sidewalk and held the gate for the young logger.

He chanced a glance at the door, but whoever had let Thomas out had closed it.

"What are you doing here?" He didn't bother to hide the anger behind his words. His gut dropped when the man bared his teeth in a failed attempt at a friendly grin.

"I had some business in town. I thought I'd pay Carrie's father a little visit."

"What business?" Simon's fingertips tingled with the rage he felt deep within his soul. Before today, Thomas had never known the Kerrs existed. Why visit now? Simon took a step toward the man. His instinct told him to pound the man into the ground, but he resisted.

Thomas flinched as if he knew Simon's inner thoughts and stepped back. "Now, now. That's between me and James."

"James?" Simon's vision tunneled on the man. He balled his fists and released them several times. Thomas was on a first-name basis with Carrie's father?

Thomas shrugged.

"That's his name. Isn't it?" He snapped his jacket open, pulled out a cigar, and popped it in his mouth, rolling it around with his tongue.

"Yes," Simon growled out. Was there any way Thomas had come now because he knew about Simon's plan to ask for Carrie's hand? Chances were slim, but it didn't stop the rage boiling in his blood. "I assume your business is finished here and you're going to return to camp on the three o'clock train?"

Thomas bumped Simon's shoulder as he walked past. "I assume I'll see you there?"

Simon inclined his head and clenched his teeth as he took a second to gain his composure, but all he wanted to do was knock the boy into next week. Why was he here? Simon spun around to give in to his basic instinct, but Thomas was already out of reach. He took a step toward him, but stopped. Chasing after the weasel would only cause a scene on the road in front of Carrie's mother's house. Which would do nothing for his cause.

The skin near his scar twitched, and he spun on his heels. He slammed the gate behind him, but that was all the anger he dared display. Showing up raging mad in front of the father of the woman he planned to marry wouldn't gain him any points.

He wasn't giving up on Carrie. No matter how many suitors approached her father first. What were the chances Thomas hadn't visited for that reason? In two steps, he rapped hard on the wood panel. Maybe a little too hard. He flinched at the noise. Within a few heartbeats, the door yanked open to reveal Carrie's father, his round belly tight against the vest he wore over his white cotton shirt, a watch chain hanging from the pocket only to connect through the button loop.

"Yes?" Carrie's father squinted as if trying to gauge the situation.

"Mr. Kerr," Simon greeted, and then cleared his throat, confident his pulse thrummed hard enough even the old coot living next door could see the movement. "I don't know if you remember me—"

"Elizabeth's brother." James frowned. "The one who got attacked by the mountain cat last summer?"

Simon flinched. *Hell*. At least he was no longer known as the reprobate of society. In this case, maybe pity instead of contempt would do him good. "Yes, sir. And I've got a proposal for you."

James lifted his head but kept his expression stern. After a few tense moments, the older man stepped back and motioned for Simon to enter.

Simon let out the breath he'd held during the strained second and walked into the entrance. He'd never been inside Carrie's home, only seen the outside while passing by on his way to an acquaintance's house next door—opposite from where the old coot lived.

What he did know was that the backyard was full of little white flowers. The same ones Carrie had brought him. Simon placed his hand over his pocket to feel for the handkerchief holding the forget-me-nots. No matter what happened today, Carrie would always be near his heart.

He couldn't lose her.

Simon would have one hell of a time convincing her to trust him with her heart and her life. She deserved to have the world laid at her feet for the choosing, not to be directed where to go in life. And Simon planned to give her everything she wanted, and more.

"This way," Mr. Kerr said, and motioned toward a nearby door.

Simon followed Carrie's father into the study. Across the room a large desk sat proud with papers piled neatly on top. To the right, a large bay window overlooked the street, and to the left two chairs faced the fireplace with an ornate oak side table in between.

Carrie's father took a chair and motioned for Simon to do the same opposite him, so he followed suit. "If you're here for my daughter, I'm afraid you're too late."

Nausea hit Simon's stomach like a train to a deer on the tracks. She couldn't be promised to anyone else. She'd spent the last few months with him. They were meant to be together. Heat at the base of his neck caused the skin beneath the collar of his shirt to itch.

Thomas.

"I'll be honest with you, sir, I did come for Carrie. I've never met a woman quite like her, but I also came to make you a business offer."

James scooted to the edge of his chair and squinted. "I'm listening."

"I find the need to take on another position in life, and it's been brought to my attention that you have a business for sale."

James frowned and sat back in his chair, shaking his head. "I don't know where you heard that, but you're mistaken."

Carrie's father stared hard, his face unreadable as the moment stretched. Simon wasn't about to let him intimidate him with the silence. He lifted his head and sat back to mimic the older man's body position. "I'll make it worth your consideration."

Sam Hill, the man kept the silent intimidation tactic strong until Simon struggled to maintain an air of confidence. Mere seconds before Simon would have given in, James shook his head. "I'm not selling."

"I can offer you a price well above what it's worth."

"No." He shook his head again. "This business is my life. I'll not give it away, no matter the price."

Blast! The man emanated pride—apparent by the hard way he stuck to his lie, even though Simon knew he needed help. "Well, then, would you consider taking on a partner? I could buy half the company and bring in a few new clients to sweeten the pot."

Good Lord, where was he going to get new business from?

James pressed his lips together, his elbows resting on the arms of the chair where he sat. His eyes slid over Simon as though to size him up. "You've been through more than a man could take, and lived. So you're a hard man, and hard men make good businessmen. But I've heard rumors of your character in town, and I'm not impressed with what I hear. How do I know you aren't going to bilk me?"

"I may have been a little on the wild side in my younger days, but I've never cheated anyone. Especially out of their money." Simon adjusted his seat and leaned forward, resting his arms on his knees. "I'm not the man I was years ago. You're right about one thing: the cougar attack did change me, but it was Carrie who showed me who I was as a man. What I'm doing isn't just for me, it's for her. I don't know who you've promised her to, but I can guarantee you that I can bring a lot more to you than whoever it is." *Especially if it was Thomas.* "I can help you build your company stronger, and I will love and provide for your daughter until the day that I take my last breath."

The look in James's eyes grew cold. "So you're the one?"

"The one?" Simon sat upright, confused at the man's sudden change in mood.

"You're the man who ruined my daughter?"

"I beg your pardon?" Simon's heartbeat sped up, and sucking in even the smallest of breaths grew difficult. *Thomas.* Simon held back a roar at the thought. If the little weasel had ruined his chances with Carrie, he'd take great pleasure in strangling the fool until his eyes bulged. "Where did you hear that?"

"Where is not important. Are you or are you not the man who compromised my daughter and any future she may have had?"

"If you've gotten your information from the man who was in here before me, you should know he has spent the entire summer vying for Carrie's attention and has failed miserably. He will stop at nothing to get what he wants. Even turning Carrie's own parents against her, apparently."

"Does he lie? I've yet to hear you deny the claim."

Simon rolled his shoulders to stretch the taut muscle forming in the middle of his back. His legs grew restless, and he fought the urge to shake them free of the sensation. What was he supposed to say to the man? He could lie and tell him they'd never so much as touched, but there was a chance he'd see right through the lie. The other was to confess, and risk Carrie's reputation and anger. Goddammit! Thomas was the only person who knew about them, or suspected he knew something about them, and the only person who'd visited her parents. So he had to be the chiseler who'd aired Carrie's personal affairs. Was that why he'd come down the mountain? To ruin any chance Simon had with Carrie?

"I think that's something you need to take up with your daughter, but I can tell you Thomas is not one to be trusted. If he's the blowhard you've promised Carrie to, you need to pull back now while you can."

"Are these the words of a jealous man or a businessman?"

"These are the words of a man who adores your daughter. One who is willing to do whatever he has to in order to persuade you to give me your daughter's hand in marriage."

James peered down at him through his wire-rimmed glasses. "Anything?"

Simon answered with a single nod.

Carrie's father frowned. "Okay, Mr. Sanders. You bring me a big fish client, and one hundred hides, and I'll take you on as a partner."

Simon leaned forward. "And Carrie?"

"If you can do that, you can have my blessing to wed my daughter. If not, she goes to the man I've promised her to."

"Even if she doesn't want to marry another man?"

James gave a large belly laugh. "Carrie's mother is in bed with the vapors because of the recent news of her irresponsibility. Once my daughter returns, she doesn't have a choice as to whom she marries. Not unless she plans to shuck out on her own. No longer a Kerr." James shook his head. "No. She's a good girl. Once she returns and discovers what she's done to her mother, she'll do whatever she needs to do to save this family's reputation."

Simon pinched his mouth shut to stop the retort burning the edge of his tongue. What sort of father willingly sacrificed his daughter to the first man who asked for her just to save the family name? And that was the man he was casting in his lot with.

But if he wanted Carrie, he had no choice. He'd find the clients, and the hides. He had to for Carrie's sake. His stomach churned. What would Carrie think of what had transpired here today? Would she be mad at him for treating her like a business deal? More than likely. The better question was, would she forgive him? Simon held his hand out for the man to shake. "You have yourself a deal."

Still with the frown plastered to his face, James stood. "Splendid. I'll give you one month to get me the goods. Otherwise she'll be married to the other man I've promised her to as soon as she returns from her little adventure."

Simon nodded as he stood, and he followed the man to the door. "Best have your lawyers write up the contract, because I will not fail."

Finally, the man smiled, but one of those business smiles that didn't reach his eyes. "Good. I'll count on it."

Simon said his goodbyes and left, glancing at the sun to gauge the time as he hurried down the dusty street. The train would pull out of the station any minute, and he was scheduled to return with Aunt June and the locomotive.

With no time to waste, he ran. Before long the train horn blasted and filled the air around him. With luck he'd make it before the engine took off down the tracks. As suspected, the rail cars jerked as he rounded the building to the platform. Aunt June's worried face stared out at him from within the second-to-last boxcar. He counted the strokes of the wheels against the track to time the jump. As his intended car slid by, he leapt, barely landing inside the car as Aunt June pulled him in—as if her tiny hands could prevent his large frame from tumbling under the wheels.

He stood and dusted his hands as the car slowly picked up speed. "I can't stay. I came to tell you to have Wall give me a few more days—"

Aunt June shook her head, cutting him off from his next words. "There's a fire."

"The chute?" His senses focused on the older woman's words, but he wasn't too concerned. The chute had caught fire before, and they always managed to put out the flames.

Her face grew grey like the ash from the fire in question. "The forest."

Simon stilled.

The dry season turned every branch, every leaf on the mountain into tinder for a fire.

"We got a wire a few minutes ago from the Mill," she said.

"Where's Carrie?"

Aunt June bit her lower lip before she spoke. "Chances are she's with Beth and Garrett. Don't you worry, they'll protect her."

Simon slammed his fist into the metal wall of the boxcar. Pain erupted from his knuckles all the way up his arm, but he didn't care. Carrie was in the middle of a raging fire alone, and he had no way to know if she'd been caught in the blazing inferno or if she'd escaped. He couldn't lose her. Not now. Not after everything she'd done for him. Not after he'd given his heart to her.

Chapter 19

Carrie coughed in her sleeve and fought her way through the haze toward the railcar. Night threatened to overtake the land while the fire heated the air around her. The fading light, combined with the smoke, made it impossible to see more than a few feet in front of her. Sweat trickled down her spine, one droplet after another, as she lugged her bag of possessions toward where she thought the train stood waiting.

Garrett had ordered her to hurry ten minutes earlier when he'd come into camp with the news of the decision to leave. They'd settled down after a somber supper when he'd entered camp and told the entire crew to hurry to the railcars so they could get to safety. They needed to escape down the mountain before the fire. From the feel of the heat around them, they might be too late.

Nots barked from where Carrie had placed her in the bag. She'd packed up her small parcel of belongings as the train horn blasted a warning. She ran. The last thing she wanted to do was miss the only chance she had of getting off this godforsaken mountain alive.

Within a few breaths, the blurred sight of the train in the distance loomed before her. Another blast, and she ran up the steps to Beth and Garrett's caboose. She set her bag down near the door and clutched her stomach as the train blasted the horn again. She grabbed the doorjamb to steady her as she caught her breath and found Beth peering out the window at the gray abyss.

"Where's Garrett?" she asked.

"Up front with the men. He gave me strict orders to stay here."

Carrie motioned toward the smoky haze outside. "How'd the fire start?"

"I don't know. There was no storm, so it wasn't lightning," Beth answered. "Plus, we haven't used the chute."

Carrie nodded as the train horn sounded once more. Nots barked at the noise and wiggled in the bag, fighting for freedom. "Stay still." Carrie bent down to try and hold her pup as the little creature broke free and bolted for the stairs.

"Blast!" Carrie shouted, and started to follow.

Beth caught her by the arm as the train jerked forward. "The train is leaving!"

Carrie flicked a glance at her pup, who followed the rails toward the engine. "She moved toward the front of the train. I'll grab her and jump on one of the railcars with the men."

"Fine, but I'll watch you. If you don't get onboard a car, then shout and I'll yank you back on the caboose." Beth bit her lip like she was apt to do when nervous.

With no time to waste, Carrie leapt from the caboose and ran after Nots.

The dog weaved in and out of the wheels as they picked up speed. Carrie's mouth ran dry and her heartbeat chugged faster than a runaway train as she followed, bending down as the pup ran in front of her, only to miss the little scamp by a fingertip.

Nots ran in front of her again, and she reached out toward the side of the train as it moved faster past her. She grabbed the pup as a long piece of metal from a boxcar sliced through the flesh in her arm. Blood began to fall. Nots wiggled from her hands, and she let the pup go as panic assailed her chest at the sight of her arm.

"Carrie!" She made out Beth's voice above the roar of the train on the tracks and looked up in time to see Beth's hand extended as the end of the train grew closer.

Carrie searched the ground for Nots, but the animal had gained a few feet from where she now stood. She could make it. She had to.

Using all the speed she could muster, Carrie ran and snatched up the pup and rushed back as quick as she could to catch the train as Beth's hands grew farther away.

"No! Beth!" she screamed when she realized she didn't possess speed enough to catch the caboose. Tears fell hard down her face, and she didn't bother to squelch them. She stopped running, clutched Nots in her arms, and bent over to try and stop the vomit threatening to expel at the thought of burning in the fire.

She sobbed, and glanced up in time to see Beth leap from the speeding caboose and roll on the ground to come to a stop.

Carrie ran to her dearest friend as she swiped at her tears. "What in Hades are you doing? Garrett told you not to leave the caboose."

"Are you daft?" Beth stood tall and dusted her pants. "I would never leave you behind in the middle of a forest fire. Garrett will come back for us."

Carrie coughed as smoke entered her lungs. She covered her mouth with her sleeve.

"Let's go." Beth grabbed her arm and ran.

"Where?" Carrie asked as she followed her friend.

"Garrett will come for us, but we need to find a way down the mountain. It might be hours before he finds out we're missing." Beth studied the mountain and took a deep breath. She sucked on one finger and stuck it high in the air. "The winds are blowing this way. If the breeze doesn't change, the fire will be here before Garrett."

Unable to hold her vomit back any longer, Carrie lurched over and released the bile burning her throat. What had she done? Put not only her life in danger, but her dearest friend's as well. She was a mudsill. What sort of person puts everyone they love in jeopardy?

"Better?" Beth asked.

When Carrie nodded, Beth grabbed her hand and towed her behind as she ran toward Aunt June's cabin. She skidded to a stop next to a shipment of supplies that had been unloaded from the returning train the night before.

"Help me!" Beth tugged at one of the bateaus that had returned to camp with the load but not yet been taken to the lake.

Carrie coughed again. She tucked Nots down the front of her bodice to keep her secure while she worked, and reached down to heave the front of the boat. She shuddered, unable to hold back her tears further. If her situation wasn't such a dire one, she might have stopped to appreciate the strength she possessed. One she never thought she'd have, but now wasn't the time. Now she needed to figure out how to stay alive. She followed Beth's direction as they made their way through camp toward the lake.

They'd made it past the cold campfire ring when Beth dropped her side of the boat. "Hold on."

Carrie set her side down and stood huffing as her friend disappeared into Aunt June's house. A few minutes ticked by before Beth emerged. She tossed a long rifle out the door and struggled under the weight of a crate as she took laborious steps outside and set the box down. She stopped to kick the door shut and yanked out a white sheet of paper from the crate. With a knife she pulled off of the nearby serving table, she stuck the paper on the door, then beckoned Carrie with a wave of her hand. "Come here!"

Carrie ran toward her. Beth plucked the gun off the ground and held it out. "Put this in the boat."

Nots wiggled in the front of her blouse as she grabbed the gun and returned to the boat. It wasn't hard to figure out Beth had formed a plan. She possessed a mind clear enough to gather supplies before they left. If Carrie had been left alone, God only knows what she would have done. Certainly not had the good sense to grab a weapon and what looked like a crate full of food, let alone figure out another escape route from the burning inferno up the mountain slope. Carrie more than likely would have hidden in the cabin and curled up into a ball until someone rescued her or she'd gone down with the camp.

Behind her, Beth lugged the heavy crate to the boat and set it in the bateau. She grabbed the front once more, so Carrie heaved up her side but rearranged her grip. Her fingers strained under the extra weight, but she clutched the edge as tight as she could to keep it hovering over the ground. "What'd you do?"

Beth peered over her shoulder at the knife and paper. "I left a note in case Garrett comes back for us. I also grabbed us some supplies."

"What are we doing? Staying in the middle of the lake until help comes?" Carrie couldn't hide the desperation in her voice, and frankly didn't want to. The last few minutes had been the worst moments she'd ever experienced. Even worse than when she spotted Simon riding into camp slumped over the saddle in front of Wall. His body covered in blood, and what skin she could see ghost white.

"We're getting off this mountain," Beth answered, and faced the trail.

It was all too much for Carrie. She was a town girl. Not cut out to be a forest-dwelling cook. Perhaps Victoria was right after all. She needed to go home. Find a life where she didn't wake up every morning wondering what sort of disaster awaited her. Or perhaps even death. She needed to find her security elsewhere. Not on the mountain.

A ranch wouldn't be bad, would it? Better than in town at least. Then she'd live on a homestead instead of rough-built cabin surrounded by wild animals and men with no respect for manners. She needed to refocus her goals.

Beth stepped boot deep into the lake with no concern for the water seeping into her clothes. What Carrie wouldn't do to be as brave and fierce as her friend. Beth had her faults, but she was the most loyal and determined friend to those she loved. She could always be counted on in a tough situation.

"We're going down the river?" Carrie asked, and set her side of the boat down on the bank.

Beth adjusted the bateau in the lake. "I'm not about to sit around and wait for the fire to reach us. I know Garrett will come for us, but we don't know how long it will take. This is the fastest way for us to get away from the flames."

"What if the river flows over by where the fire is?"

Beth shook her head and climbed in to take up the oars. "The fire is northwest of us. The way the wind is blowing now, the flames are coming straight at us. If we're lucky, though, the wind will shift north, or blow back on the fire to turn it away. Either way, we should be good. Unless the winds shift south."

"Then we're in even more trouble?" Carrie climbed in opposite Beth. The crate full of food and supplies sat square in the middle of the boat. Nots wiggled again, and popped her head out of the top of her dress. Somehow the warmth she gave calmed Carrie enough to at least follow Beth's orders. Without the pup, she'd be in a swirl of emotions. Unable to think straight enough to get off the mountain alive.

"Let's pray that it doesn't." Beth shoved off from the bank and rowed the small boat toward the mouth of the river.

Carrie took a deep breath and clutched the side of the bateau as it rocked. She wasn't cut out for this. Didn't have the adventurous soul her friend before her possessed. Wasn't usually willing to take risks with her life the way Beth seemed to do...until today. "What if Garrett comes back for us? He's going to be in danger."

"Garrett will bring the train up so he can have a straight shot back home. Once he reads my note, he'll either go back down on the engine or bring the second bateau down the river to find us. If the fire is far enough away by the time we reach The Thirsty Woodsman Saloon, we'll see if we can go in and find help."

"The Thirsty Woodsman?" Carrie asked. She knew the place. Last year when they'd taken the drive down, they'd stopped near the filthy saloon to unjam a blockage in the river. Because of the way the river wound around and leaked into other lakes, the ride to the saloon was days away from where they were now. At least. "Are there no homesteads or other stopping points before there?"

Beth shook her head as the boat caught the current and shot into the mouth of the river. "That's the closest we can get. We'll plan to make it there, and then see if we can't get us a horse to take the remainder of the trail to the mill."

Carrie's chest tightened to an almost painful level, and her breath grew shallow. They'd never make it out alive. "I don't like this plan, Beth," she shouted over the water.

"It's too late now, and it's a helluva lot better than burning to death in the cabin." Beth maneuvered the bateau around a rock, then slid her a quick glance. "It'll be fine. We'll row through the night. If the river's fast enough, we will be there before the end of the day tomorrow. We don't stop and we'll be fine."

Beth had a point, but that didn't make the plan any more enticing—not that she wasn't grateful for her friend jumping off a train to rescue her. But a plan to put her trust in a winding river to get them down the mountain faster? Carrie's only hope was to make it off the mountain alive. The only thing she wanted was to see Simon again. Feel the strength in his arms as he held her. Feel his lips against hers. She had to live. Even if only long enough to tell him, despite her plans for her life, that she loved him.

* * * *

Simon jumped from the train before the screeching wheels even had a chance to settle. His legs burned as he ran, but he didn't care. He searched the throng of loggers in the mill yard, disembarking from the train with Garrett's caboose. They'd made it down before the fire.

Where was Carrie?

Aunt June appeared beside him and stood on tiptoe to survey the crowd. Her brows pulled down in worry. Not waiting to see if she planned to follow, he headed toward the caboose. Chills raced down his spine and his stomach grew heavy with each second he didn't see Carrie's blond hair shining among the men. She had to be here.

Garrett's large frame stood out amidst the men milling around the train yard, and Simon motioned to him. "Oy, Garrett!"

His friend raised his head in greeting.

"Have you seen Carrie?"

"I saw her get in the caboose with Beth before we pulled out."

Simon walked past Garrett and fought his way through the crowd to the back of the train.

"Everything all right?" Garrett's voice sounded behind him, and Simon looked back to see his friend following.

"I want to check to see if she's here before I relax."

"I watched her get on myself. Otherwise I wouldn't have given the engineer the go-ahead to leave."

Simon nodded, but his chest tightened. Something wasn't right. Carrie and his sister should have stepped out of the train by now. Perhaps he was overreacting? But then again Carrie had been left alone with his troublesome sister.

He took a few deep breaths and leapt onto the back of the train. Normally he would have yanked the door open, but it was locked in the open position. His fingers grew cold. No sound came from within, and he doubted he had missed them disembarking.

Where the hell were they?

"Carrie!" he called as his heart dropped to the empty pit in his stomach and a lump formed in the base of his throat. He leaned in and spotted her bag half open near the wall. It took him no time at all to search the backroom, but there was no sign of either Carrie or Beth.

"Carrie!" he shouted louder.

"Beth," he heard Garrett call from outside the railcar. His friend leaned over the side and searched the crowd. He waited for a second, then shook his head. "They're not here. What the hell happened to them?"

Garrett's jaw flexed and his chest rose and fell as if he too felt the tightness that gripped Simon's heart like the coupling of a train. His friend's question burned in his mind. Where were they?

He couldn't lose the only women in his life who cared about a mudsill like him. He couldn't lose them. Either one. For the first time in his life, he felt the need to cry, but he fought the urge. Replacing it with sheer rage instead. He slammed his fist into the wall of a railcar for the second time today. A piercing ache spread from his knuckles to the inside of his elbow, but he didn't care.

Garrett took a step inside the caboose. "They've got to be up the tracks somewhere."

Simon studied the track leading up the hill. "Let's go. I'll not lose them. Not now."

"It'll take hours to get the tracks cleared and a train ready to go up. We don't have time."

Simon waved toward the middle of the train as the workers brought the livestock out of the stock cars. "We'll ride. Follow the tracks."

Garrett gave a single nod and leapt off the train. Simon ran behind his friend, only to be yanked back by a weak hand. He turned, ready to knock out whoever had tried to stop him from going, only to see Aunt June staring back at him. She frowned. "Where are they?"

Simon shook his head. When she let him go, he gave her a reassuring squeeze. "I'll find them."

"Come back with my girls." Aunt June's chin quivered, but he didn't stay long enough to see if she cried. He pivoted and ran after Garrett. A few railcars down, Garrett and a logger readied two horses with saddles. Simon approached as the logger checked the cinch and stepped back.

The mount's reins dangled, so Simon scooped them up and swung them over the horse's neck as he mounted. He adjusted the leather straps in his hands and kicked the horse into motion.

The sound of Garrett's horse behind him pounded in conjunction with his own mount's hooves. The noise helped Simon focus on the task at hand instead of the frantic emotion bubbling in his gut. He counted the beats of the hooves in time with his own breaths to keep from spiraling mentally.

It would take them hours to ride to where the camp was, and by the looks of the fire, they might not make it in time. He planned to try, though.

Where were they? Had they fallen from the train or stayed behind for some ridiculous reason? No reason would ever be acceptable for staying behind in the midst of a forest fire. He didn't know if he could ever forgive either one, but first he needed to find them.

The men rode hard up the mountain—a task that would have been more difficult through the smoke had they not had the tracks to follow. Simon coughed, and then pulled his handkerchief from around pocket and tied it around his face. Taking his cue, Garrett did the same. Before long the thick air around them grew dark as the sun set. To his left, high in the forest, the bright orange of the fire illuminated the smoke around the flames.

"This way!" Garrett shouted, and turned down the wagon trail that led straight to Aunt June's cabin.

Simon's bones chilled at the eerie silence of camp. No sound of timber falling, mumble of the loggers, train whistle or grinding of the tracks, not even the gentle clank of the cook dishes filled the trees as they normally did. Nothing but the far-off roar of the fire as it ate its way toward the logging operation.

"Victoria's going to be furious," Garrett said, and dismounted next to the cabin. "If this fire eats up not only the trees but all of the equipment, Great Mountain will be left with nothing but the hauls we got down."

Simon shook his head and tightened his lips. Although he wasn't one of Victoria's greatest followers, he didn't want to see her suffer.

"What started it?"

Garrett stared at the far-off flames. "Dry lightning. We think. There's been rainless storms in and out over the last week. None down here, but there was one further up the mountain a few days ago. Lightning can strike from miles away."

"Where are the women?" Simon dismounted, and tromped about the camp, searching for signs of Carrie.

"Over there," Garrett called, and pointed toward the cabin door as he ran.

He got to the missive before Simon, and swiped it from the piercing grip of the knife.

"They've gone down the river." Garrett handed the note to Simon, and Simon ran a quick eye over his sister's swirly scribble.

"She thinks you brought the train up. Told you to go back down on it. She plans to try and get to The Thirsty Woodsman." Simon slapped the paper against his thigh. "What in God's name is she thinking?"

"We've two choices," Garrett said, heading toward his horse. "We go down the tracks and wait, or follow the river and hope to find the women."

Not bothering with the stirrups, Simon swung onto the saddle and adjusted the cougar bone tucked into his belt. "I'm not leaving my sister or Carrie to fend for themselves on the river."

"If they left shortly after the train, they'd be by The Thirsty Woodsman tomorrow afternoon. We can't pick our way down the bank in the dark, and I'm not willing to stay and wait until morning." Garrett mounted his horse as well.

"So tonight, we ride the tracks until the saloon. Then when the sun comes up, we'll head up the river and head them off."

Garrett frowned, but nodded. Simon agreed. He didn't like the plan any more than his friend, but it was all they had to go on. They'd both found out the year before how dangerous searching the banks of the river at night could be. Their best chance was to go down far enough to head the women off on the river. Once the women were secure with them, they could high-tail it down the mountain to safety. For now, they had to ride. And pray.

Chapter 20

Carrie concentrated on keeping her breath even. The night had long since closed in around her, but that didn't make each bump of the boat on the rocks and riverbed beneath them any less frightening. *Oh God*, what she wouldn't give to be wrapped in Simon's arms back at Mother Goose's Cottage—with no threat from the fire and no one else in the world but them.

Would spending a lifetime with a man like Simon, even with his gruff flaws, be so bad? Not when days, and nights, were as amazing as the time they'd spent together. Would he give up logging and get a job on Wall's ranch as a cowpuncher so they could be together?

Carrie silently chuckled at the thought of Simon riding fences. He'd find a job in a bank before taking up as a cowboy. Was there something else she could do in town for a job? She needed to remember that Simon was nothing like her father. He'd never put his pride before family and common sense.

Then again, Simon wasn't the type to marry. Plenty of Missoula women could claim to have experienced the way he loved women, but not one of them could claim he'd ever been on the verge of marriage to any of them. He was a proud bachelor. Would he give up his status for her? It wasn't like she was any different from the other women in town. She'd fallen for the same man that they had.

"There are rocks ahead." Beth's voice pierced her thoughts.

Carrie examined the river before them. Moonlight glittered off the white of the rapids, and her heart sped up to pump blood through her veins as fast as the river current flowed. She must forge her own path without a care to the consequences. No matter what happened tonight, she was going to fight like Beth always did. Fight for her life, for Simon, and for her freedom. Could she have all three? Maybe, if the stars aligned and she fought like hell.

God, she hoped fate was in her favor tonight.

Carrie clutched her seat with one hand and placed the other over her chest where Nots slept. The boat rocked and swayed. Bumping into rocks as it pinged around the river like when she would throw a flat rock across a glassy lake. Only this lake wasn't glassy. It churned and bubbled.

"Hold on!" Beth yelled and, through the faint light from the moon and forest fire, she dipped low and dug the oar into the water, alternating sides until they were clear of the rapids.

The boat slowed, and Carrie sat back with a sigh.

Only one woman she knew could have navigated a white-water rapid safely in the dark. If they ever got to town alive, she would buy Beth a wardrobe—or new pair of logger's boots—for jumping off the train to come to her rescue.

They floated with the current fast, then slow, only to speed up again, using the feel of the river, faint light from the fire, and moonlight to guide them until the sun peeked out from behind the mountains. The daylight illuminated everything with a bright sheen. The tense ache in Carrie's shoulders eased, and she slouched back in her seat.

She grew tired as they floated through a lake and another river, taking breaks every so often to stretch their legs and take care of business. Beth pushed the boat into the water one last time. Carrie's gaze stopped on the small box of food Beth had had the good sense to pack, and her stomach growled. With a quick glance at the sun to gauge the time, she scooted toward the box and searched the contents. "I don't know about you, but I'm starving."

Beth nodded. The weary gleam in her eye and lack of her usual smile were telling signs as to how exhausted she too had become. Her friend must be ravenous after the work she'd done to get them down the mountain. "Maybe some food will give us some energy."

"Do you want me to take over while you eat and then rest?" Carrie shoved a large piece of dried meat into her mouth. The savory substance wasn't quite enough to squelch her hunger, but that didn't matter. They were alive. And far enough away from the fire to relax, but not far enough away to want to stop.

Beth studied the river ahead. "There shouldn't be any big rapids. I suppose I could give you a quick lesson and then rest my eyes for a spell."

"Simon let me try a little when we went out on the lake." She reached for the oars. "I promise not to tip us over."

Her friend gave a faint smile, handed her the peavey and oars, and snatched up the food like she'd never before had something so delectable. Carrie chuckled. "You're quite rabid with that meat."

"I'm starving. For a few weeks now, I can't seem to eat enough, and half of the food I eat makes me nauseous, and I end up tossing it out."

"Have you got a little Jones in there?" Carrie teased, but the words penetrated her thoughts. Had she put not only her best friend, but her friend's unborn child in danger?

And what about herself? Could she be with child? She wasn't overly hungry, but then again she was the cook. She tasted virtually everything she made, and she ate quite frequently. Nothing made her nauseous. At least nothing but the moment the train left them behind. How long had it been since she had had her womanly time? *Good heaven above.* Had Simon left her with something more than a memory?

Best not get ahead of herself. She wasn't even certain Beth was with child, let alone herself. Chances were slim.

Carrie maneuvered the boat around a large boulder as she watched Beth inhale the food, then sit back and close her eyes. Beth would make a perfect mother. Despite all of her adventures, Beth was one of the most caring people she'd ever met. Would Carrie be as perfect a parent as Elizabeth? Not if she had to work hard just to keep the both of them fed. She'd have no time to raise a child.

No.

She wasn't pregnant, and life would continue as she had planned. Maybe she could live through Beth and her babe. She'd spoil the little peach rotten until her dearest friend begged her to let the child alone for behavior's sake.

Get over your fantasies, she scolded herself. Best concentrate on the task at hand—making it to the Mill alive. After all, neither one of them could have a baby if they were dead.

She floated in silence as Beth slept hard on the floor of the bateau. The only sound besides the bubbling of the river beneath them was the gentle whines from Nots. Beside her feet the little pup lay next to the crate, her eyes sad as though she pleaded for a reprieve from the confines of the bateau. "I know, I know. I could use a stretch too."

Carrie studied the mountain where the fire blazed. Although smoke still floated around the mountainside, they were still safe to stop. Carrie spotted a sandy bank down the river and dug deep in the water to move the boat toward the shoreline. In a few hard-fought minutes, she landed the little vessel with a thump.

Beth woke with a start and searched the river frantically before easing her shoulders at the scene. "How long have I been asleep?"

"Maybe an hour." Carrie motioned to her pup. "Nots needed a break, and so did I."

Beth nodded—her face ashen and hair disheveled. Was that what Carrie looked like as well? She imagined it was, though maybe not as rough. What a sight they must be. Two proper women run ragged from almost two days in a little boat, fleeing for their lives.

Beth jumped from the boat and eased it farther onto the bank, securing the line to a nearby tree stump. As Beth took up the rifle and checked to ensure it was loaded, Carrie picked Nots up and clambered out of the bateau. She wobbled to get her balance as the solid land seemed to roll beneath her feet. The routine they had whenever they stopped for a break barely changed from one stop to another: Beth confident in the role as protector and Carrie the mothering hen who watched over the pup.

Carrie stretched her arms above her head. "Are you certain we're going down the right rivers? Shouldn't we see any signs of civilization by now?"

"We're getting closer to The Thirsty Woodsman. Should be there by tonight," Beth said, then perked up to stare hard in the brush.

The bone-chilling click of the gun sent her stomach rolling, and Carrie searched where Beth stared. Nots barked at her feet and took off into the vegetation. Carrie flinched to follow. "Nots!"

"Stop!" Beth commanded, and pointed the gun toward where Nots had disappeared. "Something is back there."

With the vegetation so thick before them, all they could do was wait and listen. A high-pitched screech sounded through the branches, and tears filled Carrie's eyes. Her love for her pup prompted her to go to her rescue, but common sense, and Beth, forced her to stay. She couldn't lose the one thing on earth Simon had given her.

Her spine prickled as the screech switched to a low growl and back to the screech as the distinctive sounds of a mountain lion filled the trees around them and intensified. Nots's barks grew frantic somewhere in the brush. Coward that she was, Carrie moved behind Beth and the gun and waited.

"We're going to die," she whispered.

"No." Beth adjusted the gun on her shoulder. "The animals are running from the fire and just as scared as us. Let's get in the boat. We might have to leave Nots behind."

"No."

"Carrie," Beth said, sternly. Even though she'd only spoken her name, the one word pierced her heart and screamed of truth. If they wanted to live, she might have to sacrifice her pet.

"Simon gave her to me." Carrie didn't bother to hold back her tears. She let them fall like the water droplets off a boulder in the middle of the river.

"Get in the boat." Beth's tone didn't leave room for argument.

With one last glance to where Nots had disappeared into the brush, Carrie scurried onto her seat in the bateau and waited. Worry dug a hole in her stomach when Beth didn't move toward the boat. Instead she stood, gun trained on the brush, as another screech filled the air.

"If he attacks and I miss, row out to the river, Carrie. Don't look back."

"No!" Carrie shouted, and tripped as she lurched upright and fought her way back to the bank as a large cougar emerged from the brush ten yards in front of them.

The sleek cat cocked his head to the side and tipped his mouth back in a scream to frighten even the bravest of men as Nots danced around behind him and nipped at the back of his heels. Her brave little pup. The cat growled deep in its chest and turned slightly to swipe at Nots with his front claws, but missed. Carrie stopped short when the cat trained his gaze on her—his eyes like the black soulless stare of the devil.

"Shoot him!" Carrie tried to shout the words, but her voice barely made a whisper of sound. Regardless, the sound drew attention to her. The mountain lion moved his head and took a step forward as Beth fired a shot.

Carrie jumped at the sound, but the bullet missed and the cougar flinched then charged. She didn't think the animal aimed at any one of them; it simply attacked. Carrie screamed and turned to run toward the boat as a second shot rang out around them, followed immediately by a third.

She turned back to the scene in time to see the cat drop to the ground and blood spread beneath the tan hide. Dead.

No longer able to hold her own weight, Carrie's knees collapsed beneath her, and she fell. Shaking as tears puddled the ground. She let herself go just for a moment. Needing the few seconds of utter silence to bring the world into focus.

Before she could gain her composure, strong arms encircled her shoulders and tugged her up. Her stomach flipped as she stood and peered up into Simon's worried eyes. He pulled her into his shoulder, and she sank into his embrace, letting the emotions flow like the river behind her. Thank God he'd been there. How he was there didn't matter. She was safe and in his arms again.

She dug her face into his chest, and he held her. Quiet as he caressed her hair. Each stroke eased the fear coursing through her veins and helped to calm her.

Below, Nots bumped at her ankles and barked, but she didn't want to break away from Simon to pick up the pup.

"You came," she said into his shirt.

"I'll always come for you, my love." He squeezed her tighter and dipped his chin down to bury his face in her hair. His breath tickled the base of her neck, but the sensation made her want to lean toward his mouth. He was here for her. At her darkest moment, he'd found her in the middle of the forest, during a fire. What man would do that for a woman they only dallied with?

Did he now mean it when he called her his love?

God, she hoped so. She'd only just realized how deeply she loved the man before her. Discovered how much she needed him. In more ways than one. No. In every way possible. He was the man who made her strong enough to face the world. She couldn't do it without him.

* * * *

Simon held Carrie so tight he thought she'd lose the ability to breathe, but for the life of him, he couldn't let her go. Sheer dread had filled his veins with ice when he'd heard the sounds of the cougar attacking. The only two sparks of warmth in his dank world.

They'd made it to The Thirsty Woodsman as the sun came up, and after a quick reprieve, followed the river upstream. Since they'd turned, they'd ridden in relative silence. Searching the banks and river for signs of the women. They'd ridden so far his heart ached as thoughts of her dead body made his fingers grow numb.

And then they'd heard the mountain lion and dog, and he knew they were close. Without a word to each other, he and Garrett had kicked their tired horses faster and come upon the scene as Beth fired the first shot. He had just enough time to yank his weapon free of the holster when his sister fired a second, but he took a third. He didn't know which bullet had killed the beast, but it didn't matter. Only their lives mattered.

"Ready?" Garrett's voice penetrated his thoughts, and Simon glanced up as his friend lifted his sister onto their horse before turning to take care of the boat.

Simon urged Carrie to lift her face from his chest, cupping her cheek in one hand. "Pick up Nots. I'm going to put you on my horse and take you to safety."

She nodded numbly and did as directed. The dog squirmed and licked his hand when he reached out to pet the little scamp. Little challenger, more like. The pup wasn't afraid to protect her mistress.

If only people showed the love and loyalty the way dogs did. Perhaps nothing bad would ever happen in this world.

The cat's tan fur moved in the breeze. Whether it was Beth's bullet or his that had stopped the cougar, he'd taken part in stopping the animal. Yanking out the bone he'd kept like a knife tucked into the back of his belt, he tossed it onto the newly deceased cougar. The bone from the one who wounded him would rot with the body of the animal slain to protect the woman he loved. On a deep, freeing inhale, he faced his mount, and Carrie.

By the time Garrett mounted behind Beth, Simon had Carrie secure in front of him, and he scooped up the reins. Kicking the horse into motion to walk behind Garrett and Beth. They had a few hours' ride ahead of them, but once they made it to The Thirsty Woodsman, they could rest until refreshed enough to ride the rest of the way to the Mill.

"What's going to happen now?" Carrie asked, breaking the silence.

"With what?" He bent down to kiss the top of her ear. She leaned back as if wanting more, so he dipped lower and kissed her neck, grateful she didn't fight. He needed the intimacy as much as he suspected she did.

"With the Mill. The camp." She waved toward the distant forest fire. "What if it's all destroyed?"

"Well, when we get back we will have to send someone after the boat you stole," he teased. She playfully shoved her back against him, so he squeezed her tighter. "And then once the fire is out we'll go back up and assess the damage. If the camp is safe, we'll start work back up, but if it's all gone then Victoria will have to decide what to do next. They can either close their doors or move their operation somewhere else."

"I've never been overly fond of Victoria, but I hope the camp is safe. For her sake."

"Me too, my love, me too." He adjusted the reins in his hands and kicked the horse up a small incline. Letting the silence take over.

A few hours ticked by with occasional conversation, but for the most part they remained ensconced in their thoughts. If the other three were anything like him, they relived the last few hours over to see if they'd do anything different.

As dusk started to settle over the mountainside, the ribbon of smoke floated into the air from The Thirsty Woodsman. Simon adjusted his horse's direction to head toward the barn. The small saloon catered mostly to mountain men and loggers. Because of the vast distance the clientele traveled, the short, stout owner had a handful of cabins built for weary travelers in need of rest and a long line of stalls where you could rent a space for a dollar a night. A steep price for a mountain man. Many simply hobbled their rides and let them loose in the nearby meadow.

Simon rode to the front of the barn and dismounted, reaching up to help Carrie slide off the saddle. Like Beth, she looked white and numb. They'd been through a lot the last few days and needed a rest.

"I'll go in and pay for the cabins and stables," Garrett offered.

Simon nodded and grabbed the reins from his sister. "I'll take care of the horses."

In no time at all, he'd brushed the mounts, locked them in two stables against the far wall, checked the water, and tossed in a few flakes of hay. Once satisfied the animals were well cared for, Simon stepped outside to find Garrett with the women.

"There's only two cabins left. Seems the fire is bringing a lot of men down from their trap lines. We're lucky two of his customers moved on down the mountain this morning. Otherwise we'd be paying for a spot in the barn."

"I suppose Carrie and I will take one cabin, and you and Simon the other," Beth said, but Simon didn't miss the disappointment in her voice. She was a married woman and had every right to sleep in the same bed as her husband. Whereas he was a single man, for now, who'd been through way less than the strong women before him.

"Why don't you two take a cabin, and Carrie can have the second one? I'll sleep out here with the horses."

Beth shook her head. "I couldn't do that to you."

Simon tossed his hands in the air with as much nonchalance as he could feign. "I'm a woodsman. This won't be my first time sleeping outside, or even in a barn for that matter."

Beth visibly relaxed into her husband's embrace and smiled her thanks.

Simon scooped Nots up in one hand and extended the other for Carrie. She leaned on his arm as if he were a lifeline, and he started toward the small abodes. Ever since they'd discovered the women, they'd all been quiet. Much more than he'd ever seen them before. He rubbed his sweaty palm on his pant leg at the thought of Carrie and Beth alone, taking the winding rivers as far as they had. "Which cabins? I'll get Carrie set up with a fire, and then we can head in to get something to eat before the men get too much whiskey in their bellies."

"The two on the far left, over in the trees." Garrett motioned with his head.

Simon made short work of getting Carrie settled, complete with blazing fire, while Garrett and Beth did the same in their cabin. He'd left the door open for her reputation, but in reality he wanted to shut it and leave them alone. Together. He knew the look in her eyes. Had felt it on many occasions, even on a good day, but never had he wanted to see it on her beautiful face. The cougar attack had gotten to her. And rightly so.

"I can sleep on the ground in front of the cabin if you want?" He took a few steps to stand before her. Hoping his presence would reassure her enough to put a smile on her face. Even a faint one would do.

Carrie met his eyes with hers and shook her head. "I'd rather you stay with me in here. I don't think any of these mountain men are going to be a problem in town. Do you?"

"What about my sister and Garrett?"

"I don't care if Beth knows about us. Not after what we've been through. I just want you."

Simon gave a deep exhale. "I was hoping you'd say that. I didn't much feel like using horse manure to cushion my head."

Carrie gave a small, breathy chuckle. "I would hope no one would want to use such a pillow."

"I thought I'd lost you before I even had you." He closed the door, and wrapped his arms around her waist to pull her toward him. "When we heard the cougar, and then Nots, I knew you were in trouble. I can't lose you. Not to a mountain lion, the forest, not even to another man."

"Right now, being by your side is all I want to do." Her weary face gazed up at him, pleading for him to take away her strife. To make love to her. To make her his. That's what he took from her expression. She needed him. He'd always been one to understand a woman's flirtatious looks, but that was about it when it came to reading a woman's thoughts.

"Only your strength could have brought me out of the hell I was living in. I need you more than any man ought to need a woman."

"You don't have to say pretty things to me anymore, Simon. You've already stolen my will to resist your embrace. Take what you can."

"I say these things because they are true. I'm lucky they happen to be words that please you." He bent down and kissed her. She melded into his arms, and his spirits soared. No matter what happened tomorrow, or once they got back to town, they had the night on the mountain. This moment—this one kiss—to take them through until death.

Chapter 21

Carrie finished what she could of the meal, but all she wanted to do was go back to the cabin. She'd invited Simon to stay not because she was afraid to be alone but because she wanted to be in his warm, protective arms once more. Maybe even feel the masterful way he tuned her body with his loving. She'd always been one to play the martyr for others, but today she wanted to be selfish and have Simon for herself. No matter the consequences.

Carrie yawned, but she didn't need to fake it like she'd intended. "I think I could sleep for a week."

Beth gave a faint smile in response. "Me too. Perhaps we should all call it an early night?"

Garrett frowned and helped Beth to her feet. Her friend had grown even paler since sitting down to eat and had only picked at the food on her plate. By the look on Garrett's face, he too had noticed. He cleared his throat. "There's no rush in the morning. We'll get up easy and get on our way."

"I'll see to the horses before I hit the hay." Simon stood and pulled Carrie's chair out for her as if they were dining at the Grande Hotel Restaurant and not The Thirsty Woodsman.

Carrie smiled.

Although he was gruff, and often difficult, one could always claim Simon to be a gentleman. Well, most of the time.

The cool air outside hit her face with welcome force, and she headed toward her cabin. With a quick goodnight to her friend, she closed herself into her cabin. Relieved to finally be alone in a warm space.

The small, one-room abode was similar to Aunt June's in style but held a number of bunks built onto the walls.

"I suppose I get to choose where to sleep," she said to Nots, who popped her head up from her paws upon hearing her voice. Although the fierce little creature had attacked the cougar with all the viciousness of a wolf, she certainly didn't move much whenever Carrie came and went from whatever cabin they were staying in. The dog yawned and laid her head back down, the necklace she'd used as a collar noticeably absent. Carrie thought back to the last time she'd seen the necklace and remembered the glimmer of the jewel before steering the boat to the bank. Somewhere between the mountain lion and here, the thing had gone missing.

For a moment, worry descended upon her. How would she explain the loss of the treasure to Thomas? She wouldn't. Plain and simple. If she had her way, she'd never have to see the man again. Not that he was a bad person, but she was done playing those games.

A few minutes ticked by of Carrie surveying the bedding options before Simon slipped through the door and locked it behind him.

He didn't smile his usual wolfish grin but kept his face like stone. Under his scrutiny, she wiggled in her seat on the bed.

"How are you doing?" He took a chair from the small table in the corner and flipped it around to straddle the seat.

"Fine I suppose. Considering."

"What are your plans when we get back to town?" He scooted higher in the chair.

"I may not have told you this, but I plan to find a job. Become as independent as Aunt June. Build my own destiny I suppose." She placed a hand over her stomach. What if she carried his child? She wasn't quite certain when her monthly cycle was supposed to happen. It was possible she'd already passed the day. How would she know? Not like Beth, who obviously needed to go into town and see a doctor.

Simon stood. The chair scraped across the floor when he moved it out of his way. "What about us?"

"Us?" she asked, then wanted to suck the words back into her mouth. She didn't want to hurt him or ruin anything they had. And the question sounded like she didn't care about them. She loved Simon, more than she'd loved anyone in the world, but she needed to think on it when she could focus again. What if he betrayed her the way her father had done to her mother?

"Do you want me in your life when we get to town?"

"Of course I do. You're Beth's brother, and a dearest friend."

"And that's all I am to you?"

Was it her exhaustion that made her hear a hint of pain in his words? Did the most sought-after bachelor in Missoula want to continue their dalliance once they returned? Could she do it without losing her heart completely? Or had she already? "Can we just be tonight? You and me, and no one else in the world?"

She stood and stepped toward him like the hussy she prided herself in not being. She would be it for him, though. At least tonight. The rest she would have to mull through until they got to town.

He let out a grateful sigh as she ran her hand over his scars on his chest and followed them up to trace the healed wounds on the side of his face. "I don't know why you spent a year hiding yourself from everyone. Even with these scars you're flawless." She smiled up at him. "They make you look rugged, like a timber beast."

"Only one woman on earth would agree with you. Aunt June. But let's not talk about her right now." He bent down and forged kisses along her neck, then stopped. His breath tickled her skin, and he tugged at the collar of her dress on her shoulder as he spoke again. "I want to see your body."

She dropped her head to the side to bare her neck to him. Every touch sent tingles radiating through her core.

"You did already."

He shook his head, and began to lay kisses along her skin again, only to stop to talk. "Not with the firelight illuminating you like it does now. I want to see your naked perfection in every light in this world." He reached behind her to unbutton her dress. "Even the moonlight dancing on your skin, making you look like a sensual wood nymph out causing mischief, would do your body no justice."

"More pretty things," she said, but inside she reveled in the description. Many potential beaus had commented on her hair, or the way her smile tipped back, but never before had she believed the man using the words regarded what he said the way Simon did. His eyes spoke to her, confirming the pretty things he said to be true.

His hands floated across her skin like a leaf on the river and made her stomach churn like the bubbles of a fierce rapid.

Simon finished his work with the fasteners on her back and slipped the dress from her shoulders. The fire on one side warmed half her body, while the slight chill of the cabin cooled the other. The sensation, so unreal, heightened every move Simon made down her skin as he felt her.

He slid his hand over her stomach and she quivered beneath his touch. Heaven above, she wanted his baby. Wanted to be with him forever, and bear him more children than even he could handle. With the way he touched her with such reverence and passion, she'd probably be nothing but pregnant, or at least constantly trying to become so. She brought her mouth to his ear, mimicking the sensual whisper he'd used many times on her. "I don't want this to be the last time we're together."

He drew his head back and searched her eyes until she smiled.

Without saying a word, he picked her up and stepped forward until the cold, hard logs of the cabin wall pressed against her back. The cool wood somehow heightened the heat and anticipation that coursed through her body. The rough fabric of his trousers chafed against the sensitive skin between her legs, but she welcomed the sensation.

He pressed his body against hers, lifting his knee to help hold her upright. The pressure against her most intimate of parts helped ease the ache she'd had since he kissed her neck. Simon pressed his mouth against her lips, and she opened them to him like before at Mother Goose's Cottage.

His breath hitched. He took the opportunity she'd offered and dipped his tongue into her mouth to run it against her teeth, and then further. She mimicked his action, and he groaned, squeezing her tighter.

After only a few moments of her taking charge, he adjusted his grip on her, and she balanced on the edge of a log beneath her derrière. Movement between her thighs brought her love-hazed attention to where he stripped himself of his trousers using only one hand. She unbuttoned his cotton shirt. Each button exposed more of his scars, and she kept her eyes on the slashes as she eased the shirt from his shoulders and let it drop. Running her hand over the wounds. She bent down and kissed his chest until he finished undressing and lifted her face to his to devour her mouth. He ran his palm up and down one leg, imprinting his warmth from her buttocks to her knee.

After a few passion-filled moments of kisses, he gently nudged his manhood into her, and she sucked in what air she could get. Each thrust of him inside her shot hot waves through her body, building until she wasn't certain she could take much more. Yet somehow, she craved the welcome torture he bestowed up on her. Needed it like the air she was barely able to get with each breath.

Her stomach quivered, and she clutched his shoulder to help keep her grounded as the tension within her tightened.

"Let it go, my love," he said, his voice rough, yet somehow soft and needy.

Even if she wanted to argue, her body refused to disobey him. Each movement intensified the waves, teasing her core until she could hold back no longer. She let her head fall against the wall, exposing her neck as the sensation flowed to every inch of her body and then ebbed.

"Yes, my love," he ground out, and with a final pump expelled his seed inside her.

She clamped her legs around his thigh. Needing him to stay inside her until her unruly body would function as she wished. After a few minutes, instead of easing her down like she'd expected, he picked her up and deposited her on the bed. Running his hand along her stomach, all the way to her curls.

She bit her lip against the new emotions he evoked with the simple touch.

How were they going to go about their lives now? They'd agreed to become lovers, but did he truly love her? Would he stray when he got bored of bedding her? Doubts in the man she had agreed to give herself to was never a great start to an affair. She didn't want to have doubts.

* * * *

Simon caressed Carrie's hair as he watched her sleep, snuggled tight against his torso. Her pale skin shone with what light was left from the faded embers of the fire. Soon they would wake and start down the mountain, and life would change for them both. He'd gotten to have her, possess her three times during the night, but even that didn't seem to be enough. He craved her like a hungry predator does its prey, only he devoured her in a completely different way and could never be satiated.

If only these moments alone with her in the mountain cabin, both here and Mother Goose's Cottage, could last forever. Nothing but the two of them and the log walls enclosing them in a protected cocoon. Life was different with her. Made sense. Had purpose. With Carrie by his side, he could deal with his demons and be better than the man he was a year ago.

He moved the hair from over her ear and bent down to gently kiss the smooth skin. He whispered so as not to wake her, "I love you." And then snuggled his face in her hair and rested his head on the pillow they shared. He knew she couldn't hear him, but it lightened the knot in his chest to confess it to her, even if she was asleep. How would she react if he told her while awake? Would she tell him the same?

His heart soared as the memory of her acceptance replayed in his mind. To Hades with Thomas. Simon would fight like the devil to secure everything he needed to keep Carrie in his arms. Forever. Not just as lovers as she believed, but as man and wife.

Simon's back muscles tensed. He needed to get contracts with several of the men outside in order to keep his promise to Carrie's father and secure their future together. He slipped out of bed, tucking the blankets behind her. In less than a minute he dressed and eased out of the cabin door, shutting it gently behind him. He'd counted over a dozen mountain men in the saloon at supper, and more were certain to have made their way out of the path of the fire during the night. With any luck, he'd get a good deal of business secured. It didn't hurt most were drunk off their rockers.

His spirits lifted even higher than Carrie had already brought them. Now all he had to do was find a new client for the merchandise.

Chapter 22

Carrie secured the pup across her lap and held onto Simon with one arm as they rode. Half to ease her incessant need to ensure he'd not left her, and half to staunch the ache she felt in her heart after having woken up this morning to a few drops of blood staining the sheet where they'd slept. She'd convinced herself she didn't care whether she carried Simon's child, but at the sight of the small stain, she knew she'd lied to herself. She wanted his baby as badly as she wanted him, but it wasn't what she needed at the present time. She'd be the outcast of society and would have a helluva time finding a position in which to support both herself and a babe.

She and Simon would have to be more careful in the future.

They'd ridden for hours down the mountain, but the more homesteads and buildings she saw, the more she knew it was a matter of time before she'd have to face reality. And her parents. The last she didn't want to do.

The smoke from the mill stacks drifted above the trees ahead of them, and she let her head fall back against Simon's chest as she took in a deep breath. There were a few months left of the logging season, but with the fire raging the way it still was, she didn't think they would go back up anytime soon.

Simon adjusted his grip on the reins and kicked the horse faster as Garrett and Beth did the same with their mount.

They entered the mill yards, which were filled with people and trains, the former waiting to find the fate of their livelihood. As the horses pulled to a stop, Aunt June bustled up to them. "Oh, thank the Lord above. I thought I was going to have to come look for all of you myself. And we don't want an old bag like me traipsing around a forest fire. My lungs couldn't take it."

"I don't think Beth's did, either," Garrett said as he dismounted and reached up to help Beth down. "She's been weak and sick ever since I found her."

Simon waited for Carrie to readjust her hold on Nots before tugging her down next to him. Carrie let down the little pup, who ran around the mill yard as if waiting for days to be free.

"How long have you felt ill?" Aunt June fussed around Beth like a mother hen.

"A week or two." Beth swiped at her pale forehead.

"Hmm," Aunt June answered, frowned, and turned to Carrie. "Miz Carrie. Are you feeling the ill effects of the smoke?"

"A little, but I'm better." Carrie sighed as a wave of exhaustion took over. "Aside from being tired."

Aunt June stared at her from head to toe with a keen eye and nodded in satisfaction. "You two women come with me. We'll get you settled in Beth's caboose, and I'll have one of the men bring you some food."

Simon bent down so only she could hear. "Go back with Beth. I'll meet you at your parents' house once I'm done with some business up here."

"How long?"

Simon lifted his head back up. "Tomorrow at the latest. Tonight if I can manage it."

Carrie nodded and followed her godmother, scooping up Nots as she walked past. Before long they were settled in Beth's mountain home, and both held steaming bowls of stew like two orphans clutching a treasure.

"I didn't realize how hungry I was until this came," Carrie said, not bothering with manners as she dug into the meal like she'd seen the men do on many occasions.

"I can only imagine what you girls have eaten the last few days. You must be starving." Aunt June pushed a plate of sandwiches toward Beth, who set her stew down as she shook her head. She slowly picked up a biscuit and nibbled on it like the squirrel who lived in the tree next to Aunt June's cabin.

Aunt June stared at her with a twinkle in her eye. The same look Carrie had on her face, no doubt. Carrie scooted closer to the edge of her seat. "Beth, would you like me to go with you to see the doctor when we get into town?"

Beth shook her head. "I think I need some rest is all. I haven't got my land legs back since we got off the river."

"Or you've got a wee one in your belly," Aunt June suggested.

"Oh…no," Beth stuttered. "There's no way. Is there?"

"You're a married woman, child. It's possible you have a little Jones growing inside you." Aunt June took a sandwich and placed it on her plate, then turned to Carrie. "But you, young lady. You better be peckish because of what you've been through."

Carrie took a drink of her water to calm the nerves Aunt June's words evoked. There was no way her godmother knew of her indiscretions. Carrie needed to keep a poker face. "Don't worry about me. It's Beth who needs to see the doctor. Can't you persuade her to go?"

Aunt June took a second of staring straight into Carrie's eyes before she turned back to Beth. "We'll both convince her once we get into town. Wouldn't want that babe to surprise her one day when she wakes up on the mountainside with a fat ol' stomach and no way to put on her logger spikes."

Aunt June chuckled at her joke, and the group remained silent while they ate their meal. A few moments later, Beth scooted back from the table and stood. "If you'll excuse me. I need to lie down."

"By all means," Aunt June said. "You need plenty of rest in the months to come."

Beth simply shook her head at the older woman's comment and disappeared into the sleeping quarters of the railcar.

After Carrie finished eating what she could handle of the soup and sandwiches, she scooted back in her chair and relaxed. "How long do you suppose the fire will last?"

Aunt June shrugged. "There's no tellin'. Could be days, could be over a month. It all depends on God and whether or not he decides to grace us with some summertime showers."

"And what's going to happen to the people? And the Mill?"

"Most of the workers are Bonner boys, so they'll go home for a spell and wait out the fire. The Missoula boys will either stick around and wait, or cut their losses and go home. Once the fire settles, Victoria plans to send the boys back up."

"Will we go with them?" Carrie wasn't certain whether she wanted to or not. Victoria had made it perfectly clear she only had a job until the end of summer, and frankly she was tired of the mountain. But what if Simon chose to go back up, and she stayed behind? Things might not be the same once he returned. He'd more than likely forget about why he'd asked her to be his lover and move on. Or she'd find a position somewhere and move out to the country. No. She needed to be wherever Simon was or break off their new arrangement.

"I'll go back up," Aunt June said, interrupting her thoughts. "You, my dear, need to get home. There's been some decisions made in your family that you might want to be privy of."

"What decisions?" Carrie wanted to massage her temples, but to do such a thing would be rude. She hated subtle hints. She'd much rather get the blunt truth and be done with the conversation.

"That's not for me to divulge. But before you go, remember everyone involved loves you dearly and only wants to see you happy."

Carrie glared. "What do you know?"

Her godmother shook her head. "I can't say, but be prepared to fight for what you want, and don't take anything less."

"Good God, woman. Out with the gossip."

Aunt June gave a simple pinched smile and sipped from her cup. Carrie tried not to scowl at the woman's halfhearted attempt at a warning. If the last few months in the lumber camp had given her anything, it was a new lack of care for etiquette. Which she'd have to check starting now. Especially if she was going to have any standing in the fight with her parents. Which, by Aunt June's hints, was imminent.

* * * *

Simon left Victoria's office satisfied. For the first time in his life, he'd given up something he loved for someone else, and it felt freeing. No longer would he work for the Great Mountain Lumber Mill, but if the stars aligned he'd be in the leather business. With the most beautiful woman in the world on his arm. Staring up at him like he didn't have a disfigurement that most people despised.

All he had to do now was secure a ride, then meet the mountain men with the money for the hides. Where was he going to get a big fish client to buy hats and shoes? Chances were the mercantile around town were already contracted out. And the Salish tribes made their own clothing. He might have to go out of town to get the client, but that would take time, and he'd already lost almost a week of the month given him to secure the clients. He needed more time.

Simon located Teddy—the chute monkey and the man who kept the horses for the camp—and beckoned him closer. In a few breaths, the man dipped his ear low as if to listen through the gentle rumble of noise surrounding them. Simon pointed to the large bay horses in the stalls nearest them. "Do these horses belong to you or the Mill?"

"The Mill," Teddy answered, and stood tall.

"Blast!" Simon cussed. He'd quit before he could borrow a horse to get the hides, and the nearest livery was ten miles away in Missoula. Most of the men he'd talked to earlier were eager to offload their pelts, and he'd arranged for a meeting this afternoon an hour up the mountain.

"But I got a few geldings down at the end that are mine," Teddy said. "Victoria lets me keep them here during the summer, and old Bartlet feeds them for me. For a price, of course."

Simon perked up and snapped his gaze to the man's face. "Could I rent both of them from you? One saddled and one with a pack if you got it?"

"I don't know." Teddy scratched his face. "They got every kinda riggin' you could need here, but I's plannin' to get back down to Missoula tonight and see my ma."

Simon pulled a twenty dollar bill from the stack of money he'd gotten from Victoria. Since he'd gone straight to the doctor the following year, he hadn't stopped to pick up wages owed him. He had stuffed two seasons' worth of pay into his pockets. He'd rent the horses, and the rest he planned to use to buy the pelts to take to Carrie's father.

With a now-wealthier Teddy's eager cooperation, he wrapped the lead rope around the pommel of the saddled horse and mounted. An hour after that, he rode into a large clearing on the top of a hill and leapt to the soft meadow grass. He'd wait all night if he had to, but he planned to buy every pelt he could find in the mountains surrounding Missoula.

Before long, the first rough, bearded man came riding into the meadow, pulling a weighed-down horse behind him. Simon made short work of buying the pelts and slipping them over the pack saddle, only to turn as another mountain man appeared, and then another. With the fire close to home, the men needed any money they could get from what they had in case they needed to move on to another mountain range. Which was good for Simon's business now, but not good if he wanted them for future supplies.

By the time the sun showed signs of fading into night, both of the horses drooped under the weight. He counted eighty-seven hides total. Although not what he needed for the business deal, he wasn't altogether upset at the haul he'd gotten that day. He'd let the men know as they left to tell others where to find him in town. With any luck he'd have the first half of the bride price by evening tomorrow.

With no daylight to waste, he led the horses as fast as he could off the mountain. Night took over the sky and the crickets chirped in the tall bear grass outside the Mill by the time he secured the pelts in the train car he'd take to Missoula the next day. He unsaddled the horses and put them in their stalls with fresh hay and water. Tonight, he'd have to sleep in the mill's bunkhouse, but come sunup he'd be on his way home.

God he wished he could be with Carrie tonight. Once he got Carrie's father's blessing confirmed, he'd beg her to wed within the week. There was no reason for them to be apart any longer.

Living in his grandmother's house with a wife wasn't ideal, but soon it would be his, and he'd much rather sacrifice his pride for a chance to have his wife by his side even sooner.

Simon stepped into the bunkhouse and hung his hat on the peg near a cot, then snatched up a pile of blankets from the linen shelf and made his bed.

"I heard you didn't work here no more." Thomas's voice penetrated his concentration on squaring away his bunk. He turned to face the weasel of a man.

"Victoria said I could stay the night to square away any last-minute things. I'm out of here tomorrow morning."

"Couldn't take it no more?" Thomas leaned on a nearby bunk and crossed his legs. A smug grin plastered across his face. "Lost your woman, and now your job. Tsk, tsk, tsk."

Simon bit his cheek and clenched his fist against the urge to plow the boy right in his gut. He adjusted the holster and gun from around his waist, not wanting to take it off just yet. "Carrie's still mine, and I quit 'cause I got myself something else lined up."

"Oh, you mean the deal you made with Carrie's father?" Thomas pulled a smoke out of his pocket and lit it. "He gave me the same deal. One hundred pelts and a contract. Seems whoever gets him the goods first gets the girl and the business. I'd like to thank you for the job, though. Already got a business partner lined up and everything. Just need to get me some pelts. While you were up there playing hero, I was securing a buyer. Hardest part of the deal, if you ask me."

Simon quickly moved his gaze away so the damned fool couldn't see the rage shining in his eyes. A thousand replies ran through his mind. Everything from sticking a knife in the man's heart to walking away, but he could do neither. "Carrie's a strong woman, and no one's property. If she don't want to marry you, no deal her father makes will make her do so."

"Oh, I think she will. I got me all kinds of ways to…how should I put it…persuade her to see my way."

Simon's scar twitched as his stomach grew hard and his heart began to thump. "If you lay a hand on her, I swear to God you won't take another breath. I'll kill you before the pain in Carrie's body ebbs from your blow."

"You won't be there. You'll be in some back-alley dump drowning in whiskey and misery while I teach your woman how to be a proper logger's wife." Thomas took the cigarette out of his mouth. "But don't worry. If she's full with your bastard child, I'll let her keep it. The kid will be a good tool to keep her busy."

Simon reached for the gun but stopped short of clearing leather. Thomas wasn't worth losing his newfound life over. Simon tapped his middle finger against the cool steel, then dropped his hand by his side.

Thomas gave a greasy smile and leaned his back against the wall as Simon envisioned sending him through the hard wood. The weasel puffed out his smoke, and moved his hand to place the cigarette back in his mouth. Clenching his teeth tight, Simon stepped forward and caught Thomas' fist midair. Which had the effect Simon had hoped for as Thomas struggled to free his hand and fear darkened his eyes. The weasel yanked hard as the cigarette caught Simon's attention. Rolled tight in printed paper with a ribbon of smoke floating up from the burnt end.

"I thought you smoked cigars."

"Cigars are for celebrating. Cheaper to roll my own tobacco."

Simon struggled to keep his voice steady when he spoke. "What a unique way to roll it."

"Yeah." Thomas gave a half-smile. "I think this is Luke 1." He drew out the words, and his upper lip twitched. "Wonder why most people haven't discovered that Bible pages make good rolling paper, and are a helluva lot cheaper, too."

Heat flushed through his body, and he slammed his forearm into Thomas's neck, pinning him to the wall. Simon had never been a religious man, but that didn't mean he didn't respect the hell out of God and the Good Book. He wanted to shove his arm into the man's throat until the life seeped from his being, but then Simon would be no better than the blasphemer before him.

What this man had done was beyond reprehensible. Beyond damaging a perfectly good read. What sort of man smokes the pages to the Bible?

Thomas started to turn red and struggle for breath. He flailed about, tapping on Simon's forearm. Simon could ease up, give the man breath. Or he could rid the earth of the likes of Thomas.

Carrie's image flashed in his mind, and he stepped back as Thomas dropped to the floor and clutched his neck. Thomas wheezed for air, and a strong sense of satisfaction pulsed through Simon's fingertips.

Simon started to turn toward his bed as Thomas's sudden movement caught his eye. In a few heartbeats the man reached underneath his cot, pulled out a pistol, and pointed it straight at Simon's heart.

On reflex, Simon cleared leather and simultaneously cocked his hammer. "What did you do to Jake?"

"That lowlife?" Thomas spit the cigarette out and crushed the smoke beneath his foot. "You should thank me. I killed him for touching Carrie."

Simon flexed his jaw. "Just now I wanted to kill you, but I held back. And I'm willing to bet I've got a faster trigger finger than you. I could kill you right now. But I won't. What gives you the right to take a man's life? Even if it was in service of Carrie."

"Jake had it coming anyway. He's wanted a few states over for crimes against women. We weren't friends. We just worked together."

"Then why hide the body and act like a concerned friend?"

Thomas gave him a look like he was daft. "I don't want to go to jail for putting some rapist where he belongs."

"You're no better than him."

"I may use questionable tactics to get ahead in life, but I'd never treat a woman the way he did on many occasions. Hell, I heard he even strangled a prostitute over in Nevada while he took her." Thomas's gun wavered slightly as though he was second-guessing his decision to take Simon on.

"What else have you done up there on the mountain? Did you start the fire?" Simon un-cocked his gun and placed it back in his holster. Hoping the weasel would do the same.

Thomas followed his lead and secured his weapon under his cot. The fool wasn't brave when up against a better man. Thomas swiped at something on his forehead. "Nope. That was an act of God."

"I thought with the way you desecrated His book, you didn't believe in God."

"I believe in him all right. I've just come to terms with the fact that most of us have little chance of making it past those pearly gates."

"What else?" Simon already knew the lowlife had spied on him and Carrie across the lake, but what other crimes had the man committed up there under the guise of vigilante justice? "What about the man at the beginning of the season? The one who was hit with the log? Some of us don't believe he was hit by a widowmaker."

Thomas shrugged and shook his head. "Wasn't me. Maybe you have another man up there tired of all the lowlife rats plaguing the timber operations."

"You aren't the judge, jury, and executioner." He could let the man get away with what he'd done based on the character behind the man he'd murdered, but there was no way he'd let Thomas stay in Carrie's life any further. "You're going to back out of the marriage deal with Carrie's father. Otherwise I'm going to take this to the law."

"And tell him what? You *think* I killed someone on the mountain? You can't prove anything. What you've got is hearsay at best." Thomas dusted off his shoulder, although Simon failed to see what offended the man so much he needed to flick it off. His jacket was as clean as fresh linens. In fact, they looked brand-new. Probably purchased in order to impress Carrie's father. Thomas's eye twitched. "I backed down from our standoff just now 'cause you ain't done nothing worth killing for. Mostly. But I ain't giving up Carrie 'cause you say to. I'll take my chances."

"If you don't back out, I'll take my chances with the sheriff." Simon straightened taller, hoping to at least scare the little weasel. "I don't know why you're so in need of a wife that you'll force one into marriage, but I can guarantee she doesn't love you."

"Not that it's any of your business, but my ma won't be in this world much longer, and all she wanted was to see me hitched to a good woman. I need to marry in a hurry. I don't have much chance to search. And it doesn't hurt that her father offered me a partnership if I take his soiled daughter off his hands." Thomas shrugged. "Carrie will learn to love me in time."

"Then you don't know Carrie." Simon relaxed against his bunk. If he knew anything about the woman he loved, it was that she'd fight until her soft little hands were torn and bleeding before entering into a marriage she didn't want to be in. Even if her father forced her, she'd never go willingly.

There was a small chance he'd have to steal her away and run, but that was a chance Simon was willing to take if it came down to it. He sat on his bunk and lounged as if no longer affected by the weasel's words, and Thomas responded as he'd hoped—by taking a step back and frowning in confusion. Simon let a smug half-grin stretch across his face. "I suggest you look elsewhere. I'd wager there's a mail-order bride you can order. In fact, I'm fairly certain I saw a flyer for an Irish wife back at the Missoula Mercantile."

"I ain't paying for no wife. Especially an Irish one." Thomas shuffled to his bunk and sat. His words were strong, but his posture showed Simon had defeated him. Or at the least planted a seed of doubt in his half-cocked plan. "Not when I have one I can profit from."

"If by profit you mean lose everything, then keep trying. Carrie will run before she'll allow some half-wit to force her into marriage."

"And you'll be leading her horse, I suppose. A woman would never shuck out on her own without a father or husband to support her."

"Goes to show how much you know the woman you aim to force into marriage," Simon said. "If she needs me, I'll be there while she runs, but she won't. That woman is stronger than Beth and Aunt June combined. Just doesn't show it much."

He wasn't going to sugarcoat anything for the fool. Carrie would run if she had to, and like Thomas suggested, Simon would be there to help her in whatever fashion she needed. Especially if she needed him to help her run for her freedom.

Chapter 23

Simon stuffed his belongings in his canvas bag and slung it over his shoulder. He squinted in the dense early morning dark to the bunk where Thomas had slept the night before, but the bed was empty. Better off. He didn't want another confrontation with the man who aimed to take away the only thing in this world that gave Simon reason to breathe. Carrie.

With no one else in the bunkhouse and no need to stifle his noise, he yanked the door open and stepped out into the cool of the mountain air. The train would leave in less than twenty minutes for Missoula, and he needed to be onboard. If luck was on his side, he'd deliver the pelts to Carrie's father as a good-faith gesture and hope it helped secure his future. The smell of burning coal mixed with freshly cut wood filled every inch of the air around him. A scent he loved dearly and would miss after today.

The release of the train brakes sounded through the darkness, and he jumped aboard the railcar where he'd stashed the pelts the night before just as the train chugged slowly down the tracks. He felt through the dark for the stack of hides but met only with the cold wood floor of the train. A sour taste in his mouth formed as a lump took residence in the back of his throat. He searched frantically around him until he'd felt almost a quarter of the railcar floor, with no luck. Where the hell had his pelts gone? His heart thumped fast, rivaling the escalating chug of the train wheels beneath him.

"They aren't there," a familiar voice said through the darkness as the train picked up speed.

"Who's there?" Simon raised his head as he spoke, even though he knew the other passenger couldn't see his movement. "Teddy?"

"Yeah," Teddy responded. "You're looking for those pelts, right? I saw you bring them in last night."

"I am looking for them." Simon plopped down in a corner of the dark railcar across from where his friend's voice originated. "What do you know about their whereabouts?"

"Can't say for certain, but this morning I was gearing up my pack line and Thomas appeared. Offered me one hundred bucks if I could take his spot on the train and let him take my horses down."

"And you didn't find it odd?"

Simon heard more than saw Teddy's shrug through the slowly lightening morning dark. "You offered me money to borrow them last night. I figured I was making out, but when I got in I noticed your pelts were gone."

"And you figure Thomas took them?" Even if Teddy didn't, Simon did. The dag-blamed weasel had gotten a jump on him and stolen his bride price. The only thing left for him to secure James Kerr's blessing to wed Carrie.

"Don't know what's going on, but I got a hunch I want you to take the lead in whatever battle you're fighting."

"In short," Simon started, and slouched to try and staunch the ache inside his gut, "we're fighting for Miz Carrie, and if I don't get those pelts back, then she's going to have to walk away from her family and struggle like hell for her freedom or be married to a curly wolf like Thomas."

"And if she marries you?"

"I love her," Simon confessed. He'd told no one but Carrie his true feelings, but there was no reason to hide them any longer. Especially now. "And if I'm reading her signs right, she loves me too. Only problem is her father wants to turn her marriage into a business deal."

"What is it with you city folk and selling your kids off for business?"

Simon shook his head in answer. If his parents had lived to see he and Beth grown, he had to believe they wouldn't have been so callous. "If I fail, all hell's going to break loose for the woman I love. She'll fight to be free and lose her whole family in the process." Simon shrugged. "I don't know. I don't want her to lose her family, but I can't live without her either."

"My sister went against my parents," Teddy began. "Fell in love with a card player from Bozeman. When my ma told her to let him be or pack her bags, she chose the card player."

"I hope he settled down. Got a job like a decent man would." Simon slid his hand over the rough floor of the boxcar and traced his fingers around a knot in the panel.

"Nah. A year later she showed up with a faded bruise on her face and a baby on her hip."

"You come from good stock, Teddy. I can't believe your ma let her stay out in the cold."

Early morning sun slanted through the open door to the railcar. The scene outside was serene. Towering hills—speckled with tall pines—cradled the logging train as the tracks sliced through the narrow green valley. The area was sparsely populated, but a place beautiful enough to steal a man's breath and make him want to move there just to wake up to see the elk feed off the hilltops surrounding him. This was perhaps the last time he'd ever see this land—a place dear to his heart, but now a part of his past.

"Ma didn't let her in. Slammed the door right in her face." In the deepening light, Simon noticed Teddy yank cash from his inside jacket pocket. "That's why I'm taking the extra money. I set my sister up at a boarding house in Missoula. She's working on finding a good job where she can raise a little one and the boss man don't care."

"I didn't know." Simon sat taller and stretched his legs out before him. "Is there any way I can help?"

"She'll be fine, but that's not the point." Teddy shook his head and stuffed the bills back in his coat. "You don't want to chance Carrie not having anyone to count on if she don't got you."

"I'm not some lowlife who's gonna leave her with a baby and no money. That's why I'm damned determined to make this deal with her father."

"I didn't say you were." His friend rested his head against the railcar, staring more at the ceiling than Simon, as men were apt to do when conversations steered toward the personal side. He looked back down. "But what if something happened to you? What if, after you gave her a few little hellions to raise, you were killed? Who would she go to? After what I've seen, I'd want my woman to have family she could count on if anything happened to me. That's all I'm saying."

"You make a good point." Simon scratched the back of his neck and studied the floor. "How am I going to beat Thomas if he's got a contract and a head start with my pelts?"

"Well, either you cut him off before he gets there and take back what's yours, or you get another loot before he gets to her father. Something even better than what he's got. What's the bargaining chip, anyway?"

"One hundred pelts, and a new client."

"Leather business?" Teddy raised his chin with the question, and furrowed his brows.

Simon answered with a nod.

"Well, there you go. Wall's looking for some leather straps for a new mechanism he invented, the one that's gonna be taking my job within the next few years," his friend gave a teasing smile. "Maybe you can get him to sign on with you. Course that's more a cowhide sorta thing."

"Yes." Simon squinted against his thoughts. There was one man he could go to for both things he needed. If luck was on his side, he could get everything he needed and get to Carrie's father before his stolen hides. He inclined his head to Teddy to get his attention. "You think you can head off Thomas and stall for me? I'd pay you."

Teddy tipped one side of his mouth back in a sly smile. "No need. I don't much like people using my horses to steal other people's belongins. He told me to meet him at the Angry Grizzly this evening."

"He'll more than likely be headed to Carrie's house first thing." Simon stretched the side of his neck at the thought of Thomas beating him to Carrie's father's home. The scar on his cheek twitched. He couldn't let it happen.

"With a pack train in tow he'll be hard to miss, and slow going in town," Teddy supplied. "I'll find him. What are you going to do?"

"I think I know how to please Carrie and her father. I just need time."

"I'll get you that. If not for you, then for Miz Carrie. I'm going to miss her cooking."

Simon knew exactly what to do, but his stomach balled with nerves he'd never felt before. He could leap out of the way of hundred-year-old pines, face cougars, even bed the mayor's wife, but he'd never been as scared as he was right now. If his plans failed, he could risk Carrie's future. Whether she chose to run or not. He had to win. Needed to give her the life she deserved. Until the moment she took her last breath, he could dedicate his life to her. If only the fates would bend in his favor.

* * * *

Carrie hid in the cool of the shadows as the train eased to a stop. Simon jumped onto the platform and stood tall. She watched him as she struggled to catch her breath against the tight bodice she wore—a piece that had fit perfectly before the beginning of the season. She thanked the Lord above that she'd chosen to forgo the corset, much to her maid's chagrin. As the sound of Simon's boots on the hard wood deck bounced off the depot building, he searched the area up and down the tracks. Lord above he was a fine figure of a man. Scar and all. Ever since she knew him she'd harbored such thoughts. She must persuade him to join her in securing a position on Wall's ranch or risk a miserable, lonely life.

But she wasn't here to see him. She was here for Wall. Chances were, being the new leader of the Devil May Cares, Wall would be among the men designated to meet the train to offload the supplies brought to town. And she needed desperately to speak with him about the position on his father's ranch.

She had returned home yesterday to the usual empty house. Her mother was off somewhere playing tea party, pretending nothing was amiss in her life, while Carrie's father busied himself with work. Late that night, as she sat with her mother and listened to the meaningless town gossip, as though financial ruin didn't threaten their lives, her father peeked into the drawing room to set up a meeting with her this afternoon. Always a meeting. Never a family gathering with comfortable chatter and passing of family business. No. James ran his family like he ran his business.

Into the ground.

No wonder they were falling apart.

Carrie had taken a single step toward Simon when Wall's head bobbed in the crowd of men gathering around one of his contraptions as the straps securing it to the railcar broke free. To her surprise, and slight disappointment, Simon failed to realize she stood among the crowd and instead moved toward the group of men around Wall.

As well as she could, she muscled her way past a burly logger and dipped under another's arm to avoid getting an elbow in the temple. Once free of the danger, she stood on her toes as Simon slapped Wall on the back and leaned close in secrecy. Wall nodded, then barked a few orders to the loggers beside him before disappearing with Simon to the outskirts of the crowd. Blast! What she wouldn't give to be strong enough to muscle through the men like Simon did.

She headed in the direction she'd seen them disappear. With a few well-placed jabs to a rib or two, she eased out of the back of the group and searched for her target. A few feet away both men stood with matching stern expressions.

She began to walk toward them as Simon's voice pierced the noise of the offload. "Just wait. Let me talk to her. Don't give Carrie the job. I know someone else who needs it more."

Carrie stopped short before the men could see her and ducked behind a logger who'd moved outside the crowd. They were talking about her. But why would Simon do such a thing? Why would he stop her from the security of a future?

She peeked around the logger to find Simon and Wall making their way toward the depot office door. She rubbed her chest to try and stop the ache within. She'd expected her father to betray her like this, but never Simon. Why would he do such a thing? Why try to force her to his will? Stop her from being independent?

Tears burned behind her eyes, but she refused to let them fall. She was as strong as Elizabeth, and as determined as Aunt June. What she needed was a defense against the controlling forces of the men in her life. What she needed was Aunt June's help.

She forced her mind to focus on the task and not on Simon's betrayal as she made her way to Aunt June's home. She knew her godmother would help her. Perhaps even take Simon to task for interfering with her plans. After all, Aunt June was the only family in her life who truly wished to see her happiness come before money.

It took her longer than she'd wanted to pick her way through the streets to Aunt June's front door. Through the large bay window overlooking the street, she spotted her godmother sitting demurely in the sitting room where they'd tricked Simon into taking the chloroform. Carrie's stomach dropped at the memory. She didn't like the deception then, and she still despised the memory. If she could go back and do things differently, she would have found some other way to get him to camp.

Sure their plan had worked. Simon grew out of his depression and once again graced them with the charming man she'd fallen in love with years ago. But at what cost? Would he forever hold her part in the scheme against her?

Not bothering to knock, Carrie hurried inside and through the door directly to her right where Aunt June sat stabbing a needle through a white linen kerchief. She pinched her lips tight as she jabbed the cloth again. Without glancing up, she said, "I could never get the hang of this."

Carrie kicked her skirts as she settled into a chair opposite her godmother. "I need your help."

Aunt June dropped her hands to her lap and finally looked up, cocking her head to the side. "Well, that's nothing new, but I'm always eager to hear what sort of difficulty you've gone and gotten yourself into. And even more eager to join in the fun."

"There's no fun involved." At that she let out all she'd heard on the platform. Not that it was much, but enough.

Aunt June frowned. "As much as I would like to, I'm afraid I cannot help."

"Why not?" She struggled to hold back the emotion from shaking her voice.

"For starters, have you spoken to Simon? Given him a chance to explain himself?"

She shook her head. "No. I came straight away to you. To get your help in organizing my life." She punctuated her thoughts hoping her godmother would see her way, but the way Aunt June shook her head and turned back to her sewing dropped all hope from Carrie's chest to the deepest pit of her stomach.

"Communication is key to a successful marriage." Aunt June gave a quick glance to the wall, then back to her sewing. "Which is probably the reason your parents haven't figured out their issues."

"My father wants to speak with me this afternoon. I only have an hour before sitting down with him."

Aunt June once again dropped her hands to her lap and gave her attention to Carrie. "Did he mention what he plans to discuss?"

Carrie shook her head. "No, but the last time he used that tone on me I was sentenced to a summer of misery at the Young Ladies Finishing Retreat in Spokane. Not that I didn't already have social graces. Worst summer of my life."

"Did your father say anyone else would be at the meeting with him?"

Carrie frowned. "No. Why? Who would be there besides us?"

At that, Aunt June stowed her sewing in a basket on the side table next to her chair and stood, straightening her skirts in the process. "Let's go. I think I will help you after all."

"You will?" Carrie followed as her godmother bustled out the doors and turned toward the route they usually took to Carrie's house.

"Yes. I'm afraid my curiosity has once again gotten the better of me, but after we speak with your father, you need to have a good long talk with that handsome beau of yours."

"I don't have a beau," Carrie lied. Did she lie more to herself or Aunt June?

"Someone should tell Simon then, 'cause that man has fallen deeply for you, my dear. If you feel the same as him, then you need to tell him. And if you don't then you're a daft fool and no goddaughter of mine."

"I feel the same," she confessed. "But unless he gives up his current life and becomes a cowpuncher, he doesn't fit in my plan." More to herself, she mumbled, "If Wall still plans to take me on."

"Life doesn't have only one path. That's why God gave us volition, my dear. Your choices determine who you become in life."

"No, but if living with my father has taught me anything, it's that I need to depend on myself for my future and not on a man."

"Simon is nothing like your father. If that man gives his heart to someone, he will change the world for her and not make her change for the world.

You should trust in him more than your plan." Aunt June rounded the corner onto the street where Carrie lived with her parents. "You may find your life plan works better with him moving obstacles out of your way."

Carrie didn't know how to respond, but it didn't matter. In front of her house sat a sight so unfamiliar to her part of the town that it gathered attention from passersby. A string of packhorses carrying piles of pelts stood swishing their tails and occasionally lifting a hoof but otherwise motionless. Their leader was tied to her father's fence.

"That's a sight that will haunt your mother's ears for a few weeks at least."

"Father's never conducted leather business at home." Carrie frowned and slipped past her godmother as she took the steps to her house. Once inside, she led the way to her father's study.

"Ah, there you are," her father said as she entered. "I believe you know Thomas from your little excursion this summer."

"Thomas," she said with a forced smile, but she couldn't hold back the confusion from wrinkling her forehead.

Before she could ask why he was there, Aunt June stepped up next to her. Her father frowned. "June. I believe my wife is in the sitting room."

"Yes. I saw her briefly." Aunt June sat in a nearby chair and settled in with defined movements. "She looks distressed."

"This is family business."

"I wonder then why Thomas is here."

"June." James voiced her name as a warning, but her godmother was even more stubborn than her father. In all their dealings in the past, her father had always buckled under Aunt June's fierce stare. Carrie hid a smile behind her hand until she could gain her composure.

"As I was saying," her father continued. "Thomas has asked for your hand."

"I'm sorry, Thomas, but the answer is still no." Carrie didn't bother to sweeten the rejection. He wouldn't have understood subtle urging anyway.

"You don't have a choice," her father stated.

Carrie tensed. "Excuse me, Father, but my future is my choice. And I choose not to wed Thomas."

"I believe you're missing a participant here," Aunt June interjected. She scooted closer to the edge of her seat.

James cleared his throat. "The deal was the first one to bring me the pelts and client."

Carrie started. "The deal?"

"Yes, dear," Aunt June said, locking her eyes with Carrie's father. "The business deal your father made in exchange for you as a wife and part of his business."

"You traded me for pelts?" Carrie balled her fists. "Like I was some property of yours to sell to the highest bidder? Like I was Victoria Harrison?"

"And apparently, your father isn't interested in waiting for Simon," Aunt June interjected.

"Simon?" He was involved? Her heart skipped a beat, but she didn't yet know how she felt.

Her father waved toward the front of the house. "The other man who approached me for your hand after you were ruined up on that mountain."

"Simon?" She repeated the question, but directed it toward Aunt June. Her chest twisted in betrayal. He'd told her father about their liaison? Felt guilty over ruining her so he offered marriage in exchange for what? Part of a business?

Aunt June leaned toward her in secrecy. "I told you. Trust in him."

"Trust him? A man who entered into a bidding war to buy me from my father? A man who—" Carrie stopped herself from spilling her secret affair. "Never mind. I'll not sit here and be bartered and traded like cattle. You can take whatever payment he's brought you, but you'll have to give him something else. I'm not for sale."

Her father stood, his chair scraping across the floor in a sound so abrupt it made her jump. "If you can't participate in this family and its business then you have no place in my home."

"Fine. I'll get my things." Without waiting for a response from anyone, she ran to her room to pack what she could carry. She didn't hide the tears from falling down her face. She couldn't stay, but she didn't know where to go. Aunt June's was out of the question, at least for the time being. She couldn't stay with her now, knowing her godmother had harbored this secret from her. She should have let her know. Warned her of the impending danger, but she'd sided with Simon, and her father.

A man she thought she could trust with her life, but one who had treated her no different from her father. With lies and deceit. She couldn't trust him as Aunt June claimed. She trusted no one but herself. And Beth. That's where she'd go. She'd call on the many favors her bosom friend owed her, and intrude for only as long as it took her to find a position.

As she rushed past Aunt June in the hallway before her father's study, she shook her head to ward off any argument her godmother was certain to give. Somewhere deep in her father's office a new voice echoed off the walls, but she didn't care to find out who the voice belonged to. She needed only to find Beth. Lose herself in self-pity for a spell, then pull herself up off whatever spare bed her friend would lend her and start her search.

   She placed her hand over the ache in her stomach—still bloated from the ridiculous meals she'd inhaled lately, as if living with the lumberjacks had turned her into one. To her irritation, the ache usually accompanied nausea that made sweat bead from her hairline. This whole summer had turned into one big pain in her stomach. The first time in her life she'd felt desolate. Betrayed by almost everyone. The worst of whom was the man she loved. She searched the yard out front for her dog, scooping her up as the little pup jumped up her leg only to tangle her nose in Carrie's skirt. The pup licked her hand. At least Nots wouldn't betray her the way everyone else had.

Chapter 24

"Are you certain?" Carrie asked for Beth as the doctor placed the stethoscope around his neck. She grabbed Beth's hand and squeezed. She'd fled to her friend's house only to find her bent over the bushes behind the kitchen sicker than she'd ever been before. Ignoring her own immediate needs, she'd rushed Beth to the doctor's. Leaving a note for Garrett to let him know they'd return shortly. Carrie mentally shook her head. Thankfully this doctor was not the one who'd administered the chloroform to Simon.

Interrupting her thoughts, the doctor nodded. "Yes, ma'am. It's going to be a Christmas baby."

Beth gave a happy giggle, but placed her hand over her mouth as if holding back the urge to vomit. "Garrett's going to be surprised. And pleased."

"You should start feeling less queasy in the next week or two. Just try to keep food down as much as possible, and stay well hydrated. And rest. Lots of rest."

"No problems there," Beth said, and stood. "It seems that lately I do nothing but expel what I eat, followed by a lot of sleeping."

"Now for you, young lady." The doctor faced Carrie and pulled the stethoscope over his ears.

"Me?" Carrie leaned away from the doctor's hand as he extended the mouthpiece to her stomach.

"Yes. I suspect you're a few weeks further along than Mrs. Jones."

Carrie shook her head. "There's no way."

The doctor frowned, sat back, and pulled his earpiece down. "Are you certain? You've got a little bump forming there." He poked at her stomach and made her wrap her hands around her middle. "Good you aren't wearing a corset. Have you felt any of the symptoms your friend has?"

Carrie shook her head numbly. The thought of Simon's child filling her belly sent a riot of emotions coursing through her thoughts. Elation. Fear. Desperation. She couldn't be pregnant.

She snuck a peek at Beth, who stared wide-eyed at her. Carrie's face grew hot, and she gave a desperate whisper of a chuckle.

The doctor adjusted the stethoscope and leaned into her stomach. "Yep. There's a little one in there. I'd say you're about to start looking less like you overate and more like you've got a baby hidden away."

"Beth," Carrie said her friend's name with distress.

"It'll be fine," Beth all but whispered.

The doctor frowned. "I take it the father isn't in the picture?"

"I…he…" Carrie stuttered.

The doctor waved off her poor excuse. "Ain't no business of mine, but you may want to consider getting hitched. Don't want your baby growing up without a male figure in his life to guide him."

"It's a boy?" Carrie asked, but the question sounded dumb, even to her.

"No telling. I was speaking generally. Point is, you need to figure things out soon." The doctor stood and motioned toward the door. Both she and Beth followed, although Beth with more of a bounce in her step than Carrie.

Once they were on their way down the street and clear of anyone who could overhear, Carrie leaned in toward Beth's ear. "What am I going to do? My father kicked me out of the house this afternoon when I rejected Thomas's hand in marriage. I can't go back there." She sniffled as tears rolled down her cheeks. "My life is falling in on me, and I can't see how to dig myself out."

"Bosh," Beth replied. "We all know whose baby that is. And don't you dare keep that little one from my brother. Else I'll never let you over to let the kids play."

She didn't know how to answer Beth's response. She needed to tell Simon. Maybe even trust in him. "Can I stay with you until I figure things out?"

"Of course, but don't wait to tell Simon." Beth locked arms with her and hugged her close. "We're going to be sisters."

Beth's excitement was contagious, but at the same time Carrie's nerves made her nausea worse. Would Simon welcome a little one as Beth suggested? Would he run or insist on marriage? She didn't want to force Simon into marriage, whether by guilt over having ruined her or because of a baby. She wanted a husband who loved her for being her. He'd yet to tell her so in person. Sure she'd heard it in her passion-filled dreams when they'd spent the night alone in the mountain cabin, but the real Simon had never confessed such a thing. And even though she was adventurous enough to venture into a logging camp, she wasn't brave enough to throw herself at him like the weak woman deep inside her—who sounded a lot like her mother—wanted to.

Carrie and Beth walked together, both consumed in their thoughts until Beth's house came into view. Simon's carriage was parked on the street out front.

"Looks like we've both got some talking to do." Beth let go of Carrie's arm as she led the way up the staircase. "You take the study, and I'll talk to my husband in our room." She peeked over her shoulder and smiled as Carrie tossed her a pleading stare. "And don't worry. Garrett will be fine with you staying here. Set yourself up in the spare room at the end of the hallway upstairs." She opened the door and ushered Carrie through. "I assume you brought bags with you before you picked me up out of the bushes?"

Carrie nodded but wrung her hands as her heart sought out the sound of Simon somewhere in the house. "I left it in the kitchen."

"Good luck with you." Beth headed toward the gentle murmur of the men's voices occupying the study.

As Carrie stepped tentatively through the door, Beth ushered Garrett out and shut the door behind her. Leaving Carrie to face her truth alone.

"Are you all right?" Simon's face dropped in concern, and he rushed to grab her hands to lead her to a nearby seat.

"No," she started. "I have something I need to talk to you about."

"First," he interrupted. "I need to tell you...Aunt June...I mean, I heard that you rejected your father's proposal."

"Proposal?" she scoffed. "Don't you mean business deal?"

Simon rubbed his hand over the back of his neck and paced before her. "Yes. Business deal. But you need to know that what I did, accepting the challenge, it was all for you."

"To rescue me?" She pinched her lips together to stop her chin from quivering.

"No." He stopped pacing and spun around to face her. "To rescue *me*. Don't you see? You are the only thing in this world that makes sense. The only person who can make me the man I'm supposed to be. Without you, I'm nothing. I know you have plans for your future, but I'm asking you, pleading for you to consider me as an alternative."

"Simon..." she sniffled as tears rolled down her cheeks so fast they wet her blouse. She no longer wanted to hold in the emotions she'd staunched for who knew how long. "Simon, I need to tell you—"

"Please." He dropped to one knee before her and scooped her hand up in his. His palm warmed the chill in her fingers and loosened the knot in her stomach. "I promise I'm not your father. You will be my partner in everything I do. We'll make all of our decisions together, no matter if they lead us down the wrong path. I love you, Carrie. I live for you, and you alone."

Her chin quivered, and she no longer tried to stop the movement. She placed a hand over the babe growing in her stomach. "I hope you don't live for me alone."

"What?" Simon paused, taking a quick glance at their hands as she took his and placed it over her stomach. He swallowed hard and fear seeped through her body. Did he understand? Immediately regret professing his love? God, she couldn't live with herself if that happened. Not when she'd finally given in to her heart and admitted to herself she loved him.

"I'm going to have your baby." She bit her lip and cried. Searching his face for how he felt.

To her surprise, he bent down and gently kissed her stomach. When he stood upright and pulled her up with him, his chest shuddered as if he held back tears.

"I stand corrected." He kissed her hard and wrapped her tight in his arms. "I live for us, and us alone."

"I love you." She finally confessed on a new wave of tears. The damned emotions were running too wild for her liking, but she suspected she'd have to get used to such a feeling.

"So you'll marry me?" He leaned back and peered down at her face. "No matter what happens in our future? You'll promise to always be here with me?"

"Yes," she all but cried out.

"Even if I went into business with your father?"

"Did you?" she asked, not knowing what answer she wanted to hear.

"Yes. I bought half of the company."

"With pelts?"

To her relief, he shook his head. "No. I had planned to. Gathered most of what I needed to beat Thomas to your father, but then the weasel stole it and beat me to your parents' house."

"So how did you buy out half of his business?"

"I brought him an offer he couldn't refuse—a deal with Wall for leather straps for his contraptions, and the cow hides from Wall's ranch to make them with. And the sheriff being there to arrest Thomas helped sway their decision. Turns out the law likes to know when someone is a thief and a murderer."

"A murderer?"

Simon nodded and gave a quick account of the conversation he'd had with Thomas the night she'd spent alone with her mother in the parlor. Relief over so many things eased the tension in her shoulders, and she leaned into Simon's embrace. "Does this mean my father doesn't want to disown me anymore?"

"I don't know, but if you want to have a relationship with him, I'll be here for anything you need."

"I don't care about my father, but my mother is fragile. She needs me. Even if it's just to listen to her meaningless prattle over tea."

"I think you'll be able to have whatever you want in life, my love."

"With you to love me, I already do."

Simon bent down and kissed her again. A kiss different from the rest. One that brought focus to the little bundle in her stomach, and one that made her feel as though her heart was free. Free to love and be loved. A mirror to the plea that had brought them together.

All I ask of you is to love me.

If you enjoyed *Wild Passion*, be sure not to miss the first book in Dawn Luedecke's Montana Mountain Romance series,

WHITE WATER PASSION

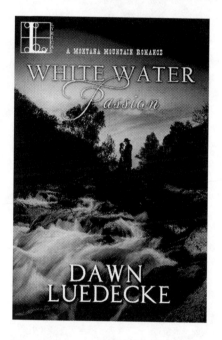

Elizabeth Sanders isn't afraid of anything, except what will happen to her beloved town if the Big Mountain Lumber Mill is destroyed. When she overhears a plot to do just that, she vows to put a stop to it, even if it means dressing as a young lumberjack to expose the saboteur. There's only one problem with her plan—her brother's handsome friend and fellow logger Garrett Jones, who arouses a desire within her soul as fierce as the river rapids.

When Garrett discovers that the odd new lad on the crew is in fact Beth, he's shocked. A logging camp is no place for a young woman—especially the spirited beauty he's admired for so long. Keeping her safe is easier said than done, however, as the attraction between them flares into true passion. As the danger mounts, Beth and Garrett must work together to survive the last log run down the wild rapids and claim any chance of saving the mill—and their chance at a future...

A Lyrical e-book on sale now.

Read on for a special excerpt!

Chapter 1

Missoula Montana, 1888

Elizabeth Sanders could vanish right now, and no one would notice. She blended in with every other woman by wearing her matching pinstriped walking skirt and blouse. Each store clerk and patron in Missoula, focused on their affairs without a care to their neighbor, would fail to notice if she walked through Higgins Street naked, let alone disappeared into thin air. They certainly wouldn't look twice when she came back this way a different person.

Hundreds of people bustled in the heat of the Montana sun doing the same old things, the same old ways, with nothing to show for their trouble but dirty shoes. If Elizabeth was going to get her shoes dirty, she preferred to have fun doing it…the Devil May Care way.

Navigating the pedestrian-riddled streets was treacherous at best. Times like this made her wish she'd taken her grandmother's buggy. At least then she wouldn't be jostled around like a dirty shirt in a churning wash bin. A deep exhale boosted her determination enough to risk a step to the side to duck around a particularly slow matriarch. The small triumph lasted only a moment before she slammed into a hard chest.

The soft fabric of a well-tailored suit skimmed her cheek a split second before warm hands reached out to steady her. The touch—firm, yet gentle—made her feel like she now balanced on the back of a high-strung and wild mustang as it fled down a hill with uncontrolled freedom. She hadn't needed the extra hand. Wasn't in danger of falling over. What sort of dullard rescues a woman in no need of liberation? She pulled away and adjusted her skirts as he let go. Her mind focused once more.

"Pardon me." She glanced up to a familiar face. One she'd seen many times in her dreams. Her breath failed as her brother's friend, Garrett Jones, peered down at her with silver-clouded eyes. Oh, how he made the world spin whenever he drew near. His handsome, yet rugged, face made her fingers ache to touch the severe lines of his jaw. The rich scent of tobacco infused with lavender and some sort of citrus drifted on the breeze. Eau de Cologne. A fragrance only the wealthiest of men in Montana could afford. A scent belying the canvas pants, spiked boots, and sturdy cotton shirt he sported every time she'd seen him on the train platform.

"Elizabeth." Did he say her name, or did she dream the word? Oh to be noticed by a man like Garrett Jones. The only man who could make butterflies flit around in her stomach and fear slide through her chest in the same confusing moment. The hem of her dress hovered mere inches from his feet. Her face heated and heart began to pound. Try as she might, she couldn't keep her eyes off the man who led the Devil May Care boys. The man who held her future in his hands if she succeeded in becoming part of his crew at the logging camp. If things went the way she planned, she'd be staring into his amber and steel speckled eyes for the rest of the season. Did he truly recognize her after all these years of no more than a passing glance?

"Terribly sorry, sir." She shifted her bag to the other hand. "I didn't see you."

He shook his head, but remained silent. The gray in his eyes shone in a color she couldn't quite name, but it softened his jagged expression enough to make her blush once more. A slight movement in his right hand caught her attention as he tapped his leg with his index finger and shuffled his feet, but his chest remained still. After a brief, uncomfortable silence with Garrett offering no more than a fleeting glance, she chewed on her lower lip.

"I suppose I should get going." She took a half step around him, and stopped.

He nodded and gave a bow with an air so refined she paused in surprise. Throughout her years in Montana, she'd grown used to the hard and less-than-mannered ruffians who usually passed her on the street. Even those on the social circuit rarely bowed in such a stiff and crisp manner. He'd certainly never shown such niceties where she was concerned. With one last look at his emotionless face, she nodded and stepped around his broad frame. She locked eyes with him, and felt his gaze follow her while she walked by. Beth forced herself to keep a steady breath as she left.

She hugged her satchel and skirted the shadows until she rounded the corner of a residential street, and all but ran the remaining distance to her friend Carrie's house. She rapped on the large pine door, and took a quick step back as it swung wide open. Finally, she was here. Now she had to force herself to follow the plan.

"It took you long enough, Beth." Carrie grabbed her arm and yanked her into the foyer.

As the huge front door closed behind her, Carrie shoved her forward, causing her to trip quite improperly into the adjoining parlor. Swinging around, Beth flinched as Carrie peeked down the hallway and slammed the parlor door. Carrie pivoted, and shifted her weight onto one leg. "Well?"

"Well, what?" Beth dropped her satchel next to the cold fireplace, trying not to smile at her friend's trepidation, letting the emotion bring her focus back to the issue at hand. She faced Carrie as if nothing out of the ordinary were about to happen.

"Well, what did he say?"

"He?" The image of Garrett on the street took over her thoughts. His strong shoulders, the stiff way he'd bowed, and the whisper of her name on his lips. There was no way Carrie could have seen the awkward exchange, was there? Beth peeked out of the large bay windows across the room, but as she already knew, the view to where she'd bumped into Garrett was blocked by several houses and streets.

Carrie rolled her eyes. "You darned well know who I'm talking about. Your brother."

"Yes, of course." Gracious be, where was her head? Stuck back on Higgins Street and Garrett's disarming gaze. "Simon said yes." Beth raised her chin, and silently dared her friend to argue. She couldn't be swayed. "Tomorrow, I will become a logger."

Carrie dropped her shoulders in defeat, but she folded her arms and glared in a blatant show of disapproval. "Please tell me you are going to help with the cooking, or at least cut the trees like your brother."

"Nope." Beth felt the lack of air plaguing her lungs. Carrie was like a sister, and perhaps a voice of reason, so it was hugely important to get her approval for this adventure—a blessing of sorts.

Carrie frowned and the disapproving look in her eyes deepened. "Don't tell me—"

"Yep, a riverman." Her heart shouldn't run away at such a statement, but it did. To be a riverman and experience the sheer sensation of total control over Mother Nature would be the boon she needed. And in her plight, she'd save not only her brother's job, but an entire town from certain destruction by a saboteur. If she could control those logs down the river, she could easily squash a snake in the grass...or rather trees. It didn't hurt that Garrett would be there. With him at the helm—the man her brother had talked about so often over the last few years—she knew she could accomplish anything.

"Didn't you see the journal last month? They did an exposé on the Missoula rivermen. They said they're ruffians...vagabonds. The men who ride the river have a devil-may-care attitude toward life, and the social skills of a spring hog."

"My brother hasn't said such things, and I'm inclined to believe him over some two-bit reporter. I am going to be a Devil May Care boy."

"I honestly don't know why you want to do this. It is pure madness, not to mention dangerous. I can't believe Simon agreed to your foolish scheme."

"Simon's word isn't law. Please don't tell me you still have that silly schoolgirl crush on my brother."

Carrie's cheeks dusted in a pink hue. "No, but he's a voice of reason."

Beth pursed her lips to stop all the dirty secrets on how she tricked her brother from spilling out like a waterfall. The secret buggy rides where he insisted he needed to go alone to clear his mind. The midnight voices in the garden beneath her bedroom window. All of which allowed Beth this small handful of leverage over her beloved brother. "I don't want to risk making him a target for the saboteur, or losing his job if I end up being wrong. I know it's dangerous, but I have to do this. You don't know how important it is I go."

"I figured you'd say that, and when you get an idea in your head, not even a blizzard in July can stop you. Just promise you'll be careful. Perhaps you should take along someone else to help you, or let me write my godmother. She is a cook somewhere up there. You can see if there are any other positions at camp, one more suitable for a woman. You cannot traipse around like a wild woman in the mountains. It isn't proper." Carrie mimicked the look of a concerned mother.

Beth shook her head and waved off her friend's trepidation. "I want to be a riverman, not a cook. I need to have complete access to the camp, including the dangerous areas. From what Simon has told me in the past, cooks aren't always allowed up there. I can't get close enough to the action while working as a cook. I'll be fine, trust me. Simon wasn't happy about letting me tag along, but after I convinced him—quite forcefully, might I add—he had no choice." She plopped down on a chair. "He or one of his friends will watch me every second of the day. As per his direction, I'm to try to stay away from trouble."

"Everything you've ever dreamed of, a man to watch over you every second of the day." Carrie's mouth twitched in an unsuccessful attempt to hold back her 'you got what you deserved' grin.

Beth wrinkled her nose and sat back in her chair. She wasn't fool enough to think this summer would be easy, but Carrie was right. She didn't want someone watching her every move, especially when she was investigating. There were ways to get around a guard. "A little imagination could serve me well I should think."

"Are you really going down the river?"

"If I can manage it, I will. The log drive is the target, and that's where I need to be."

"You do realize the men who do that particular job are considered wild and touched in the head. Most aren't allowed in polite society."

"I can't go into the upcoming season without helping to secure a future for my brother. I'm to be presented to every eligible bachelor this year." She took a deep breath, and shook her head. "We've always been close, and I don't want to see him suffer while I go off to a life of marital bliss. He needs this job, and I need to know he's happy."

"Why would Simon need you to help? He's done fine at the lumber camp without you so far." Carrie rolled her eyes. "Really, Beth. You must think these things through."

"I have." Beth dropped her shoulders and wiggled to the edge of the seat. "There was a man. On the platform a week ago."

Carrie scooted to the edge of her own chair, and furrowed her brows. "What man? A handsome one? Are you in love already? Oh, I knew it. Just the other day I…"

Carrie's words were lost on her as the memories of the man on the platform flooded back to her.

The early spring chill had penetrated her wrap, and she'd snuggled deep into the fabric as she waited for her brother to return from his pre-season meeting at the mill. Off in the distance the train bellowed and made her sit up tall to look for the engine.

That's when she heard the man with the drawl. A voice she'd never forget. "And they are willing to pay one thousand dollars if the drive never gets to the mill. Destroy the drive, destroy Big Mountain Lumber Mill. The mill will have to pay severance, and they won't be able to recover."

The deep mumble of another man's voice sounded, but he spoke so low she couldn't make out his words. Was that a hint of a Spanish accent? She couldn't be certain.

After the man with the possible Spanish accent finished speaking, the first man continued, "I suppose the families of Bonner will be forced to find a home elsewhere?"

There was a hint of sadness in the man's words—or was it cold-hearted malice? Who were these men?

Beth's breath grew shallow. Whoever they were, they planned to destroy the mill without a care to anyone else involved. What would Simon do for work? What would the families who lived in Bonner do once the mill closed and their livelihood was torn from them? Dear Lord, she had to do something.

"Well, is it?" Carrie's voice penetrated Beth's thoughts, but the question was lost on her.

Is it what? Blast. What was the best response when faced with a question you didn't hear? "Yes."

"So the man from the platform is the man you danced with from the Mayfield's ball?"

Oh good Lord. Beth waved her had across her face. "No, no, no. I overheard two men plotting on the train platform the other day. After they finished their vile conversation, the man with the cane hobbled around the corner with a smug smile. As if he hadn't been plotting Great Mountain's downfall. A place my brother loves dearly. Not that he knew Simon works there, but that's beside the point. Someone wants to destroy the Big Mountain Lumber Mill. Imagine what would happen to all of the families if the mill were shut down. The babies would starve. The fathers would have to leave their homes and families behind to find new work, and who's to say they will? There's an evil plot afoot, and I'm the only one who can identify the culprit."

"Oh my God!" Carrie's eyes flashed in concern. "You need to tell Simon."

Beth nodded. "I will. Eventually. After I've found the man in question, I'll let Simon know. As I said before, I don't want to risk his life, or job, if I'm wrong. I'll go up and identify the culprit, and then tell him once I'm certain. My brother has done so much for me since our parents' deaths. I need to do something for him in return. If I tell him now he'll only leave me behind, and they may never find the saboteur."

Carrie slouched in a show of defeat. "Promise me you'll take care to not get into trouble. If you see the man from the platform, tell Simon. Don't go getting yourself killed."

"Of course. I'm not a fool. I have no intention of getting myself into trouble."

"But how will you pass as a man? With your curves and long hair, you're the perfect example of a woman." Carrie waved toward Beth's hair, piled high on top of her head in the latest fashion.

With a secretive smile, Beth reached into the satchel and searched through the clothing within to pull out her mother's old silver-handled scissors. She reached up to her perfect coif, a style she often worked hours on perfecting. How would she feel without the familiar weight of her hair?

Carrie eyed the sharp tool. "Please tell me you brought those to cut paper."

"Not paper." Beth forced a smile. If she was going to do this, she would do it right. Although set in her decision, she reached up to touch the silky tendrils she'd grown to love. Her best feature. She forced back the tears burning behind her eyes. The sacrifice of her hair was worth saving her brother and his job. She firmed her lips, and held the scissors out to Carrie.

"What will your nana say?" Carrie asked.

"She has taken to her bed as of late, and only leaves to visit her matron friends for tea on Tuesdays. Her maid is there with her every second of the day, so I'm of little help. I asked her if I could accompany you to visit your sister for the spring, and she agreed. I'll come home after the drive, and she'll be none the wiser. My hair will grow again, and I'll either pin it back, or I'll say your little niece Tawny cut my hair while I slept because she wanted it for her doll. Your niece is quite the troublemaker. Nana will have no trouble believing me."

"Tawny's done worse, I suppose." Carrie pinched her lips shut and stared with a calculating, but disapproving, look. Beth smiled as Carrie plucked the scissors from her hand with a sigh. She could always count on her dear friend to cave when logic and passion were at the heart of her arguments.

Two hours later, Beth sauntered down the stairs and out the door like she'd seen her brother do on many occasions. She enjoyed the feel of the trousers tight against her legs. The harsh scratch of the blue denim a vast difference from the soft cotton of her dresses—not to mention a distinct lack of a bustle strapped to her backside. The sensation of nothing but the rough work pants lent a sort of wicked freedom she could get accustomed to. The satchel swung as she walked, and she ignored the odd looks from the women passing by on their way to the shops—a few of which she recognized from the Missoula Women's Society tea three weeks past. Did they recognize her? Even if they did, she didn't care. In a few days she would be on her way to Bonner to work for the Big Mountain Lumber Mill.

Beth rushed home and snuck up the stairs leading to her room. After she made certain no one was around, she eased the door shut.

She tossed the satchel on the bed, stared into her long dressing mirror, and ruffled her short, spiky hair. Turning to her armoire, she took out an old petticoat and plopped down on the side of her bed to tear the strips of cloth that would bind her breasts. What would the gossiping ninnies of the town think of her now? Scandal followed Beth's family like a hungry dog. Not that she personally deserved the stigma, but with her parents' deaths, and Simon's debauchery whenever he was home, the town gossips painted all the Sanders in the same tainted light. An escapade like this wouldn't come as a surprise.

A knock sounded, and she scrambled to stuff the cloth under her pillow and yank on the hat from atop her dressing table. She pulled the brim over her ears. "Come in."

The door slid open, and her brother Simon peeked in.

"Hey, Lizbe. It's all set through the big bugs at the mill. I thought maybe we could go out and practice tonight. My secret's safe, right? You aren't going to tell the mayor?"

With a sigh of relief, Beth pulled her hat from her head. "It's safe for now. Practice what? And you know I hate that nickname. It makes me sound like I'm twelve."

Simon grimaced as his gaze skimmed her head. "Practice being a man. Meet me by the front door after Nana goes to bed." He studied her a moment longer, and then frowned. "Did you steal those trousers from the twelve-year-old neighbor? You look like a blacksmith's errand boy."

Beth stuck out her tongue as Simon twisted on his heels. She could hear the angry click of his boots as he disappeared down the hallway. She had no idea what he'd planned, but she wasn't about to let his reluctance or insults get in the way. Simon had no clue about the saboteur and catastrophe in the making. Eventually he'd appreciate what she'd sacrificed, after she saved his job, the lumber camp, and the entire town.

Meet the Author

A country girl born and bred, **Dawn Luedecke** has spent most of her life surrounded by horses, country folk, and the wild terrain of Nevada, Idaho and Montana. She enjoys writing historical and contemporary romance and spends as much time as she can working on her current manuscript. For more information visit www.dawnluedeckebooks.com.

Printed in the United States
by Baker & Taylor Publisher Services